GUARDIANS OF THE MIRROR

John D. Fennell

Books by John D. Fennell

THE MYSTICAL MIRROR Trilogy:

Book 1: The Boy in the Mirror
Book 2: The Book of Mysteries
Book 3: Guardians of the Mirror

THE ROMAN TIME MACHINE Series:

Book 1: Vesuvius
Book 2: The Prophecy
Book 3: The Druid of Britannia

Copyright © 2020 John D. Fennell
All rights reserved
ISBN-13: 9798652868857

www.johndfennell.com

For Mum

Without your love and encouragement none of this would have been possible

Chapter One

The Never-ending Storm

Porthgarrick, Cornwall

It was the loudest clap of thunder any of them had ever heard. Even far underground in the gloomy cavern below *Morladron House*, the noise shook the massive stone pillars holding up the roof high above them. Tiny particles of stone fell down from the blackness above and skittered across the rocky floor. Somewhere nearby, a metal object was shaken from a table and clattered noisily to the ground, and a baby began crying, sending eerie, echoing cries through the cavern.

Instinctively, many of the remaining survivors from Porthgarrick peered anxiously up at the roof, praying it was not about to come crashing down on top of them. Mercifully, the enormous pillars ceased their disconcerting tremors moments later and, for the time being at least, remained as solid as before.

Molly was beginning to lose count of how many times she had experienced these terrifying storms in the last few months. With every week that passed, they were becoming more and more frequent, the gaps between them shorter and shorter. How much longer would it be before they simply joined together and became one continuous, never-ending storm? But no, she had to stop thinking like that. *Take each day as it comes*, she chided herself.

'Penny for your thoughts,' said Tom, and gave her a comforting squeeze with the arm he had around her shoulders. They were sitting huddled together in the dark on a frayed blanket on the cold cavern floor. A solitary flickering candle, which stood on what had once been a small bedside table, was the only meagre light near them.

As if defying her to respond, another deafening peal of thunder shook the entire chamber. A few paces away from them, dozens of candle flames guttered violently for several seconds. The shrill, unsettling cries of the baby grew even louder.

Instead of speaking, Molly gave Tom a weak smile and then snuggled closer into his body where she always felt safe, or at least safer than anywhere else. Now that her parents were missing, he was all she had left.

Ahead of them, in the ghostly light cast by the candles, Molly could see many groups huddled together, couples like her and Tom or whole families, all seeking what little solace they could find in the arms of a loved one. All those nearby faces that she could see in the pale light looked white with a mix of fear and shock.

'I've got a present for you,' said Tom brightly, when the latest peal of thunder had finally abated. He then rummaged around inside his coat and presented Molly with a pristine green and red apple.

She sat up and looked askance at him. 'Where did you get that?'

'Never mind about that, babe,' he smiled. 'Just take it.'

'You didn't steal it, did you?' she whispered.

Tom frowned. 'I think you know me better than that.'

Molly sat back into his comforting embrace. 'We'll share it,' she insisted.

'No, Molly. It's yours. Look on it as a belated birthday

present.'

'Thanks, Tom,' she said, and took a large bite out of it, which made a satisfying crunch in her mouth. It tasted so good. She had not eaten fresh fruit in days. In fact, she had hardly eaten anything at all in ages, save for the meagre rations, which were handed out every two days.

With around a third of the juicy apple still left, she handed it back to Tom, even though her stomach was still growling with hunger. Despite his repeated protestations, she eventually persuaded him to eat the remainder.

'Thanks again, babe,' said Molly. 'That was divine.'

'Now that you're fifteen, you need all the energy you can get,' he grinned. 'Besides, an apple a day keeps the storms away. Isn't that what they say?'

She elbowed him lightly in the ribs. Then after a pause she asked: 'Do you think we'll still be around to see my sixteenth birthday?'

Tom chuckled lightly. 'Of course we will. We'll sort this out one day, you'll see.'

She smiled and hugged him tightly. That was one of the many reasons why she loved him: he was always optimistic, always seeing the positive in everything, however gloomy the outlook may have appeared. In short, he always managed to make her feel better.

A few minutes later, the dark shadow of a man trotted up the steps that were set into the sidewall of the cavern. When he reached the top, he eased open the thick door and cautiously peered out for a moment, before closing it and scurrying back down the steps. 'All clear!' he yelled when he reached the bottom.

A collective sigh of relief rose up from the hundred or so

people sheltering in the cavern. Even the cries from the baby seemed somehow less piercing. Chattering began to break out, even a couple of chuckles, while most people rose stiffly to their feet.

'Come on,' said Tom. 'Let's get some fresh air. While we can.'

Molly stood up and smiled warmly at him. It would be good to escape the murky confines of the cavern, which at times felt more like the terrifying underworld from Greek mythology than a sanctuary from the storms. Yet equally, she felt as apprehensive at the thought of going outside once more as she always did these days, worried about what new signs of devastation they would see this time.

Only about twenty or so people headed towards the steps. The remaining occupants of the cavern tended to their frightened children or tried as best they could to smarten up their makeshift shelters. But neither Molly nor Tom were interested in tidying up their tiny part of the chamber. What few possessions they had left were stacked in a corner, largely hidden under a few flimsy sheets and tarpaulins for privacy, and none of it needing any attention. Besides, getting outside, even if it would only be for a few minutes, was infinitely more appealing to them.

As Molly stepped through the doorway at the top of the stairs and out into the open, she was greeted by a cold gust of winter air. The rain had stopped, but everywhere was still dripping wet from the recent downpour. Tom turned and gave her a hand negotiating the blocks of masonry, which lay scattered around like tombstones in what had once been the downstairs of *Morladron House*.

She looked up at the sky where dark clouds were scudding

by, as if trying to flee from the approach of the next storm, which was no doubt already building somewhere nearby. She and Tom passed through the ruins of the front door, where the remains of the stone walls stood no more than chest high, and stepped into the grounds of the old house.

In the distance, to their left, the storm could be seen receding towards the horizon, where the sky was as black as coal except for when frequent bursts of lightning lit up the low-lying cloud. Three or four massive tornadoes gyrated at the edge of the storm, as though they were escorting it away from the house. And each time that more lightning erupted out of the cloud, several more whirlwinds could be seen swirling in the heart of the storm. It looked as though the whole vast mass of cloud were being carried along on top of a dozen giant tornadoes.

Thankful that the latest terrible storm had finally passed, Molly quickly turned away and looked to her right, down at the remains of Porthgarrick. Over the ruined and abandoned town, the sky was grey, but showed no immediate signs of a new storm.

'We should be all right for a little while,' said Tom, who was by now also looking up at the sky. 'Come on. Let's see if there is anything we can do to help.'

Holding Molly's delicate hand, Tom led her into the garden by the side of the crumbling remains of the house. A middle-aged man and woman were treading carefully through a large patch of earth, stooping down regularly to pick up pieces of torn greenery from the ground. As Molly and Tom approached them, a pale shaft of sunlight managed to penetrate the cloud and briefly cast weak shadows across the scene.

'How's it looking?' asked Tom, hopefully.

The man glanced at the two teenagers, then screwed his face into a frown and shook his head. 'All ruined,' he sighed, and picked up a shrivelled plant from near his feet. 'It's all ruined. We just can't grow anything with these wretched storms passing through every few hours. It's hopeless.'

'We've got to keep trying, though,' said the woman, and smiled weakly at them. 'Otherwise, we're all going to starve.'

'Well, let us know if there is anything we can do to help,' said Tom.

Tom's offer seemed to go unnoticed, since neither the woman nor the man said anything further but continued their forlorn inspection of the ground.

Feeling uncomfortable, Molly pulled Tom away. 'What are we going to do, babe?' she asked. 'If the crops won't grow ...' The fear caught in her throat, made her unable to speak.

Tom gave her a hug. 'I don't know. I really don't,' he replied.

'If only we could use the mirror to escape from all this,' suggested Molly. 'And take everyone with us.'

Tom sighed heavily. 'We know that's not an option. For one thing, we'd be arrested as soon as we got through to the other side.'

'Surely, it's better to be arrested than to stay here, isn't it?'

Tom shook his head. 'They would just send us straight back here,' he said bitterly. 'That's what they do. They don't give a damn about us here.' His face suddenly looked angry, as it always seemed to, whenever he spoke about the other world. It was the one subject, thought Molly, that was guaranteed to make him lose his composure.

She wiped away a tear and found it impossible to speak for

a moment or two.

'We've just got to take each day as it comes,' continued Tom, regaining some of his cheerful demeanour. 'And hope we can find a way through this.'

Just then, a loud voice called out. 'I'm looking for volunteers,' announced a tall, thin man. 'To come with me down into the town. We'll have a look around, see if we can find anything useful to bring back with us.'

'Come on, babe,' said Tom, pulling Molly gently towards the small group of people gathering around the man. 'We haven't been down there for a couple of days. Must be our turn.'

Once ten or so people had assembled around the gangly man, they set off down the hill. As they walked along, a man next to Molly took out a pistol from his pocket and seemed to check that he had enough bullets in the cartridge. He glanced across at Molly's horrified face when he realised she was staring at him. 'Can't be too careful,' he said with a wry smile. 'There are still one or two undesirables living down there.'

The thought made Molly uneasy, so she focused on the way ahead instead. Before them, down in the valley, the ruins of Porthgarrick came into view. Several screeching gulls circled in the cold December air above the town, no doubt as starving as every other living thing seemed to be in this barren world. Not that there were many signs of life anymore. With winter holding the whole area firmly in its grip, even the vegetation seemed to have given up the fight for survival.

As the small group entered the outskirts of the town, the seagulls flew away, leaving nothing but an eerie silence. The cold wind blew through the deserted streets, while the faint echos from their footsteps on the road made it sound like their number was much greater than ten. But otherwise, there was no sound. And no one spoke a word.

The empty, crumbling remains of houses could be seen everywhere. No building had been left untouched by the storms, with not a single roof still in place. Only sections of walls here and there now remained, while debris lay strewn across the roads and paths: bricks, roof tiles, wooden beams, fragments of furniture, fallen trees. They passed the twisted and battered remains of a vehicle, which looked as though it had been picked up by passing whirlwinds time and again, until all that was left was a crumpled mass of contorted metal.

Even though Molly had been down into the town only a few days previously, the changes, the signs of new destruction were horribly stark. A few more weeks of this, she thought, and Porthgarrick would be erased from the land.

As the group continued down into the valley in silence, their eyes scouring the landscape for anything that might be of use to their small community, the occasional dark figure would appear briefly next to a section of wall, eyeing them warily, before disappearing back into the shadows. Where these few scavengers went during the frequent storms, Molly could only wonder at. Perhaps like so many people these days, they no longer cared for their own safety.

At last, they had reached the river in the centre of the town, and now that the road bridge had long since been destroyed and washed away, this would be the end of their trip. For there was no way to cross the river, which now flowed past at a terrifying speed. A scattering of branches, large and small, was swept along in the swirling, muddy waters. When Molly looked closer, she could also see dozens of dead fish floating on the surface, racing past towards the sea.

Guardians of the Mirror

By now, Molly was so shocked she could not speak. It was horrifying to witness the death of her once much-loved hometown. It was a terrible nightmare, from which there seemed no possible way to wake.

After a few minutes' scouting around through the rubble, the small group had found nothing but a few pieces of cutlery and crockery and other small items, which they stuffed into holdalls. Their tall leader then declared it was time to head back when he looked up at the sky. Molly followed his eyes to the east and saw black clouds building in the distance over the far side of the valley.

While they trudged back up the hill with their few meagre findings, the deep throbbing of a helicopter quickly rose up behind them. Molly and Tom turned their heads and saw the large military Chinook approaching over the valley.

'Food drop!' yelled one of their group above the noise. 'Quick! Back to the house.'

And so, they all hurried up the side of the valley while the helicopter flew low over their heads towards what was left of *Morladron House*. By the time they had reached the ruins of the old building, the Chinook had landed, and soldiers were heaving a large wooden crate out of the cargo bay, while the propellers still whirled noisily above them.

Lightning erupted out of the sky to their right, splitting into many jagged tentacles, which then ripped into the ground nearby. As their small group hurried towards the soldiers, Molly realised the helicopter was preparing to take off again.

'Wait!' she yelled above the sound of the propellers and ran forwards. One of the soldiers who was rushing back to the cargo bay turned to look at her. 'You can't leave now,' she continued. 'How are we supposed to survive with just that?'

she added, waving a hand at the single wooden box the soldiers had left behind, which was little more than a cubic metre in size. 'It won't be enough — there are over a hundred of us.'

'Sorry, luv,' shrugged the soldier. 'But you're not the only ones in need of supplies.' Whereupon, he turned around and disappeared into the Chinook.

Molly felt so cross, so scared at the same time, that she was about to scream at the soldiers some more, but Tom seized her gently by the arm and coaxed her away. 'Come on,' he urged. 'Let's help get this food inside before the storm gets here.'

By now, others had emerged from out of the ruins of *Morladron House* and were hurrying towards the crate. While a dozen of the strongest men moved the box towards the house, Molly turned around and saw that the sky behind them was now as black as night. Lightning was beginning to flash at regular intervals, some alarmingly close by, others further away, but all accompanied by deafening explosions of thunder.

The helicopter was finally beginning to lift off, thrusting a gale-force wind towards them as it rose. Someone was yelling at everyone to seek shelter in the cavern as soon as possible, but the voice was barely audible above the roar of the Chinook's engine and the frequent peals of thunder.

The helicopter had only risen a few metres into the air when it was struck. A dazzling trident arrowed down from the dark cloud, as if an angry god had cast the lightning intentionally at the Chinook. A vast bouquet of sparks erupted in all directions. The helicopter tilted to one side and then crashed back down to earth, like a giant beast that had just been slain. The propellers dug into the ground, buckled like cardboard

Guardians of the Mirror

and then ceased to rotate. One of the helicopter's engines exploded, issuing a small fireball into the air.

More lightning cracked across the sky all around them. Molly was about to run towards the door to the cavern when she realised Tom was heading in the opposite direction. She turned sharply and grabbed his arm. 'What are you doing, Tom?' she screamed.

'I need to help,' he said. 'There are people still in that helicopter. We can't just leave them there.'

'There's nothing we can do, Tom,' said the tall leader, who was standing nearby. 'Hurry up. We need to get back inside.'

'No!' cried Tom. 'I'm not leaving them there.' And with that, he ran towards the stricken Chinook, part of which was now on fire.

'Tom ... no!' yelled Molly.

But there was no stopping him, as he raced across the grass towards the burning wreck. The man nearby grabbed Molly by the arm. 'We have to go,' he insisted, as yet more lightning erupted before them.

But Molly could not move. Her eyes were fixed on her beloved Tom, who, by now, had almost reached the helicopter.

Another single bolt of lightning was unleashed by the coal-black heavens. It arrowed down and struck Tom. In the blink of an eye ... he had gone.

Molly froze, then sank to her knees. She went to speak but nothing would come out. The rangy leader of their community picked her up and carried her into the safety of the cavern. But by now, she was numb, unable to move, to speak, to think.

Tom had gone ... and was never coming back.

Chapter Two

The Birthday Party

Some days earlier

From nowhere, the flame burst into life, chasing away the shadows. Before long, more fire flared into existence. Thin wisps of smoke began to climb, whilst the heat from the flames began to dance on his skin.

Tom was nervous. He had never felt anything like it before. If he made a mistake now, the consequences were unthinkable. His eyes studied the flames, mesmerised by the dancing fingers of red and orange.

To his left, a door burst open, causing him to start. A mop of blond hair appeared from behind the door.

'Hey, Tom,' said Jake. 'Have you finished lighting those candles yet, mate? We're all desperate for a slice of this cake, you know.'

'Nearly done,' replied Tom, striking a final match and holding it to the last pair of candles. With fifteen bright candles now lit, he proceeded to lift up the circular cake and carried it nervously in front of him at arm's length, as though it were a bomb in danger of exploding at any moment. It was Molly's birthday, and he owed it to her to make sure everything was perfect.

When he brought the cake into the next room, the lights had already been dimmed so the candles glowed brightly in the dark. As he crept cautiously forwards, terrified he was going to drop the cake, everyone began singing "Happy Birthday".

Guardians of the Mirror

Molly was grinning broadly, and her eyes sparkled as brightly as the reflection of the candles in her glasses.

As Tom placed the cake down onto the small table in the centre of the room, everyone waited with anticipation. As well as Molly and Jake, there were Tom's grandfather, his cousin Izzy and Tony Singh. It was only a small, clandestine party, but given that Tom and his grandfather were still wanted by the police, they did not have much choice.

After she had blown out the candles, cut the cake and made the customary wish, Tom handed her a small present, which she unwrapped with relish. Inside was a small box containing a sparkling pendant attached to a delicate silver chain.

'It's beautiful!' gasped Molly, holding it up.

'It's blue zircon,' said Tom. 'Your birthstone.'

'It's lovely,' said Molly, and then gave Tom a peck on the cheek. They both flushed scarlet.

'Oh, dear,' mumbled Tom's cousin Izzy with a twisted smile. 'I think I'm going to be sick.'

'But how could you afford it?' asked Molly, fastening it around her neck. 'And how did you ever manage to get to the shops?'

'Ah, well,' began Tom. 'When you're a wanted criminal, you get to meet all these dodgy characters in the criminal underworld ...'

'Aye, that and the paper round you've now got,' smiled Jake.

'You have a paper round?' gasped Izzy, all wide-eyed surprise.

'Er, well, yes,' admitted Tom. 'I've been living a double life these past couple of months. Passing back and forth through the mirror. One minute I'm a nerdy schoolboy with a paper round and a drunk for a father in Jake's world. The next, I have the most amazing girlfriend in the world, I'm wanted by the police and have a completely different father banged up in a maximum-security prison in this world. Just a normal teenager's life really.'

'Well, however you managed it,' said Molly with a grin, 'I'm very grateful.'

While the others in the room proceeded to give Molly their presents, Jake moved next to Tom and mumbled in his ear. 'So, what's it like dating an older woman, eh?'

Tom laughed. 'It's wonderful. We've only been together a few months, but I just can't imagine my life without her, to be honest. Bit scary really when I think how much I ... well, you know.'

Jake patted his friend on the shoulder. 'Aye, I know, mate.'

'You didn't want to bring Clare along, then?' asked Tom.

Jake gave a wry smile. 'She won't come within a mile of the mirror these days. Not surprising really, after being kidnapped by Harry that time. It's probably best, anyway. Clare has a double lurking somewhere in this world, so it would be a bit dodgy her being here as well.'

'Not something you and I have to worry about these days,' said Tom.

'Aye,' agreed Jake thoughtfully. Both Sean and Michael, Jake and Tom's respective doubles, were now dead, which did at least mean that the two of them could now move freely between the two worlds without setting off a storm.

'Anyway, it's cake time,' said Jake brightly, rubbing his large hands together and moving back towards the table.

'You did well, Tom. Molly loves her pendant,' said another voice in his other ear this time.

Guardians of the Mirror

Tom turned to see a grinning Izzy now standing next to him and smiled back. But then he looked rather thoughtful. 'Shame Tony can't give her a pendant like his one. Then Molly could come with me now and again into the other world.'

'Yeah. He's only got the one, though. And he can't really lend it to her, can he? He'd be putting his own life in danger if he did.'

Tom nodded pensively, knowing that as long as Tony's double, Harry Singh, remained in their world, Tony's life would be in danger if ever he removed his protective pendant.

He then sighed heavily. 'When is all this hiding from the police ever going to end, Izz?'

'I wish I knew, Tom. I really do.'

'I just want to do something simple, like take Molly to a café for a drink, or go for a walk along the beach with her. But I can't do any of that, can I? Not without fear of being arrested.' He watched his girlfriend, who stood a few metres away with a lovely smile on her face, as she unwrapped a present and shared a joke with Jake and Tony. 'Molly deserves better than what I can give her.'

'You don't have to worry about Molly,' said Izzy, giving Tom a playful punch on the arm. 'She thinks the world of you. You know that, don't you?'

'I hope you're right. I just want us to have a normal life. And to get my dad out of prison. If we could just hack into the Internet and broadcast to the country — to the world in fact — just how bad it is here, show everyone just how evil this government is, there'd be a revolution, surely.'

'Well, I am working on it, Tom. I've got a whole laptop full of evidence — photos, videos, documents. That's not the problem. The hard part is trying to broadcast it on the

John D. Fennell

Internet.'

'You'll find a way. There's nothing *you* can't hack into.'

Suddenly, Izzy's face turned unusually grave, which looked odd on a face where a mischievous look never seemed to be far away. 'Tom, it's one thing to hack into the bungling local police force. To be honest, they are pretty amateurish when it comes to their on-line security. But hacking into the central government systems, breaking through their firewalls, is a whole different ball game. If I'm honest, at the moment, I've got absolutely no idea how to go about doing that.'

'Dad's depending on us,' said Tom quietly.

'I know, Tom,' sighed Izzy. 'I won't give up, I promise you that. I just want you to realise it's not going to be easy, or quick.'

'Well, if you need any help, just let me know.'

'Thanks, but probably best if you boys stick to the manual stuff and leave the intellectual bits to me and Molly.'

Tom laughed and then pulled a face at her. 'Seriously though, Izz. If anyone can do it, you can. I believe in you ... even if everyone else thinks you're rubbish,' he added with a grin.

'Oi, cheeky!' replied Izzy and gave him another friendly punch. 'That reminds me: I need a new partner to practise my kendo on.'

Tom laughed and then wandered out of the room. He needed some time to think. He had not seen his father since he had been arrested in the cavern under *Morladron House* two months previously, and they were still no nearer knowing where he was being held. Tom had made a promise to his dad that he would find a way to get him out of prison, and yet that idea was feeling increasingly like nothing more than a pipe dream.

He walked into the small kitchen at the front of the cottage, which overlooked a lake as large as a football pitch. Outside, it was a miserable December day with an icy wind, which blew through the bare trees and shoved sullen, grey clouds across the sky. A few spots of rain pattered against the window as he gazed out.

Tom and his grandfather had been living in what was called *Lynn Cottage* for several weeks now. It belonged to Izzy's family, but had not been lived in for many years. Although small, rather musty and rundown, it was situated in the middle of nowhere, making it a perfect hideout for the two of them.

Checking for any signs of movement outside, Tom briefly looked at the laptop, which lay open on the kitchen table. Even knowing that Izzy had set up all manner of sensors and cameras, which would instantly alert them to the approach of anything larger than a fox, he still felt he needed to check every now and then, in case Miss Doomsday and the police had discovered his latest hideout. But on such a cold and gloomy day, nothing was moving outside.

After he had finished looking out across the windswept lake a short distance away, Tom turned around and looked at the tall cheval mirror tucked away in the corner of the room. He moved closer until he could see his own reflection in the glass. A slightly melancholy face stared back at him, and he pondered all the incredible changes that mirror had brought to his life since he had discovered it some six months previously.

'Hey, mate,' said Jake, walking into the kitchen. 'What are you doing in here?'

'Oh, you know me,' replied Tom, still studying his

reflection. 'Just thinking.'

Molly followed Jake into the room, moved next to Tom and put her hand straight into his, until all three of them were staring side by side at their reflections.

'Oh, dear. I know that look,' said Jake in his pleasant Scottish lilt. 'You're planning something. I really hope you're not thinking of trying to destroy this mirror, or anything daft like that.'

Tom smiled. 'Something tells me we are not meant to close the portal between the two worlds. It seems like it wants to remain open, no matter how hard we might try to close it. So maybe we shouldn't even try to shut it down. We should just police it, guard it. Perhaps we should become the new Guardians of the Mirror.' He laughed as soon as he had spoken the words.

'Steady on,' chuckled Jake. 'I think we should leave all that superhero stuff to Tony.'

'Yeah, I guess so,' conceded Tom. 'But as long as we have this thing, we should use it, make it work for us. For one thing, we'll always be able to escape from Miss Doomsday and her cronies. I just wish there was some way we could use it to help us bring down the government and get my dad out of prison.'

'We'll find a way, Tom,' said Molly and smiled at him in the mirror. 'We always do.'

Just then, Izzy, Tony and Sam entered the kitchen.

'Why does everyone always end up in the kitchen?' asked Izzy with a grin.

'We're just trying to escape from you, Izz,' said Tom.

Izzy simply stuck out her tongue in exaggerated fashion.

As the tall figure of Tony Singh stood behind them, Tom caught sight of the pendant strap around his neck. 'Is that

Guardians of the Mirror

thing still glowing, Tony?' he asked.

Tony fished it out from behind his shirt, to reveal an almond-sized stone, which was emitting a faint yellow light. 'Yep,' he replied. 'Looks like Harry Singh is still alive and well in this world ... more's the pity.'

'Do you think he's told Miss Doomsday everything about the mirror yet?' asked Jake. 'We could be in trouble if he has.'

'We have no way of knowing,' sighed Tony. 'I've seen no sign of her looking for the mirror. So hopefully, she's just forgotten everything she saw back at Trethek Cove.'

'Somehow I very much doubt that,' snorted Tom. 'And you, Tony? No signs they know it was you who rescued me and imprisoned Harry on the beach?'

'None at all. I'm back at school now. And so far, I've not even had so much as a funny look from the deputy head. Not that she seems to be in school much these days.'

'Good. Let's hope it stays that way.'

'Anyway,' said Molly. 'This is supposed to be my birthday party. Yet somehow we've ended up crammed in the kitchen talking about my least favourite person in the world.'

'Quite right,' said Tom, turning away from the mirror. 'Come on, everyone. Let's go party!'

With every passing day, Miss Doomsday was growing more and more impatient. Things were not progressing as fast as she had hoped.

With a purposeful stride and a face of thunder, she headed towards the operations room in the Porthgarrick police station. When she burst noisily through the door into the room, several of the police officers, who were sitting at their desks, glanced round to see who had entered, but then hurriedly returned to their work when they spotted who it was.

The far end of the room was made up entirely of a giant video wall, split into multiple screens, showing images from the many security cameras dotted around Porthgarrick and the surrounding area. In recent months, Miss Doomsday had insisted that even more cameras should be installed in the town, so that now she could be more confident than ever that there was nowhere left for criminals to hide.

She briefly studied the moving images on the wall, but when she saw nothing of interest, she turned to one of the seated officers and demanded: 'I want to see the footage from Trethek Cove from last October. Bring it up on your screen now.'

At that moment, a middle-aged police officer came out of her nearby glass-walled office and headed towards the deputy head. Dressed in her smart black uniform, she moved rather regally across the room, but then a look of unease flashed across her face when she approached. 'Morning, Commissioner Doomsday,' she said. 'Is there something I can help you with?'

'Yes, DCI Prideaux,' replied Miss Doomsday somewhat impatiently. 'I want the footage from Trethek Cove that was taken in October to be reviewed again.'

'Well, things are a little busy at the minute. But I'm sure we can get round to that when we have a spare moment.'

The squat deputy head turned to stare up at the much taller police officer. 'I am not asking you, DCI Prideaux. I am ordering you.' She then tapped the back of the chair of the officer, who was sitting rather uncomfortably between the two women. 'Bring it up now.'

The seated officer glanced up at his superior officer, who

nodded back almost imperceptibly. After some furious typing, the dark images from Trethek Cove appeared on his screen. Miss Doomsday tapped the screen with an impatient finger and ordered the officer to play one of the pieces of video footage taken by the soldiers, who had filmed the confrontation between Harry Singh and his unknown assailant.

When a blurred image of Harry's opponent appeared on the screen, Miss Doomsday pointed swiftly and said: 'There! Freeze that image. Now, I want to know who that is,' she added, tapping the screen once more.

'It's very difficult to get a clear picture,' said DCI Prideaux. 'We have tried, but it was dark, and we only have partial images.'

'I don't care how hard it is,' replied the deputy head through clenched teeth. 'I need to know who that is. Now, put all your resources into this, and I mean all.' She then began walking away but continued talking over her shoulder as she moved. 'Tell me who that is. Or I will find someone else who can. Someone more competent. Understood?'

'Yes, ma'am,' mumbled DCI Prideaux, who by now looked more nervous than angry.

Sighing heavily, Miss Doomsday returned to her office in the police station, slammed the door behind her and then sat behind her desk. She drummed her fingers impatiently on the top, lost in thought.

It had now been many weeks since Harry Singh had been arrested and thrown in prison, but so far, he had proved to be of no use to her whatsoever. He could tell her nothing that she had not already read in the two books now in her possession. The one was a translation of the so-called Book of Mysteries, written two hundred years ago by her ancestor from a parallel world, Augustus Doomsday, while the other was a diary written by that Doomsday's right-hand man Albert Trevaskis. The books told her in great detail how to control the severe weather events that were unleashed when two identical people existed in one world. However, it had become apparent that to master these powerful forces she needed what was called an Iris. But what the books did not tell her was how to acquire one of these mysterious objects, other than to state that she needed to access the mirror to do so.

It was all so very frustrating. Yet her determination to find one of these Irises had not dimmed one iota since she had first learned about them many weeks previously. For she was desperate to get her hands on the powers she had witnessed being used when Harry had fought, and ultimately been defeated by, his unknown opponent in Trethek Cove. And the more she read both books the more she craved the powers they described.

She had been in her office, alone with her swirling thoughts, for at least an hour, when there was a knock at the door, which made her start.

'Come in!' she barked with such ferocity that her visitor seemed to hesitate several seconds before entering.

Eventually, in walked DCI Prideaux. 'Excuse me, ma'am. I think we may have identified your man.'

'Well?'

'With the poor quality of the images, it's difficult to be one hundred percent certain, but we think—'

'Just tell me who you think it is!'

'We think it could be Tony Singh. He's a sixth-former in Porthgarrick Senior School.'

Guardians of the Mirror

'Yes, I know who he is,' snapped Miss Doomsday, glaring at the police officer. But then her face broke into a wry smile. 'Of course. Tony Singh. I should have realised. It makes perfect sense. Well, what are you waiting for? Let's go and arrest him.' She glanced at her watch and stood up, as DCI Prideaux turned to leave. 'He should still be in school at this time of day. Let's go and have a nice little chat with Tony Singh, shall we?'

Chapter Three

The Speeches

Feeling rather frustrated, Izzy stood up to stretch her stiff neck, back and shoulders. She had been sitting at her desk in her small bedroom, dancing her fingers over the keyboard for what seemed like hours. She had even skipped a maths lesson, so determined was she to break through the government's firewalls and gain access to the Internet. But once again she had been defeated. Together with her small group of like-minded on-line friends, she had tried everything she could think of but all to no avail. She would never give up, but it was proving to be immensely frustrating.

She had been pacing up and down the cluttered room for just a few minutes, when a loud continuous beep jolted her from her thoughts. She leapt over to her desk and hurriedly brought up a new window on one of her many screens.

'Oh, no!' she muttered, as she sank back into her chair. She then shoved the headset onto her flowing blond hair and brought up a list of phone numbers on the screen, before dialling one of them. 'Come on, come on!' she said as the phone rang and rang.

When the call eventually went to voicemail, she hung up, then frantically typed 'EMERGENCY' and send it as a text. Then she typed it again, and again, and again. At last, her phone was ringing.

'Tony!' she yelled before he could speak. 'Where are you?'

'In school,' he mumbled, clearly trying to keep his voice low. 'Where you're supposed to be.'

Guardians of the Mirror

'Right. Get out, now!'

'What are—?'

'They're on to you, Tony. The police are coming to arrest you — right now. You need to get out. Just listen carefully and do exactly as I say. I'll guide you out of the school.'

'Yes, miss,' chuckled Tony.

While she had been talking into her microphone, Izzy had been bringing up a dozen images on the screens in front of her, all showing live footage from various cameras in and around the school. 'Right,' she said. 'I can see the police cars heading towards the school. They'll be turning into the car park in a few seconds. Where are you now?'

'I'm going down the stairs,' replied Tony, beginning to sound a little breathless. 'Yes, I can see the police cars coming now.'

Izzy noticed Tony appear on one of the images in front of her. He was heading fast down a corridor, mobile phone pressed to his ear. He then glanced up at the camera, as if sensing that Izzy was watching him.

'Head towards the tennis courts,' she ordered.

'Are you going to tell me how exactly you know they're coming for me?' asked Tony, sounding a little irritated. 'Because I've just walked out in the middle of a lesson. And that alone is likely to get me into trouble.'

'I have a program set up to constantly monitor all messages from the local police force,' replied Izzy. She found herself talking fast, so anxious was she. 'It monitors phone calls, text messages, emails. If there is any mention of you, me, Tom, Molly, Sam and a few others, I receive an alert. And your name just popped up — an order for your immediate arrest. It doesn't say why, but it states that you should be considered highly dangerous. That tells me they suddenly know all about you and what you can do.'

'Well, I'm flattered to be on your VIP list. You must really care about me.'

'Oh, I don't really,' she laughed. 'But you know that Tom and Sam are hiding in my grandparents' old cottage. So, I can't afford for you to be arrested, in case the police torture you and you reveal their hideout.'

'Fair enough,' laughed Tony, but then suddenly went grave. 'Oh, no! There's a teacher coming. She'll want to know why I'm not in class.'

Izzy tapped away at the keyboard and brought up the image from the corridor down which Tony was striding. In the distance, another figure was approaching him. 'Just stay calm, Tony. Say you're running an errand for someone.'

'Or I could just run,' replied Tony, and without warning, he turned around and sprinted out of shot.

'What are you doing, Tony?' demanded Izzy, whilst she frantically tried to follow his progress on the school's cameras.

'Just get me out of here, Izzy.'

'Head to the sports hall,' she replied, bringing up image after image.

On one of her screens, she could see police officers entering the main foyer at the front of the school. There were at least five of them, all carrying handguns. On another screen, five more officers were circling around the back of the school. Izzy cursed.

'What is it?' asked an increasingly breathless Tony.

Izzy watched him appear on one screen, turn sharply around a corner and then disappear down a different corridor. Seconds later, he reappeared on yet another screen, running

Guardians of the Mirror

towards the camera.

'The police have entered the front,' said Izzy. 'And another group are heading round the back. When you approach the sports hall, turn right, not left, then go out the emergency exit, towards the tennis courts. And be quick!'

'I'm going as fast as I can!' replied Tony, panting. 'Right. I'm outside. Where to now?'

'Once you get to the tennis courts, head for the line of trees at the back. Go into the trees. You should then see a small gap in the fence leading to the farmer's field at the back.'

'Izzy. Don't forget, I've not been at this school for long. I don't know my way around as well as you do.'

Izzy cursed again. 'Okay. I'll come and meet you. Just head for those trees. There are no cameras pointing in that direction, so you should be safe for a little while.'

With several further taps on her keyboard, she then transferred the call to her mobile, threw off her headset and ran out of the bedroom, phone pressed to her ear.

Even though she could still talk to him, she felt helpless, even scared, that she could no longer see what was happening at the school. If Tony was arrested now, Tom and Sam would have to move themselves and the mirror to yet another new hiding place. Yet it was more than that, she realised, as she ran towards the school, exchanging flippant remarks with Tony over the phone. The idea that he might be arrested filled her with more dread than she felt was surely rational, considering she had not known him long.

She covered the mile or so from her house to the school in only a few minutes. Avoiding the front of the school, she skirted round the back, ran through the farmer's field until she finally arrived at the line of tall trees, which ran along the back perimeter of the playing field. After ducking through the low gap in the fence, she whispered urgently into her phone, trying to locate Tony.

A group of black-suited police officers came jogging out of the main school building. They split up and began hurriedly raking their eyes across the tennis courts, the playing field, the trees. On such a cold winter's day, there were no children outside, no leaves on the trees, making it harder to find a place to hide.

At last, Izzy came up behind Tony, who was crouching down behind a tree trunk, peering out across the playing field, phone still to his ear. She cancelled the call, put her mobile away, then held a finger to her lips when Tony's head spun round to see her.

'This way, quick,' she muttered, glancing nervously at one of the police officers who was striding dangerously close to where they were.

As quickly, but as quietly as she could, Izzy led him towards the gap in the fence. Through they climbed out into the field on the other side. After a quick look back to check that they had not been seen, Izzy tugged his sleeve and pointed across the field towards a line of trees in the distance. And away they ran across the grass.

Only when they had reached the far side of the field and the safety of the trees did Izzy stop running. While she got her breath back, she looked back towards the school. There was no sign of any police in the field.

'I think we're okay,' she said, breathing heavily.

'So what now?' asked Tony, whose chest was heaving just as much.

'You, my friend, are now a wanted man. You'll have to go

and live with Tom and Sam in the cottage for the time being. Come on. We'll head there now. It'll take us a while to get there from here.'

As she turned to leave, Tony stopped her gently with a hand on her arm. 'Thanks, Izzy,' he said with a warm smile. 'You just saved my bacon. I owe you big time.'

'You're right, you do! Jewellery's always nice,' she replied with a grin.

He was still smiling at her, that pleasant, strangely innocent smile of his. Feeling herself blush, she quickly turned away. *Oh, no!* she thought. This was not supposed to happen. Falling for Tony would only complicate matters; there was just too much work to be done.

Despite all the doubts flooding through her mind, she found herself grinning stupidly as they walked away in silence.

After spending a quiet and pleasingly uneventful day in Jake's Porthgarrick Senior School, Tom and Jake wandered up the hill in the failing winter light towards *Morladron House*. The mirror in Jake's world was still safely hidden in the old but still largely intact house, and there seemed to be no immediate reason to move it. Using a medallion, the two boys passed through the mirror into Tom's world, where his mirror was tucked away in a shadowy corner of the small kitchen in *Lynn Cottage*.

As they did most days, the two boys had agreed to meet the others in the cottage. Sam and Tony were already there, since they were now both in hiding from the police, whilst Molly and Izzy were expected to turn up later that afternoon.

'Crikey!' said Jake, looking through the window across the

lake, where a keen wind was rippling the surface in the twilight. 'It looks even colder here than it was in my world.'

'You should be used to the cold, mate,' said Tom. 'Coming from the wilds of Scotland.'

'Aye, but I've become soft, living down here for so long. But, hey. Maybe it means we'll get a white Christmas this year for once.'

'What — in Cornwall?' laughed Tom. 'No chance. It never snows in Cornwall. Trust me. Ah, look. Here come the girls.'

Trudging across the grim and grey landscape were two dark figures, wrapped in their coats, hugging themselves against the cold.

'Looks like they're in a bit of a rush,' said Jake, squinting into the twilight.

Sure enough, the two figures hurried towards the cottage and then burst through the front door, where Tom went to meet them. While they unwound their scarves and unbuttoned their coats, Izzy spoke in a hurry. 'Tom, have you heard? Miss Doomsday's going to broadcast some announcement shortly.'

Tom rolled his eyes. 'Well, that should be worth watching,' he said, and then gave Molly a quick embrace, before Izzy dragged him into the lounge by the arm.

She hurriedly opened up her laptop, then switched on the television, while everyone gathered round to watch on either screen.

'Goodness!' she said, looking intently into her laptop. 'This is going to be on the TV, the Internet, even on the billboards across town. Must be something important. She hasn't done this sort of broadcast for a couple of years.'

A message appeared on the television screen, replacing the cookery program that had been on. It read: *There now follows an*

Guardians of the Mirror

important message from Commissioner Doomsday from the Porthgarrick Regional Bureau for Security.

Presently, Miss Doomsday's familiar, grim face appeared on both the television and on the laptop screen. Those piercing, unnerving eyes stared out from behind her thick-rimmed glasses, while her swept-back hair looked as immaculate, as raven-black as ever. With a smart grey jacket, she sat at a desk like a surly newsreader.

'Fellow, law-abiding citizens of Porthgarrick,' she began in a slow, precise manner.

'Ouch!' said Tony. 'Was that a dig at me?'

'Or me,' chuckled Tom.

'Or me!' said Sam, after which they all laughed briefly.

'Ssh!' admonished Izzy.

'I am addressing you today,' continued Miss Doomsday, 'on a matter of the utmost gravity. Whilst I appreciate that the vast majority of you in this town and the surrounding area are decent, upstanding members of the community, who are only interested in the common good of all, there is, as many of you will already be aware, a small number of criminals who live among us. These despicable individuals have only one interest in mind, and that is to trample over those values we hold most dear. They show no regard for the laws that we have put in place for the protection of all. They demonstrate nothing but contempt for our cherished way of life. In short, they seek nothing but revolution by whatever heinous means their deprived minds can conjure up.'

'Ooh!' said Tom. 'She sounds a bit cross to me.'

'She just needs to eat more chocolate,' said Jake. 'It always works for me.'

'Chief among these criminals,' resumed the deputy head,

John D. Fennell

'are Samuel Tranter, his grandson Michael Paget, sometimes known as Tom, and Tony Singh.' As she spoke the names, images of them appeared on the screen. Everyone in *Lynn Cottage* jeered one another and cracked jokes about who was the worst criminal amongst them, while Miss Doomsday's rant continued.

'These three individuals and their associates are working together with the sole aim of trying to bring down our society. They will stop at nothing to achieve their evil goals. They have committed an endless litany of crimes: murder, theft, vandalism, violent crimes against innocent children. They should be considered highly dangerous and should not be approached under any circumstances.

'However, we have decided to offer a sizeable reward to anyone who can help us bring these criminals to justice. We are certain that some of you out there know where these individuals are currently hiding. Perhaps some of you have helped them in the past, in the misguided belief you were aiding freedom fighters. Or perhaps they coerced you into helping them. But be under no illusions: these are extremely vicious criminals. And anyone who is found harbouring these individuals, or offering them support of any kind, will receive an automatic life sentence in one of Cornwall's maximum-security prisons.

'I reiterate: do not approach any of these aforementioned highly dangerous felons. Instead, I urge you to come to Porthgarrick police station with any information you may have regarding their whereabouts. Alternatively, you can email me directly at the below address.

'And remember: together we can catch these lawless thugs and thereby make our community a far safer place to live, work and study. Thank you for your time and attention.'

After displaying the contact details for several more seconds, the screen went black, then returned to the cookery program.

A few mocking comments flew across the room. But Tom stared in silence at the television, without seeing what was on the screen. Her words had left him feeling cross.

'Are you all right, Tom?' asked Molly.

'She said we were murderers,' he replied, feeling the anger rise. 'That we had committed crimes against children.'

'Just words, Tom,' said Tony.

By now, the room had fallen silent, all eyes on Tom. 'Yeah, but some people — many people will believe that stuff.'

'Nothing has changed, Tom,' said his grandfather. 'We're in hiding and we'll probably have to remain in hiding for some while yet.'

'But now she's offering a large reward. And threatening life imprisonment for anyone helping us. That could easily change people's minds. There must be some people who know we're here, or at least will now be tempted to follow Molly and Izzy in the hope of finding us.'

'We're always really careful when we come here,' said Izzy. 'We'll just have to be even more careful from now on.'

'But Izzy, I don't want to get your relatives into trouble. We're really grateful they have let us stay in this house. But I don't know how much longer we can safely remain here.'

'Surely you can just escape through the mirror,' said Jake, 'if ever Miss Doomsday comes knocking on the door.'

'I'm not sure that's safe anymore. We have to assume that she now knows all about the mirror and what it can do. I fear this is really all about her trying to find us so she can get her hands on the mirror.'

For a short while, there was nothing but the ticking of a clock, while everyone digested what Tom had just said.

'I agree with Tom,' said Tony at length. 'Doomsday has upped her game. She's trying to turn the town against us. Trust me, there is currently still a lot of sympathy for what Tom's father and the rest of you were trying to do, but that sympathy could evaporate in a moment if there are rewards and threats of imprisonment. We need to fight back ... somehow.'

'Yes, but how?' asked Tom.

After a brief pause, Izzy said: 'Well, I'm able to hack into the local police operations. So, I reckon I could hack into the billboards around town, maybe even into the local TV network, which is controlled by the police. Maybe we could broadcast our own message to Porthgarrick.'

'If you can do that, why not broadcast to the whole of the country?' suggested Jake.

Izzy smiled. 'One step at a time. I can get into the Porthgarrick police, but gaining access to the countrywide network will take a lot more work.'

Tom sighed loudly. 'So what could we broadcast?'

'If only we could impersonate Miss Doomsday,' said Jake, looking thoughtfully up at the ceiling.

A few seconds later, he and Tom suddenly stared at one another, grins growing on their faces. 'Are you thinking what I'm thinking?' said Jake.

'Mrs Meadow!' said Tom, grinning broadly.

'Oh!' said Jake. 'I was thinking about a giant bar of chocolate.'

Both boys laughed so much that the others stared at them,

thoroughly bemused. Then Molly's face brightened with understanding. 'You're going to ask Mrs Meadow to record a speech as though she were Miss Doomsday. Brilliant!' she said, suddenly clapping her hands like an excited little child.

Tom darted out of the room to fetch a notepad and pen. 'Right,' he said, jumping back onto the sofa. 'Let's think what we could say.'

Jake stood up. 'What about: Hello, my name is Miss Dumbsday!' he said in a pompous-sounding impersonation of the deputy head.

Everyone laughed. Then Tom said: 'My name is Miss Dungsday!'

When Jake had finished laughing, he added, in his exaggerated Miss Doomsday voice: 'I am speaking to you today from on top of my high horse here in ivory towers. And I warn you, I should be approached with extreme caution, as I have exceedingly bad breath.'

Clutching their stomachs, he and Tom fell about laughing, whilst everyone else in the room joined in, as much because of the boys' reaction as because of what they were saying.

'She is going to be so humiliated,' said Tom, his face red and contorted with laughter.

After several more flippant remarks had flown between the two friends, Izzy stepped between them. 'Enough, you two,' she said, smiling. 'I don't want to be a killjoy, and it is funny what you're suggesting. But, if I can make this work, we have a unique opportunity, which we might only get one crack at. It might not be funny, but I think we should focus on making very serious points. Like the fact that Tom's dad and Tony's mother, and so many others are in prison, without having had a trial or any prospect of ever being released. Also, we probably won't have long. Once the police realise what's happening, they will try to shut us down as soon as they can. Sorry to spoil the fun, but that's what I think we should do.'

'Yeah, Izzy's right,' added Molly. 'Sorry, guys.'

Tom smiled ruefully. 'I guess you're right.'

'Shame,' mumbled Jake.

'Right, let's think what to say,' said Tom. 'Then tomorrow we'll go and see Mrs Meadow. I just hope she's happy to play along. Oh, and we'll need some good pictures of Miss Doomsday.'

'You mean, Miss Dumbsdung, don't you?' suggested Jake, which sent him and Tom rolling around with laughter once more.

'How do I look?' asked Mrs Meadow, smiling rather uncertainly.

For a moment or two, both Tom and Jake stood gawping, unable to speak. Covering her normally greying hair, Mrs Meadow, the kindly double of Miss Doomsday in Jake's world, was now wearing a black wig, swept back to form a bun at the back of her head. She had removed much of her make-up and was now wearing a pair of black-framed glasses.

'Stop smiling, Mrs Meadow,' said Tom, glancing between the teacher and a photo of Miss Doomsday on his phone. 'And put on your most serious face. Imagine I've just failed to hand in my homework.'

'Or you've just overheard him tell someone you're a rubbish teacher,' suggested Jake.

Instantly, Mrs Meadow's face hardened — and there, standing before them in Mrs Meadow's small office, stood the spitting image of the terrifying Miss Doomsday.

Guardians of the Mirror

'Oh, my!' mumbled Jake. 'That is scary. I mean, really scary.'

'I will try to look as fierce as I can,' said Mrs Meadow, without smiling.

Tom had already shown her a video on his phone of the recent speech made by Miss Doomsday, so she was now attempting to make her voice adopt the same icy, menacing tone.

'I think we're ready,' said Tom, moving behind the camera. He had set up his mobile phone on a tripod in front of Mrs Meadow, who was sitting behind her desk. They had already made sure that there was no writing in view, which to the viewers back in Tom's world would have appeared back to front.

Tom smiled at the pleasant deputy head, who by now was fully in character and scowling back at him. He then counted down and pressed record.

'Fellow law-abiding citizens of Porthgarrick,' she began. 'I must begin by apologising for the previous broadcast I made a few days ago. It has since come to my attention that the information I gave you was incorrect. Samuel Tranter, Michael Paget and Tony Singh are not in fact criminals at all and are entirely innocent of any wrongdoing that has been levelled at them. All they are guilty of is attempting to secure the release of their loved ones, who, like so many people in this country, have been wrongfully arrested and imprisoned for no other reason than they voiced their objections to the way this current government is abusing our human rights.'

Tom found her performance chilling. It was just like watching and hearing the real Miss Doomsday, even if her apologetic tone sounded so completely alien.

John D. Fennell

'This corrupt and evil government claims to be representing us and to be acting in our best interests, when in fact we all know they will stop at nothing to suppress the knowledge of all their heinous crimes. They believe themselves to be above the law, to be wholly unaccountable for their unlawful actions.

'It is therefore time that we stood up to this despicable behaviour, and made it clear we will no longer allow our loved ones to be imprisoned without trial, to be tortured, to be treated like enemies of the state. No one should have to live in fear just because they want to voice their opinions. Criticising the government and any of its actions should not be an offence in a free and open democratic society. But unfortunately, as we all know, we do not currently live in a free and open democracy.

'Yet it does not have to be this way. If enough of us are willing to stand up in the face of this blatant wrongdoing, the government will have to take note.

'For my part, I can only apologise for all the wrongful arrests and false accusations that I have made over recent years. Many mistakes have been committed, but now is the time for us to begin a new chapter in our history, to return to democracy.

'Thank you once again for your time and attention.'

Tom stopped recording, then turned to look at Jake. They smiled at one another, then high-fived, before the Miss Doomsday lookalike came over, smiling incongruously.

'I can never thank you enough,' Tom said to her.

'Well, I only hope it can do some good in your world,' she said. 'And that I haven't just made things a whole lot worse for you.'

Guardians of the Mirror

Miss Doomsday was writing a report on her laptop when there was a knock at the door. She huffed and ordered the person to come in.

'Ma'am,' said DCI Prideaux, rather nervously. 'I think you need to come and see this.'

'What is it now?'

'You appear to be making a speech across Porthgarrick.'

'What are you talking about?'

DCI Prideaux swallowed hard. 'It's on the television, the local Net and on the billboards across town.'

Miss Doomsday huffed loudly again and called up a window on her laptop. 'You're not making a lot of ...' She froze, and her jaw dropped momentarily. On her laptop, staring back at her, was her own image talking about wrongful imprisonments and the evil government. Her jaw hardened. 'Shut it down,' she muttered.

'We're working on it, ma'am.'

Miss Doomsday sprang to her feet, sending her chair tumbling over behind her. 'I said, shut it down — now!' she roared.

'Yes, ma'am,' said DCI Prideaux, and then scurried out of the room.

With a fearful grimace, the deputy head followed her into the operations room, where her huge face was spread across multiple screens. One or two sniggers could be heard in the background, before a deathly silence descended on the room, broken only by the harsh voice broadcasting from the screens.

'How are they doing this?' demanded Miss Doomsday.

'We're not sure, ma'am,' replied DCI Prideaux. 'It is very sophisticated ...'

'Who exactly are the amateurs here? Is it them ... or us? *We* are supposed to be the ones in control, *not* these criminals.'

'Ah!' said one officer. 'I think I can block it now.'

'Well, do it!' yelled Miss Doomsday.

A few seconds later, the screens went blank just when the speech seemed to be coming to an end. Though it would be hard to prove, she suspected that certain individuals in the room, who were sympathetic to the views that had just been broadcast, had delayed shutting it down on purpose.

'Find out who did this,' demanded the deputy head, pointing at DCI Prideaux. 'If you do not, heads will roll!'

The police officer stiffened. 'I understand how humiliating that—'

'Humiliating?' snapped Miss Doomsday. 'I am not in the least concerned with how humiliating that may or may not have been for me. What really, really concerns me is that these criminals can hack into our systems at will. It has been going on for far too long now. Unless something is done, and done soon, we are all going to be looking for new jobs. Do I make myself clear?'

With that, she turned and stormed out of the room.

She had never felt as angry as she did now. Those responsible for this would pay dearly. She would make sure of that.

Chapter Four

An Unfortunate Accident

Molly had always enjoyed swimming. Indeed, her school swimming instructor had told her on numerous occasions that if she were to put in more practice, she had the potential to represent Cornwall. However, swimming for Molly had always been more about escapism than competition. As much as she loved reading and studying, sometimes it was a relief to just dive into the sea or the school pool and focus her mind on nothing more than propelling herself through the water. The fact that she was better than most was neither here nor there for Molly.

Today was such a day. The moment lunchtime had arrived, she had headed straight for the school pool, keen to empty her cluttered mind for half an hour. As she glided smoothly through the water, with the swimming instructor, the athletic Mrs Nichols, watching on approvingly, she was completely oblivious to the three other children in the pool. Two of them were boys, who seemed intent on racing her at every opportunity. But Molly barely even registered their presence. Today was all about perfecting her front crawl and nothing else.

However, she could not fail to notice when a short but dumpy figure dressed in a frumpy grey suit appeared poolside. The woman's keen eyes seemed to be scrutinising the swimmers as though looking for someone in particular.

As Molly drew near, she slowed her pace a fraction so she could throw a brief glance out of the pool. As she had suspected, it was Miss Doomsday, brows furrowed.

'Can this not wait?' Molly heard the swimming teacher ask, rather irritably. 'She's only got a few more lengths to go.'

Molly reached the end of the pool, flipped over and then sprang off the end wall, propelling herself underwater for several metres. Miss Doomsday could indeed wait, she decided. At least under water, she would not hear that awful, belittling voice echoing through the room.

After a few seconds, she resurfaced and continued swimming away from the deputy head. But when she turned to her left, there was Miss Doomsday striding alongside her, waving her arms about, calling out her name. As Molly was in the lane closest to the edge of the pool, it was hard to ignore her. After a few more strokes, Molly finally glided to a stop and stared up at the teacher, whose face looked even more grotesque than usual when viewed through her swimming goggles.

'I'd like you to come out now, Miss Trump,' ordered Miss Doomsday.

'But I've almost finished, Miss Doomsday,' said Molly quietly, not wishing to sound too difficult. 'Could I please just finish? I'll come straight to see you when I have.'

Miss Doomsday squatted down and glowered at her through those menacing glasses. 'I have asked you to get out, Miss Trump. Kindly comply immediately.' She then reached out a hand and grabbed Molly's upper arm.

The next few moments then seemed to proceed in slow motion.

Molly heard Mrs Nichols call out: 'I don't think there is any need for that.'

At the same time, Molly felt herself get cross at being seized in such an aggressive, not to mention unnecessary, manner. Swiftly, she pulled her arm away, felt Miss Doomsday's grip weaken, then completely release, as the deputy head lost her balance and fell headfirst into the pool. As the short, round figure hit the surface, a great spout of water erupted next to Molly, causing her instinctively to cover her face.

For a second or two, Molly was frozen with fear at what had just occurred, the terrible consequences already racing through her mind.

Miss Doomsday's drenched face exploded out of the water, her glasses gone, and her face contorted with fear. 'Help! Help me!' she screamed, before disappearing once more. Then her arms began thrashing about in a wild panic. 'I can't swim!' she yelled when she briefly resurfaced. 'Help me!'

Molly dived towards her. But by now, the swimming teacher had already jumped in and was wrapping her slender arms around the deputy head. She and Molly then helped to manoeuvre Miss Doomsday towards the steps at the side of the pool. When Miss Doomsday reached the steps, she scrambled up them out of the water with the frenzy of someone who was being pursued by a crocodile. Dripping wet and eyes wide, she hurried out of the room, but not before she had bellowed: 'Make sure the Trump girl is in my office in ten minutes.'

Mrs Nichols looked at Molly, shrugged and then gave her a brief knowing smile. 'I'm sorry if you get into trouble, Molly,' she whispered. 'But that has just made my day.'

'If this is about what just happened,' said Molly, as she entered Miss Doomsday's office, 'it was hardly my fault you fell in.' She fully expected a severe dressing-down but refused to just sit there and take it.

The deputy head was sitting behind her desk with a towel curled up on her head. Slowly, she put her glasses back on her nose. But to Molly's surprise, the teacher simply held up a hand to silence her, then gave her a frown that almost bordered on a faint smile.

'Don't worry, Miss Trump,' she said, indicating with a hand that she expected Molly to sit down opposite her, across her desk. 'This has nothing to do with that. I am willing to overlook what just occurred in the pool, if you will help me with a little problem I have.'

After an initial, brief feeling of relief, Molly suddenly felt nervous again.

'I just need you to tell me where Michael Paget is? Or is it Tom these days? I never know what he calls himself.'

Not again, Molly thought. How many times had the deputy head summoned her to her office in the past few months, asking this same question. She swallowed hard but tried not to show her anxiety. 'I've told you before — how should I know where he is?'

Miss Doomsday's eyes narrowed as she studied Molly with that horrible, intimidating stare.

'Look!' said Molly, trying to sound calm, even though her heart was pounding faster by the second. 'He used to pick on me, to bully me. Ask anyone in the school who knows me. Even some of the teachers will tell you. So why on earth should I know or even care where he is? To be honest, I shan't shed a tear if I never see him again.'

A thoroughly unnerving half-smile played at the corners of Miss Doomsday's mouth. 'Let's not play games, shall we, Miss Trump?' she said, linking her fingers together and leaning forward. 'Harry Singh has told me he killed the real Michael Paget when Michael tried to steal the Iris box from him. So, as we are both trying to be honest here, I will confess that I know it's Tom I'm really after, not Michael. And I'm guessing that Tom keeps evading me by disappearing through the mirror to the other world.' She then stared smugly across the table, eagerly anticipating Molly's response.

Molly felt herself go ice-cold. How on earth could Miss Doomsday know all that? And now that she did, what terrible consequences lay in store for her and the others?

'I have no idea what you are talking about,' she mumbled. Her throat was so dry she could hardly speak.

'Come now, Miss Trump. Don't be coy. I could make your life a misery, as well you know. Tell me where he is, and you have my word I will make sure you are kept out of all this.'

'I'm sorry,' replied Molly, trying to make herself feel angry to suppress the fear she felt. 'I have no idea where Michael or this Tom is. I really don't know what you are talking about.'

Miss Doomsday grimaced and sat back. 'You have been seen with Tom on several occasions over the last few months. Some are even saying you two are an item, as you youngsters call it. How sweet! Now, for the last time, tell me where he is.'

Molly really was beginning to feel angry now. Did the deputy head truly think she would betray her friends and loved ones, and Tom of all people? 'If your little spies have seen me with anyone, they are badly mistaken,' she snarled.

For a few moments, Miss Doomsday continued to eye her coldly without words or movement, while Molly's heart was pounding uncomfortably. At length, the teacher said: 'Very well, Miss Trump. I will begin by giving you detention. Let's see if that changes your stubborn mind. If not, we can always move onto more severe punishments.'

'Why are you giving me detention?' asked Molly defiantly.

Miss Doomsday shrugged. 'Assaulting a teacher, I suppose. I don't really know yet. I'll think of something.' She then began typing into her laptop. 'Just make sure you turn up after school today. You don't want to make matters worse, now do you?'

While the light began to fade around the isolated *Lynn Cottage*, those inside sat in front of the log fire, which was just beginning to take hold. As long as they waited until after dark before lighting a fire, Izzy had told them, the smoke from the chimney was very unlikely to attract attention. Besides, all those hidden security cameras she had installed in the surrounding countryside would give them ample warning of any unwanted visitors.

Tom, Jake, Sam and Tony were sharing a joke at Miss Doomsday's expense, wishing they could have seen her face when her second speech had been broadcast across Porthgarrick. Yet, as heartily as Tom laughed, he also felt nervous. Now that Tony had had to flee into hiding, the police's attention would surely turn more than ever to Molly and Izzy. Whilst he, Jake, Sam and Tony could easily disappear through the mirror into Jake's world and, in the worst case, stay there indefinitely, Molly and Izzy could not. Since they both had a double in that other world, their presence there would sooner or later trigger a terrible storm, which would ultimately put them in mortal danger.

Presently, Izzy entered the cottage, barely recognisable under her layers of thick clothing. As she unwound her scarf and removed her winter coat, Tom asked: 'Where's Molly?'

Guardians of the Mirror

'Nice to see you, too, darling cousin,' she replied, shaking loose her long ponytail. 'We had to split up because we were being followed. And we're late because Molly had detention.'

'What?' said Tom.

'Molly has detention?' asked Jake. 'That must be a mistake, surely.'

'Well, yes, kind of,' said Izzy, moving into the room and flopping onto the sofa next to Tom. A wry smile then spread across her face as she related the story of how Molly had inadvertently tipped the deputy head into the school pool. 'I wish I had been there,' she added. 'I'd have paid good money to see that. Two humiliations in one week. Doomsday must be absolutely seething.' She then studied the small images on the laptop on the coffee table. 'Molly's on her way, but she's still being followed, so she's having to take the long way here.'

Tom stood up. 'I'll go and help her.'

'Sit down, Thomas,' said Izzy, pulling on Tom's arm till he lost balance and slumped back onto the sofa. 'She's better on her own. She knows what to do. If someone else turns up — like you — those tailing her will find it much easier to track her. Just trust her, Tom.'

Anxiously, Tom waited for several more minutes, finding it hard to join in the conversation while he fretted. At last, Molly came through the door, her mouth and nose hidden behind a scarf, but her unmistakable glasses and strands of black hair still visible under the hood.

When her face finally emerged, she broke into a smile as Tom embraced her. 'Phew!' she said. 'That was close. It's getting harder to shake them off now, you know.'

'So come on,' said Jake excitedly, 'tell us about how you tried to drown Miss Doomsday.'

'I wish I could have seen that,' said Tom.

Molly grinned. 'Oh, it was good. Well worth getting detention for.' But then her smile faded quickly. 'That evil woman is going to use this as an excuse to hound me.' She then told them about her unpleasant visit to the deputy head's office. 'She knows everything. All about the mirror, the Iris box. Harry Singh and those books she has, have told her everything.'

After a brief, awkward silence, during which everyone pondered the consequences of Miss Doomsday knowing about the mirror, Izzy spoke up. 'She's rattled, that's all. All that anyone is talking about at the moment — in school and in town — is that second broadcast we did. Some people think it really was her, that she has had a sudden change of heart. A lot of others know it was a spoof, but either way, it seems to have given people hope that some sort of positive change is on its way. And that must be driving Doomsday absolutely mad.'

'Well,' said Jake. 'Maybe this is the beginning of her end.'

After a brief exchange of jokes and laughter, Molly cut in. 'I'm really worried.' The room fell silent. Tom held her hand and found it was shaking. He was about to comfort her when she spoke again. 'I really don't think some of you realise just what Doomsday is like. Over the last few years, she has arrested countless people, made others just disappear to who knows where. She will stop at nothing to get what she wants. We have to be so careful from now on.'

Every time that Tom heard mention of people being arrested it was like a stab to the heart. And with Molly beside him, clearly shaken, he could feel his anger rising once more.

'Tony,' he said. 'Isn't it about time we used your powers to help us?'

Guardians of the Mirror

Tony smiled weakly. 'I've told you before. I would need someone here, some other double in order to use my powers.'

'Or you could take off that pendant.'

Tony looked a little uncomfortable and slowly shook his head. 'No, I can't do that.'

'But if you did,' persisted Tom, his voice rising, 'with Harry here in this world, there'd be a storm in no time at all. You could then control that. Unleash all sorts, couldn't you? Break out all the prisoners. No one could stop you.'

'As I've said many times before, I will not use my powers to break out my mother, your father or anyone else for that matter. The Guardians have a strict code that says we cannot use these powers for our own use. For one thing, the temptation to abuse that power is just too great.'

Tom could feel his hackles rising at Tony's stubborn refusal to help. 'So, you're happy to let your mum and my dad just rot in prison, are you?'

'Tom!' said Molly, turning sharply to look at him.

'Of course not,' continued Tony. 'But violence is not the way. It never is. We bring down this corrupt government by peaceful means, and then all of our loved ones can walk free.'

Tom rose to his feet. 'And just how do we do that, eh? We need you and your powers to help speed things up. Otherwise it could take years.'

Tony stared back at him, then averted his gaze. 'Sorry, Tom. It's not going to happen.'

Tony's calmness was beginning to infuriate Tom. He wanted to shake him. What was the matter with him? Did he just not care? 'Sorry?' he snapped. 'How is sorry going to get my dad out of prison?'

Izzy stood up and took a step towards Tom. 'That's enough,

John D. Fennell

Tom,' she said firmly but calmly. 'You know Tony is right.'

He looked around the room as everyone stared at him in silence. 'You all think like that, do you? Am I the only one here who thinks we have a guy in our midst who is basically a superhero, but who is too scared to use his powers to help us?'

'Tom, just calm down and sit down,' his grandfather said.

'Oh, for goodness' sake!' muttered Tom, and then stormed out of the room.

By now, he was breathing hard, his pulse racing. Over the last few months, he had found himself getting angry more and more frequently. The slightest things seemed to set him off. Even knowing that it was probably just those infamous teenage hormones raging through his body was no comfort at all. The feeling that, at times, he was no longer in control of his emotions was at times terrifying.

He strode into the kitchen, yanked open the side door and stepped outside. Even though he was only wearing his jeans and a thin top, he did not notice the cold wind blowing through the darkness. He could just about make out the large black surface of the lake, some twenty paces away, rippling gently in the wind. He turned to his right, and in the distance, he could see the tall black finger of a chimney, silhouetted against the last remnants of colour in the sky over the sea. The long disused tin mine suddenly felt like an ideal place to go and brood, while his bubbling fury simmered down.

He was about to walk towards the crumbling brick building when Molly burst out of the kitchen door and walked over to him. For a brief second, he resented the idea that she was about to chastise him for the way he had spoken to Tony. But instead, she put a gentle hand on his arm.

'You all right?' she asked quietly.

Guardians of the Mirror

Tom looked at her and sighed. 'Yeah,' he mumbled.

'Look, Tom,' she continued. 'I can see Tony's point of view.'

Tom rolled his eyes. 'Just me then, is it?'

'I would much rather we had a pacifist like Tony, than a monster like Harry. If Tony was willing to just fly off and start killing police and soldiers in our name that would really scare me. That's not what we want, surely.'

Tom looked over at the tall and slender chimney once more. 'I guess so.'

'We all want to get rid of this government. But not like that.'

'That's easy for you to say,' snapped Tom. 'It's not your dad in prison.'

Molly said nothing, but simply stared back at him through her small glasses. She then reached out and held both his hands in hers, till he turned to face her. 'Tom,' she said. 'I know this is hard. I can't imagine how I would feel if my dad were in jail and I had never known my mother. But please, let's not turn on one another. We're in this together.'

'I'm sorry, Molly,' he said. 'It's just ... I can't see how I'm ever going to see my dad again. I just feel so powerless.'

'You will, Tom. We won't stop until we get them all out.'

As he stared at her face, which even in the gloom was as pretty as ever, he could feel his anger melting away. 'What would I ever do without you, eh?' he smiled.

'Come on. Let's go back inside. I'm getting cold.'

When they walked back into the lounge, the place felt wonderfully warm and comforting after the bitter cold outside. The log fire was now raging brightly, casting dancing shadows all around the room.

Tom walked over to Tony, who was sitting next to Izzy.

John D. Fennell

They both looked up at him suspiciously. 'Tony. I'm sorry, mate. I was out of order.'

Tony broke into a smile. 'It's okay, Tom. I understand. In fact, I understand exactly how you feel. When my mother was arrested, I went berserk, ransacked my bedroom. I pored over mum's books, looking for a way to free her and exact my revenge on those who had arrested her. It was dad who calmed me down in the end. He said simply: "Is this what you mother would want?" Of course, he was right as he usually is. Mum would never want me to do anything stupid, like go on the rampage on her account.'

'Yeah, I know,' said Tom.

'Look, Tom,' continued Tony. 'What I have been doing recently is studying mum's books again. There is mention of travellers who came to this world many, many years ago. They appeared not through the mirror but using some sort of portable mirror they carried with them.'

'Bah!' said Sam suddenly. 'That's nothing but a myth, a silly story. I've never seen anything like that, and nor had my father.'

'Maybe,' conceded Tony. 'But even so, I thought I might try visiting the other worlds to see if I could find such a mirror. We could appear in prison, then out again without anyone knowing. And I've always wanted to visit some of the other worlds, but never thought I would get the chance. But I guess, as I can't go to school for the time being, I've now got the opportunity to go exploring.'

For several seconds, there was silence in the room. Only the crackling of the roaring fire could be heard.

Finally, Tom spoke. 'Sorry, Tony. Did you just say — other worlds?'

Chapter Five

A Million Stars

Sam let out a rather dismissive laugh. 'Other worlds?' he said. 'That's also a myth. That one's been around for years. There are no other worlds, just these two.'

Tony was looking bemused, clearly surprised at Sam's reaction. 'Er, surely you know about the multiple worlds, Sam.'

'Okay, then,' said Sam, spreading his arms wide. 'Where are these other worlds? How do you get to them? There is no evidence they exist at all. It's just a theory.'

Tony looked around at all the pairs of eyes gaping at him expectantly. 'I'll show you if I can. I've only read about this, but we might as well give it a go.'

'Oh, goody,' said Izzy. 'Do I finally get to go through the famous mirror? About time. Can't have you lot having all the fun.'

As they all headed towards the kitchen, Jake tapped Tom on the arm and whispered: 'Have you any idea what on earth he's on about?'

'I haven't got a clue,' replied Tom. 'But I can't wait to find out.'

After a short delay, Tony came into the kitchen holding his golden Iris box. He stood opposite the mirror, opened the box to release the Iris, which shot almost immediately into the face of the mirror, turning the glass into a rippling rectangle of what looked like water. Then all six of them stepped into the void one after the other.

John D. Fennell

Walking in single file, they strolled slowly along the shimmering multi-coloured path that stretched between the two mirrors. Both Jake, who had only ever travelled between the two worlds by using a medallion, which by-passed the void altogether, and Izzy were staring in awe, open-mouthed at the scene around them. Even Tony, who had also never been in the void before, seemed dumbstruck by what he was seeing. Dozens of Irises the size of silk handkerchiefs floated about in slow motion, drifting aimlessly and casting their spectrum of bright colours on the visitors' faces. The mini rainbows swam around in front of a backdrop of a million stars, twinkling in a black sky.

Tom, who had seen it all many times before, moved up close behind Tony. 'So, Tony,' he said, jolting the tall, slender boy from his trance. 'There's this rainbow path between the two mirrors, hundreds of Irises and millions of stars. And nothing else. What else am I supposed to be looking at?'

Still partially distracted, Tony moved only slowly, but then stared quizzically at Tom. 'Those are not stars, Tom,' he said smiling. 'We're not in space.'

Tom frowned. 'Then what are they?'

'Those are the portals to other worlds. If you stood far enough away from us, near one of those other portals, and looked back at our two here, they, too, would shine like stars in a night sky.'

Tom gazed around him, past the slowly twisting Irises, and looked at the distant stars. 'But there are thousands of them — millions even.'

'I know,' replied Tony. 'Amazing, isn't it?'

By this time, Molly, who had also been in the void with Tom twice before, had come up behind the two boys. 'But they

Guardians of the Mirror

seem so far away,' she said. 'How do you reach them?'

'Well, from what I remember, it's all to do with the Irises. They are the source of the energy needed to make all this work. And as you know, if you take one out of the void, it will always try to find a way back in. But they are also the pathways between portals, waiting to be activated, just like the one we are standing on. The moment our portal is opened, an Iris is transformed into a path between our world and Jake's.'

Tom looked down at his feet. Now that he thought about it, the pathway between the two mirrors was indeed just like an enormous, elongated Iris.

'But how does this all work?' continued Molly. 'I mean, our two worlds are the mirror image of one another. How can you have more mirror images?'

'They exist in pairs,' replied Tony. 'They balance one another out, apparently.'

By now, the others had all grouped close to Tony, hanging on his every word.

'But how do you actually get to these other worlds?' asked Tom. 'There's only one path.'

Tony reached into a pocket and fished out a small cube, which he placed carefully onto one open palm. 'Well, clearly I've never actually done this before. But apparently, I need this thing.' He studied the cube carefully. It was only about five centimetres high, made of gold and had a different simple shape traced into each of the six sides: a circle on one, a triangle on another, a pentagon on top and so on.

'What on earth is that?' asked Jake.

'You'll see,' grinned Tony. 'I've always wanted to try this thing out. The book warns you to never activate this little cube outside the void under any circumstances. It doesn't say what would happen, just never to do it. So, the child in me has been itching to see what it does.'

Tony turned it over until the circle was on top, held it up close to a passing Iris and then pressed the top of the cube with a finger.

At first, nothing happened while everyone held their breath in anticipation. Then the shapes on the sides of the cube began to glow, before the object vanished behind a silent explosion of dazzling light. All the colours of the rainbow erupted out of the cube in a display that was so bright it could only be viewed through half-closed eyes.

All the Irises were struck one by one in quick succession by blinding shafts of light until, in no time at all, a vast web of rainbow paths was bursting into life all around them. Everywhere they looked, paths snaked off into the distance, linking all the stars around them.

When the cube had finally stopped projecting its arrows of light, all the Irises had been transformed into a shimmering, impossibly vast network of pathways.

'Wow!' said Tony. 'I'm not sure the description in the book I read did that justice. That is amazing.'

'Incredible,' said Tom. 'But how do you know which path to take?'

'You don't. As far as I'm aware, they have never been mapped. All I know is the nearest paths will take us to a pair of worlds that are similar to our own. But the further away from your own world you travel, the greater the differences will be. So these ones here,' he added, pointing at a pair of stars, which, now that they had paths leading to them, actually seemed to be quite close, 'will be fairly similar to our own worlds. While those that are miles away will be almost nothing at all like ours.'

Tom marvelled at the sight. Some of the criss-crossing paths did seem to lead to portals that were not that far away, while others seemed to snake away for miles and miles. And now that he looked, really looked closely, he realised that all the stars were indeed arranged in pairs. How had he not noticed that before? Maybe because, without the network of paths, it just looked like a clear night sky.

'This is all very lovely,' said Jake. 'But how exactly can we use this to help us?'

'Well,' began Tony. 'I'll come back another day and then head off to some of these other worlds to see if I can locate one of these portable mirrors I mentioned. Or maybe there's something else out there we could use.'

'But that could take you years,' said Izzy.

'Yeah, maybe. But it's got to be worth it. Even if I only try for a short while. Now that I'm in hiding, I've got nothing else to do.'

'Maybe some of us should come with you,' suggested Sam.

Tony thought for a moment, then said: 'No, I think I should go alone. I've only got one pendant to protect me, so we have no idea what problems we might cause if we travel around, popping in and out of other worlds.'

'How would we get hold of you if we needed you?' asked Tom.

'Why would you need to get hold of me?'

'Oh, I don't know,' scoffed Molly, 'because of a certain Miss Doomsday, perhaps?'

Tony laughed. 'We don't need to worry too much about her. Granted, she has an Iris box but no Iris. And she may have a medallion but no mirror. She can't do too much damage at the moment.'

'Maybe so,' said Tom. 'But she has the two books and therefore all the info you have.'

Tony shook his head. 'No. Augustus Doomsday only translated those parts of the Book of Mysteries that concern the wristbands and controlling the weather. He wasn't interested in anything else. Whereas my family has been studying the book for generations. We know way more than is written in Doomsday's translation. None of this stuff, for example,' he added, waving a hand about, 'will be in there.'

'I hope you're right,' said Tom.

'Well, I think it's time we went back,' said Izzy. 'I love rainbows as much as the next girl, but now I've seen enough to last a lifetime.'

'How long will these paths stay in place?' asked Tom, as they began wandering back towards the rear of their mirror.

'As soon as we exit the void they should disappear,' replied Tony. 'Apparently, they're only in place when a portal is in use.'

'So, is using an Iris the only way to get into this place?' asked Jake.

'Yes. As far as I know.'

'Or if you and your double touch mirrors at the same time,' said Tom. 'That also works.'

'Well, yes,' conceded Tony. 'But the chances of doing that are very remote.'

'Michael and I managed it. Several times.'

'Yeah, I know. But I think you were just lucky,' said Tony, as he stood opposite the back of the mirror.

'And getting out again,' continued Jake. 'You must have an Iris, I presume?'

Guardians of the Mirror

'An Iris or a medallion,' replied Tony. 'You can just place a medallion right against the back of the mirror and hey presto, the portal opens,' he added, getting a medallion ready to show him.

'Wow!' said Jake. 'That's interesting. Although I can't see we'll ever need to exit that way. Good to know, though, I guess.'

Miss Doomsday was spending more and more time in her office in the Porthgarrick Police Station. Her determination to gain access to the mirror and thereby obtain an Iris was becoming all consuming, leaving her work at school to feel increasingly like an irrelevance.

As she sat back in her chair, contemplating how to coax information out of Molly Trump, she heard the approach of several vehicles outside. She looked out of the window just in time to see four police cars pull into the car park at the front of the police station. They arrived in single file escorting a fifth, much larger car in the middle, which was black, sleek and looked expensive.

The electric cars purred to a graceful halt. Immediately, all the car doors sprang open and armed police officers emerged, casting their heads left and right. A few seconds later, the doors to the black car opened, and out stepped a slim man of average height in a smart suit.

Miss Doomsday's eyes widened, and she found herself momentarily holding her breath. With the man's round glasses and neatly-trimmed red hair, she knew at once who it was.

After quickly checking her own hair in a small mirror she kept in her desk, she took a couple of deep breaths and sat upright in her chair, waiting. When the anticipated knock on the door came, it still managed to startle her.

DCI Prideaux opened the door. 'There is someone to see you, ma'am,' she said, and Miss Doomsday thought she detected a faint smirk on the police officer's face.

Without waiting to be invited in, the suited figure walked into the room.

Immediately, Miss Doomsday stood up. 'Prime Minister,' she said, trying to make her voice sound measured and in control. 'A pleasant surprise. Please, do come in.'

The Prime Minister waved a hand behind him dismissively. 'Leave us,' he ordered his bodyguard, who then closed the door behind him, leaving just Miss Doomsday and Christopher Sheeran in the room. Without being invited to sit down, he then lowered himself into the chair opposite the deputy head, eyeing her suspiciously whilst his mouth had a suggestion of a cold smile.

'Good morning, Commissioner Doomsday,' he said at last. 'Although I understand you prefer the title Miss. I would have thought someone like you would be a Ms Doomsday.'

'I cannot abide that term,' replied Miss Doomsday. 'I have always been a teacher, so the term Miss seems much more appropriate. If you don't mind.'

'Perfect! Perfect ... Miss Doomsday.' The Prime Minister sat back and crossed his fingers on his stomach. 'The problem is, you're not really a teacher these days, are you? You work for me, helping to keep this part of beautiful Cornwall and its beautiful people in order. Something you have been exceptionally good at in recent years. In fact, I would go as far as to say you have been one of my best commissioners in the whole country.'

'Thank you, Prime Minister.'

'Until now, that is.' His eyes narrowed whilst the faint smirk remained. 'Just what on earth has been going on in this normally peaceful part of the world?'

Miss Doomsday opened her mouth to speak, but the Prime Minister held up a finger, much as a teacher might to stop a small child from interrupting.

'All these destructive storms in recent months,' he continued. 'Then in October, you had to call out the army for reasons I'm still not sure I quite understand. But then of course, we come to the elephant in the room, don't we? Which has absolutely nothing to do with the shape of you, I assure you.'

He chuckled to himself whilst Miss Doomsday clenched her jaw, fighting to contain her temper.

'The two broadcasts you made a few days ago—'

'I only made one of those,' insisted Miss Doomsday.

'Well, I've now seen both, and they certainly look and sound like you.'

'The second one was done by a group of local dissidents ...'

'So, you're telling me that these dissidents are able to hack into and access your local network, to access what is supposed to be a secure police network? Is that what you're telling me? Because if it is, that is very disturbing indeed.'

Any trace of humour in his face had now completely gone. He sat staring at her coldly across the table.

'I must admit,' she began, 'the local IT specialists around here are not up to the job. These criminals have a very, very clever person in their midst. As it happens, I was in the middle of drafting a letter to your Minister for Inland Security, requesting assistance to combat this pernicious threat.'

'But you should have called for assistance sooner.'

John D. Fennell

The Prime Minister continued to scrutinise her through his small, round glasses. With lips pursed and a furrowed brow below his fiery-red hair, he looked ready to explode at any moment. The rumours about his short and hot temper were rife. It was then she realised she had no option but to tell him everything. If she did not, she was likely to lose her job. Or maybe there was even a chance she would simply be thrown into prison like so many others who had crossed him.

She returned his stare, refusing to show any sign of weakness. 'I need to tell you something in the strictest confidence,' she continued.

'Perfect!'

She took a deep breath and began. 'There are some sort of magical, supernatural forces at work around here, which I fully realise sounds completely preposterous.' It was now her turn to look a little smug, for she knew she had ample proof, should he request it. She paused while the Prime Minister's eyes widened in surprise. He was clearly taken aback by her statement.

'Of all the excuses I thought you might come out with today,' he said, 'I can honestly say I did not expect that.'

'Before you dismiss me as a lunatic, let me show you something.' Miss Doomsday typed into her laptop, brought up a video recording and turned the laptop around to face the Prime Minister. She then pressed play and watched his confused face as his eyes flitted from the screen to her face and back again.

The footage, whilst taken at night, clearly showed Harry and Tony Singh battling it out in Trethek cove. Explosions of lightning erupted at regular intervals, whilst giant hailstones and even a fire tornado could be seen.

Guardians of the Mirror

'What is this?' demanded Christopher Sheeran. 'The trailer for some ridiculous Hollywood blockbuster?'

'No, Prime Minister,' replied Miss Doomsday calmly. 'This was filmed back in October when, as you say, I had to call out the army. There was a whole company of soldiers with me at the time. One hundred men and women or thereabouts, all witnesses to what occurred. Interview them if you like.'

The Prime Minister continued to watch, his face even more shocked than before, now that he began to realise that what he was watching appeared to be real. After the fighting had reached a blinding crescendo of lightning bolts, the beach went dark and nothing much appeared to happen for several minutes. He threw Miss Doomsday a quizzical look; she in turn urged him to keep watching. Then, on the laptop, he heard the teacher issue an order, and suddenly, bright lights lit up the whole beach. In the middle of the sand, glistening in the headlights, stood a tall, bizarre-looking structure made of jagged, interlocking arms of glass.

Dozens of soldiers poured down onto the beach towards the large sculpture and two nearby figures. In the blink of an eye, more lightning rained down in front of the soldiers creating a barrier between them and the two people.

Miss Doomsday stopped the recording. 'That's it,' she said, sitting back. 'That strange-looking cage on the beach contained one Harry Singh who is now in custody. The other one, who defeated Harry, is called Tony Singh. We have only just identified him and are still trying to locate him.'

'What on earth is this all about?' demanded the Prime Minister, his face contorted with confusion.

'It all comes back to *Morladron House* ...'

'Ah, yes, the castle on the hill?'

John D. Fennell

'Well, more of a house, really, but yes. A mirror was found there some while ago. A mirror, which is actually a portal to another dimension, another world, very similar to our own. With the right items,' she continued, whilst taking out her golden Iris box from a drawer and placing it on the desk between them, 'it is possible to travel back and forth through the mirror between these two worlds. The only drawback is that if I, for example, travelled to the other world and stayed there for more than a few hours, I would cause a terrible storm, much like the one that destroyed parts of Porthgarrick last summer. This would be caused by the presence of both me and my counterpart existing together in the same world.'

With his eyes not blinking and his jaw slack, the Prime Minister sat staring at her, as though she were speaking an incomprehensible foreign language. 'You have surely gone mad. Am I really supposed to believe any of this nonsense?'

Undaunted, Miss Doomsday ignored the question and continued. 'Now, back in October, Harry Singh learned to control, to manipulate the elements of these storms, using them as his own superpowers, if you like. In so doing, he brought down a police helicopter and killed a number of police officers, as I have no doubt you have already read about. Some of this was caught on police cameras and CCTV, if you would like to view the footage sometime.'

She stared at him, eyebrows raised, feeling very pleased with herself. Now that he was the one looking shocked and uncomfortable, and knowing that she had all the proof in the world to back up her account, she was enjoying herself immensely.

'But just when it looked like Harry was unstoppable,' she continued, 'along came his double, Tony Singh, and defeated him, using the same ability to control the storm.'

The Prime Minister's mouth moved several times, but nothing came out, until finally, he asked: 'How exactly do they control the weather?'

'By using these,' replied Miss Doomsday, and proceeded to remove the wristbands from the lid of the golden box. 'However, I would also need what is called an Iris to be in this box, and for that, I need the actual mirror I mentioned.'

'Which is where?'

'Well, this is where we come back to our friends, the group of criminals here in Porthgarrick. Tony is one of them, hiding with, we presume, a boy called Tom Paget, who came here in the summer from the other world. They have the mirror hidden away somewhere. I have spent the last few months trying to track it down.'

'Ye gods!' muttered the Prime Minister, and sat back in his chair, staring into space.

'Imagine,' continued Miss Doomsday, leaning forward, 'what we could achieve if we could harness this power. The means to eradicate all criminality, not to mention a way to protect this country from outside threats.'

The Prime Minister frowned. 'So, it seems to me you need to locate this mirror. I presume you have a plan.'

'I'm beginning to piece one together, yes. I think I have identified the fifteen-year-old girlfriend of this Tom Paget. If I threaten to kill her, I'm sure he will soon co-operate.'

The Prime Minister broke into a supercilious smile. 'Now just a minute, Miss Doomsday. You're right, it sounds like we do need these powers but not at any price. I cannot be seen to be threatening to murder our own citizens. That would make us no better than the criminals we are chasing. And for one thing, what if this Tom Paget calls your bluff? We can't have the news leaking that we tried to kill a potentially innocent fifteen-year-old girl. It would only take one policeman with misguided principles to leak that little story, perhaps with some accompanying photos. Our society is in a delicate balance at the moment. We don't want to tip it into open revolt.'

Miss Doomsday sighed. 'It will be very difficult to find this mirror without resorting to some unsavoury tactics.'

Prime Minister Sheeran drummed his fingertips together. 'Look: off the record, do whatever it takes to get that mirror. But I suggest you avoid threatening to kill someone; that will not end well. And if something does go wrong, I will have to deny any knowledge of all this, and you will be left alone to suffer the consequences. Do you understand?'

'Of course, Prime Minister.'

'Perfect!' he said, and then stood up. 'Make this a priority. I need to return to London, but I will send some specialists down to help you out with your little IT issues. Report back to me once you have any news. Goodbye, Miss Doomsday.'

Once he had left the room, Miss Doomsday smiled to herself. A fresh plan was already beginning to form in her mind.

Chapter Six

The Plan Unfolds

A figure appeared on one of Izzy's security cameras, triggering an alarm. The beep was quiet enough not to alert the whole house, but loud enough that she stopped what she was doing to investigate. Moving from one laptop to another, she checked out the screen, but relaxed when she saw that it was Molly approaching the house. She tapped a combination of buttons, which then caused Molly's mobile to start ringing.

'Come straight up, sweetie,' she said, speaking into a microphone.

A few seconds later, Molly entered Izzy's cluttered bedroom. Aside from one or two posters of celebrities on the walls, it was not a typical teenager's room. There was a single bed and wardrobe against one wall, but then the rest of the room seemed to be completely filled with electronic equipment, all apparently interconnected by a whole spider's web of cables. Under the window, which looked down onto the street, was a long desk covered with multiple screens and flashing boxes. The first time Molly had visited her in her bedroom, she had stood looking around in awe and had demanded to know how on earth Izzy knew what all the equipment did.

'I was just passing,' said Molly. 'Just thought I'd see what you're up to.'

'Well, Molls, you've come at just the right time. I think I've made a major breakthrough.' Izzy hurried back over to her desk and began typing away on a keyboard. 'I'm pretty sure I've found a way to access the national network through the local police network. If I can get into that, it opens up the whole Internet. We can then broadcast anything we want to anywhere in the country.'

Molly moved up behind her to peer over her shoulder. For several more minutes, Izzy was so focused she typed in silence, her keyboard rippling at great speed. Then her heart leapt. She sat back, glanced up at Molly behind her, before staring intently at the screen in front of her.

'I think I've done it, Molly,' she gasped. 'I think I'm in.'

After so many months of trying, of so much frustration and so many failed attempts, the sudden feeling of success, of elation was almost overwhelming.

'Now all I need to do ...'

Then her heart sank, her blood ran cold, her breathing seemed to stop.

'No!' she yelled. 'No, no, NO!' She pounced on her keyboard and began frantically stabbing her fingers onto the keys.

'What is it?' asked Molly. 'What's the matter?'

But Izzy could not respond while she typed furiously, her breathing shallow. She felt sick.

'Molly. Quick — phone Tom. Tell him to turn his phone off. Then turn yours off, too.'

'Why? What—'

'Just do it! For goodness' sake, Molly, do it now!' While Molly called Tom, Izzy continued typing. But it was no use. 'Oh no! Oh no! What have I done?'

'Just turn your phone off, Tom,' Molly was saying behind her. 'Because Izzy says you need to!'

Guardians of the Mirror

Izzy dived under her bed and pulled out a bag and began cramming all sorts into it: clothes, a laptop, a book. 'Molly, I've been so stupid,' she said, looking up at her perplexed friend. 'They set me a trap. Once I got into the police network it downloaded a virus onto my computer. It's got into the app that I use to track all your phones, the one that tells me where you all are. And now they'll be coming here any minute to arrest me. We've got to go.'

'Will they be able track down where Tom is?' asked Molly, as she followed Izzy out of the room.

'I don't know,' muttered Izzy. She was fighting back the tears. 'I tried to delay their progress as much as I could, but they're all over my data now. Oh, I've been so stupid, so arrogant to think they would never catch me out. They dangled me a carrot and knew I wouldn't be able to resist biting into it.'

As they rushed down the stairs, Molly said: 'What about the others?'

'Sam'll be fine. As you know, old people never keep their phones turned on anyway, unless they actually need to use them. And ... oh, no. Tony!' The realisation was like a punch in the stomach, forcing the air from her lungs. She whipped out her phone and tried calling Tony. But the call just rang and rang, before diverting to voicemail. 'He's not answering,' she said, almost in tears.

Knowing he was now wanted by the police, Tony knew he had to be extra vigilant. The middle of December it might have been, but covering his nose and mouth with a scarf whilst riding his bicycle was not necessary to keep his face warm, but was necessary to conceal his identity. He knew it was risky

John D. Fennell

cycling along the quiet country lanes in broad daylight, but he needed the exercise, the fresh air. And besides, staying for hours on end in the stuffy old *Lynn Cottage*, he decided, would be little better than being in prison.

When he breasted a hill, he pulled over to the side of the road and admired the view. A fiery, orange sun was close to disappearing below the horizon, casting vast black shadows across the landscape. Thousands of diamond-like sparkles glistened on the sea to his right, but much of the land was now fading into dusk.

The road ahead snaked down into a dark valley, such that the rare car headlights that appeared shone brightly.

And so too did the flashing blue and red lights of a police car.

It appeared over the top of the far hill, coming out of the setting sun, before plunging down into the valley before him, its lights dazzling in the gloom and its siren wailing. Shortly afterwards, another one appeared behind it.

Whilst Tony had no reason to believe that they were after him, he decided it was time to move. He turned his bike around and was about to race back down the hill when he noticed another pair of police cars appear in the distance on the opposite side of the valley. Now he really was beginning to feel concerned. Even if they were not after him in particular, there was every chance they would stop and search him anyway.

Hurriedly, he scanned the land around him. To his right were large, empty fields. Even on a mountain bike, progress would be slow on the muddy and open ground. To his left, the land sloped gently towards a large patch of woodland, which bordered the rocky coastline. At least he could hide in a wood

Guardians of the Mirror

if he had to, so off he sped.

With the piercing sirens getting ever louder, Tony raced down the hill towards two of the oncoming police cars, but then veered off to his left onto a dirt track, while they were still some way off. As he disappeared into a stand of trees, the menacing sound of the police cars began to fade behind him. He slowed his pace, skidded to a halt and looked back along the track he had cycled down. Through a gap in the trees he watched as one of the police cars came to a juddering halt right where the dirt track began. An officer leapt from the vehicle and began studying something in his hands, perhaps a mobile phone. He then pointed down the track towards the trees where Tony was hiding.

Tony cursed under his breath. Surely this meant they were after him, were tracking him somehow. Without a second thought, he thrust down on his peddles and began cycling out of the trees away from the cars. There was a short patch of open ground, which he covered in seconds, and then he plunged into the relative safety of the woods. The trees and bushes were all bare, but they would at least afford him somewhere to hide, particularly as the light was now fading fast.

Once more, he stopped to look behind him. He could hear anxious voices coming down the track, which was at least too narrow for a vehicle to use. Slowly, he shook his head. There seemed no doubt they were after him. But how? He took out his mobile and immediately saw there were several missed calls from Izzy.

He was about to call her back when he heard a deep buzzing sound above. Looking up, he saw a large police drone gliding into view. With no leaves on the trees, he would be easy to spot from above, especially if the drone had night vision, which Tony knew it would.

Off he cycled once again, zigzagging between trees, looking for somewhere else to hide, somewhere dark where the drone would not find him.

After a couple of minutes of frantic riding, he glanced up. The drone had now been joined by another. When he looked to his left, a third was also fast approaching, until there were three drones circling above him like large birds of prey scouring the land, looking for a mouse to devour.

He cursed, realising the police were tracking him as easily as if he had a large neon sign on his head. As he continued racing through the woods, it occurred to him they had to be using his phone to track him. For a moment, he considered tossing it as far away as he could, to throw the police off his tail. But after glancing up at the drones once more, he realised they no longer needed to trace his phone, for the drones now had him firmly in their sights. He had seen footage on television of criminals being tracked from above by helicopters, where the body heat from those on the ground made them stand out as clearly as snowmen against a black background. Unless he could find a cave or a building to hide in, he was doomed to be caught.

By now, he was hurtling through the woods, weaving past trees at speed, pumping his legs as fast as they would go. Every few seconds, he would throw a glance up into the greying sky, but always they were there, hovering, following his every move.

He hit a stone or a tree root, something hard and unforgiving. Before he could react, the bike fell from underneath him and he was tumbling through the undergrowth. When he came to a painful halt, sprawled on the woodland floor, gazing up into the mass of branches and twigs, he groaned. His limbs were stiff and aching, his breathing frantic. While the drones looked down at him like gigantic hoverflies, he ran through his options. He was not ready to give up just yet.

Awkwardly, he pulled himself to his feet, examined his bike, but immediately noticed he now had a buckled front wheel. So he simply ran, crashing through the undergrowth.

He stumbled once more, skidded onto his front, knocking the air from his lungs. All around him, dusk was drawing the light from the landscape, turning the woods into a world of eerie shadows.

Dogs barked in the distance, no doubt on his trail, too. As he hauled himself up, the pendant slipped out of his jacket and dangled in front of him. It glowed faintly in the gathering darkness. For several long seconds, the idea raced through his mind. If only he had the golden bracelets with him, he could remove his pendant and wait for a storm, then control it. As Tom had said, he would be unstoppable. Could he make it back to *Lynn Cottage* before they caught him? If he sprinted, and was lucky, there was a chance.

But no. His mother would surely be mortified if he used the powers for his own benefit. So he sighed, closed his eyes, tucked the pendant away down his top and chided himself for even being tempted by the idea of unleashing those forces.

He was running again, scouring the wood for somewhere to hide. The sound of the surf pounding on the rocks nearby was getting louder. He was running out of places to go. Still the drones buzzed above him, while the barking dogs drew ever closer, perhaps only a matter of seconds away now. He slowed down to a walk, then stopped altogether. He took out his phone and contemplated calling someone: Tom or Izzy. But that would be too dangerous for them. He therefore shut it down so the police could no longer track it and hurled it through the trees towards the cliffs, where it clattered out of sight.

There was nothing more he could do. He sat down against a tree and waited to be arrested.

As Izzy approached the cottage, Tom rushed outside to meet her. Even in the encroaching twilight, he could see she had been crying and looked to be on the verge of doing so again.

'Izzy. What is it? What's happened?'

'I've been hacked, Tom,' she said, her voice faltering. 'The police have hacked into my laptop. I've compromised us all.' She was barely able to look at him, as though she had committed some terrible crime.

'Where's Molly?'

'We split up again, so we would be harder to follow. Anyway, Tom, get some stuff together. We need to move out of the cottage.'

'Are the police coming here?'

'I don't know, Tom,' she snapped, her jaw trembling. 'I don't know anything anymore. We just need to get out in case. Let's go to the tin mine for now. We can watch what happens next from there.' She then hurried past him towards the cottage and dashed inside.

While Izzy darted around the cottage, picking up items and turning off some of her electrical equipment, anything that could help the police locate the cottage, Tom quickly told Sam what had happened.

Guardians of the Mirror

'We need to move the mirror, then,' said Tom's grandfather.
'Yeah. And the Iris box. Come on. Everything else can wait.'

While Izzy traipsed towards the dark silhouette of the tin mine, a stuffed rucksack over each shoulder, Tom and Sam carried the bulky mirror between them like a stretcher. Once inside the ruined brick building, they all sat down in the dark. Some weeks previously, they had prepared the place for just such an occasion. They had cleared the floor of debris in one of the rooms, repaired part of the roof and installed some basic furniture. It was only a cramped space with a small square hole overlooking the sea where once a window had been, but the room was at least out of the cold wind.

Tom lit a candle, the only light they dared use. Opposite him on a wooden chair, Izzy sat with her head in her hands. She looked up at him, eyes red.

'I'm so sorry,' she said.

Saying nothing, Tom moved closer and put an arm around her.

'I was so stupid. They laid a trap for me, knowing I wouldn't be able to resist, and I fell straight into it. And now I've ruined everything.'

'You've got nothing to be sorry about, Izz. How many times have you saved us in the past? How many times have you got me out of scrapes?'

Her anguished face looked across at his. 'I can't get hold of Tony. If he had his phone on, they'll be tracking him now. I've really messed up, haven't I?' She buried her face again.

Tom looked across at Sam and shared a frown with his grandfather. Losing Tony would be a disaster, but Tom said nothing, not wishing to make Izzy feel any worse than she already did.

'You'll make this right, Izzy,' said Tom. 'You always do. If anyone can sort this out it's you. You have to believe that. *We* have to believe that.'

Tom's cousin looked up and dried her eyes on her sleeve. 'First thing we need to do,' she said, standing up, 'is go through the mirror. On the other side, we can turn our phones and the laptop back on without fear of being traced. I can then clear the virus out of them. It's all I can think of doing right now.'

'Come on, then,' said Tom. 'Let's go. Molly will know where to find us. And Jake should be along any minute. He can help.'

The room was small and windowless, with only a single bright light directly above him. Tony was sitting at a small table, his hands cuffed behind his back. Even though he was now firmly in custody, the police were still clearly wary of what he was capable of doing.

The single door opened and in walked Miss Doomsday, a rather self-satisfied expression on her face. She approached the table and sat down opposite him. 'Well, now I have both you and Harry Singh,' she said.

'Lucky you,' mumbled Tony, returning her gaze with defiance.

'Before I ask you any questions and give you the opportunity to come out with ridiculous denials, I shall inform you now that I know everything. I have read the book written by Augustus Doomsday and the diary written by his friend Albert Trevaskis. I also have Harry's Iris box, his bracelets and a medallion in my possession.'

She smiled knowingly at her captive, no doubt hoping Tony

would look shocked at her knowledge. Tony gritted his teeth, however, determined not to give her the satisfaction of showing any such emotion.

'However, what I don't yet have,' she continued, 'is an Iris. And I would really like to get my hands on one.'

'Well, good luck with that.'

'Where is your Iris?'

'I don't have one,' replied Tony evenly.

'Come now, Tony. I witnessed you getting the better of Harry back in the autumn in Trethek Cove. After you had imprisoned him, you released what I now know was his Iris. And I have since learned that to defeat him you used the power from your own Iris inside your own Iris box. Am I wrong?'

Though he kept his emotions hidden behind an inscrutable mask, Tony's stomach was churning, his heart thumping. They had badly underestimated Miss Doomsday, dismissed her as little better than a bumbling fool. But now it was clear she knew everything.

'So I shall ask you again,' she resumed. 'Where is your Iris?'

He responded to her icy gaze with one of his own. 'Somewhere you will never find it.'

The calm stare Miss Doomsday gave him was thoroughly unsettling, not because it was in any way threatening but precisely because she looked so serene, as though his defiance concerned her not one jot.

'If I understand all this correctly,' she continued after a pause, 'the fact that you and Harry Singh are in the same world should be triggering a storm. But, clearly, it is not. Why is that?'

Good, he thought at last. Did it mean she was unaware of

his pendant? If so, that was one small advantage he held. 'I have no idea what you're talking about,' he lied.

Miss Doomsday snorted, perhaps a sign her patience was waning. Her fingers tapped the table between them, while she continued to eye him coldly. 'Your mother is in prison, isn't she? As lawless as her son.'

Tony did not respond but guessed what was coming.

'Co-operate and nothing will happen to her ...'

'Oh, I see,' spat Tony. 'Is that what you'll stoop to, is it? Threatening violence? You lot are despicable. And you're surprised that people like me are willing to stand up to the likes of you, even though we risk prison? Well, do your worst. You'll get nothing from me. My mother would never want me to give in on her account.' He glared at her, then looked away, expecting the deputy head to explode with rage.

However, she simply sniffed, then let out a brief mirthless laugh. 'Very well,' she said. 'The funny thing is, I don't really need your co-operation. I hoped you might help me speed things up a little, but I suspected you would not.'

She stood up, scraping the chair loudly on the floor. Feeling more and more uneasy, Tony glanced up at her.

'No matter,' she said, as she headed for the door. 'Back to plan A.'

The *Morladron House* in Jake's world was dark and cold, as the winter evening descended rapidly into night. In an upstairs room at the back of the house, Izzy sat at a small table, typing away furiously into her laptop by the light of a few candles, which they kept in the room for just such an occasion. Tom, Jake and Sam were pacing the room, mainly to keep warm since a cold draught was whistling through countless unseen holes in the old house.

Tom had never before seen his cousin work so fast, so intently, not stopping to utter a single word as she battled to remove every last shred of the virus on her laptop. In theory, now that they had run to the safety of Jake's world, she could spend all the time she needed to neutralise the threat. But in reality, her time was limited. Somewhere nearby in Porthgarrick itself lived her counterpart in that world, so Tom and Sam kept peering through gaps in the boarded-up windows, scanning the dark sky for any signs of a gathering storm. As soon as one appeared, which it inevitably would the longer Izzy stayed, she would have to return immediately to her world.

But for now at least, the storms stayed away, leaving Izzy to risk straining a muscle in her fingers with the speed of her typing.

'She'll be all right,' mumbled Jake, as he came close to Tom. 'She knows how to get away.'

Tom smiled briefly. It was typical of his best friend to guess what he was thinking. Tom may have been constantly peering over Izzy's shoulder, then glancing outside at the sky, but Jake knew Tom's mind was elsewhere. Until Tom knew Molly was safe, he could never truly relax.

'I hope you're right, mate,' he replied.

'She's a clever girl, Tom. They won't catch her.'

Without looking up, Izzy held out a phone. 'Tom, this is yours. I've removed all the nasties. They won't be able to track you now, but they will have your number. So, we'll all need to get new numbers soon. Now go back, check Molly's okay.'

'Thanks, Izz,' he said, taking the phone and heading straight over to the mirror. He put a medallion around his neck and then pressed its reflection in the large cheval mirror. At once, he was standing in the near-pitch black ruins of the old tin mine's engine house, his back to the other mirror.

He hurriedly went outside into the cold, windswept night, throwing his eyes left and right. But there were no flashing lights, no helicopters, no drones. Perhaps they had succeeded in turning off their phones in time before the police had located *Lynn Cottage*.

Tom looked at his phone, which now had a signal. Should he try calling Molly, or was that just too dangerous?

The phone beeped, making him jump. He had several missed calls from a number he did not recognise. Perhaps Molly was using a different phone.

Then his phone rang. Within a second, he accepted the call, expecting to hear Molly's sweet voice. Instead, a much deeper voice spoke. 'Tom Paget — don't hang up ... if you want to see your girlfriend again.'

Tom's blood ran cold. 'What do you want?' He asked, his voice barely a whisper.

'Molly Trump has been arrested,' said Miss Doomsday. 'We need to have a little chat, you and I, face to face. There's something I want. And in return I will release Molly.'

'You expect me to trust you?' snorted Tom.

'No. But you don't really have a choice, do you? Unless that is, you never want to see Miss Trump again.'

Chapter Seven

The Exchange

When the others came through the mirror into Tom's world, he was sitting in the tin mine, his head in his hands. A solitary candle was burning on the table, casting flickering shadows around the small, dark room.

'You all right?' asked Jake.

'They've got Molly.'

For several seconds, no one said a word. The wind moaned like a ghost through a gap in the brickwork, while a large wave broke onto the rocks down below.

'Miss Doomsday phoned me,' said Tom, looking up at them. 'She wants me to meet her.'

'Well, clearly it's a trap,' said Jake. 'She'll arrest you as soon as you appear.'

'Quite possibly. But she says she wants to make an exchange.'

'What does she want?' asked Izzy.

'She didn't say,' replied Tom.

'I can guess,' said Sam. 'The mirror, the Iris. Or both. Things she can't have.'

'Whatever it is, I have to go,' continued Tom.

'You can't,' said Izzy.

'I'm not asking you guys. I'm telling you, I'm going. I have to. If she wants me in exchange for Molly, then so be it. But if there is a chance, however small, that Molly could be set free, I have to take it. I won't let her rot in prison.'

John D. Fennell

An hour or so later, Tom was heading towards *Morladron House*. Miss Doomsday had said they could meet at a place of his choosing. But as no meeting place seemed any safer than another, he had chosen the old house. He could arrive early and check for an ambush, and besides, he knew the area well. As well as being in the open, there were countless places to hide if he needed to. There was every chance he would be caught if they really wanted him, but at least here, he would have a slim possibility of evading capture.

Wrapped up against the cold, he trudged towards the house. A near-full moon kept winking brightly through the scudding, silvery clouds above. Flickering shadows of twisted, bare branches flashed onto the ground in front of him as he walked. If these were to be his last moments of freedom, it somehow seemed appropriate that it should all end in something resembling the scene from a ghostly horror film.

As his feet crunched across the gravel driveway in front of the lifeless house, his eyes flitted about, but as far as he could tell he was alone. He headed for the stone porch, made sure the thick wooden door was still open and then stood stock still in the shadows, waiting and watching. Behind him, apart from the wind sighing intermittently through the derelict house, there was not a sound.

A quarter of an hour after he had arrived, a car pulled into the driveway, its headlights dazzling in the dark. It came to a halt a short distance from the house. A lone figure stepped out onto the gravel.

Tom activated and then adjusted the miniature camera he was wearing in a buttonhole. Izzy had insisted he take it, so they could at least gain evidence of her underhand tactics, she had said. Feeling he had nothing to lose, he stepped out of the shadows. The noise of his footsteps was enough to attract the attention of the silhouette in front of him.

'Tom Paget,' said Miss Doomsday. 'It's good to see you again, after all this time.'

Tom said nothing while he stood watching her, tensing his muscles, ready to run at the first sign of trouble.

As if noticing his unease, Miss Doomsday said: 'Don't worry, Tom. I've not come here to arrest you. I'm alone.'

'Then who are those two in the car?' Even in the dark, Tom could make out two dark shapes inside.

'Oh, just my bodyguards. In case you and your criminal friends tried to kidnap me in return for Molly. But I assure you, they will stay in the car unless I need them. You see, I am no longer particularly bothered about you, Tom. You have become rather insignificant compared to what I now want.'

'Which is?' asked Tom, though he felt he already knew.

'The mirror. That is all. Nothing else.'

For several moments, nothing further was said. Tom had expected a list of demands, not just one.

'Bring me the mirror and I will let you and Molly Trump go.'

Tom snorted his derision. 'You honestly expect me to trust you? Even if I were to bring you the mirror, I'm supposed to believe that you'll let me and Molly just walk away?'

'Well, it may not mean anything to you, Tom, but I give you my word ...'

'Which, you're right, at the moment means absolutely nothing to me.'

The deputy head chuckled briefly. 'You'll just have to trust me then, won't you? You don't really have much choice, assuming you want to see your girlfriend again.'

'What makes you think I care about her?'

'Oh, Tom,' scoffed Miss Doomsday. 'Let's not play silly games. I have suspected for a long time that she was your girlfriend. I should have gone with my instincts sooner. But as soon as we hacked into your phones, it became immediately obvious just how much she means to you. And your cousin Isabelle as well. I should have worked that one out, too. Silly me. But she was so clever at covering her tracks, wasn't she? An uninspiring B in computer sciences, eh? She made all the teachers think she was nothing special. Well, now we know. That's the problem with amateurs — they always slip up in the end.'

'Molly has done nothing wrong,' snarled Tom. 'What are you charging her with?'

'Oh, I don't know. We'll think of something. Unless of course you bring me the mirror. Then all this will just go away, and you two can be together again.'

Even in the dark, Tom could see she was smiling, an unnerving smirk that declared she held the advantage and she knew it.

'Unfortunately for you,' said Tom, 'this is not my decision alone to make. I will need to speak to my friends.'

Miss Doomsday spread her arms wide. 'Of course. Take all the time you need. Well, let's say twenty-four hours, shall we? After that, Molly will be charged with harbouring known criminals, or some such. And by the way, there is no chance of breaking her out. None what-so-ever.' She turned and walked back towards the car. 'You have my number now. Call me when you're ready. Goodbye, Tom. We'll speak again soon, I'm sure.'

Guardians of the Mirror

'It's out of the question,' growled Grandpa Sam, when the video had finished. They were gathered around Izzy's laptop, having just watched the footage of Tom's conversation with the blatantly smug Miss Doomsday.

'But we can't just abandon Molly,' said Izzy.

'Oh, don't worry,' said Tom. 'I have no intention of abandoning her.'

Sam sniffed loudly. 'Sorry, Tom. There is no way I can let you hand over the mirror. That is just too dangerous. Someone like Doomsday could cause untold damage to both worlds.'

'And her word doesn't mean anything, Tom,' said Jake. 'The moment she has the mirror, she'll arrest you. You know that, right?'

Tom frowned. 'In a strange kind of way, I don't think she will. What really, really scared me the most, was how she seemed more interested in the mirror than in me, or in any of us for that matter. She didn't even ask about Izzy or Sam. She has read those books and seen what Harry and Tony can do with the bracelets. And now I fear she is only interested in what all this stuff can do for her.'

'All the more reason not to let her have it,' said Sam.

'The odd thing is,' continued Tom, 'she only wants the mirror. She didn't mention the Iris or anything else. Just the mirror.'

'Maybe she doesn't know about the rest,' suggested Izzy.

'Oh, she knows about everything all right,' replied Tom. 'I just wish I knew what she was up to.'

'She can't really do a whole lot of damage with just the mirror, though, can she, surely?' asked Jake.

'Apart from set off a storm that could destroy half the town,' scoffed Sam.

John D. Fennell

'Why would she, though?' countered Tom. 'And besides, we would still control the other mirror, the other end of the portal in Jake's world.' He rubbed his chin. 'Just what does she hope to achieve?'

'Well, it's a moot point, anyway,' growled Sam. 'You're not giving her the mirror, and that's that.'

Silence fell in the darkened tin mine. Tom could feel at least one pair of eyes on him. He sighed. 'Look, what if we give her the mirror—?'

'No, Tom!' snapped his grandfather. 'There'll be no more talk of that. I'm sorry about Molly, I really am. But there are far, far greater things at stake here than one person's freedom. Even Molly would recognise that, I'm sure. Now, there is still no sign the police have located the cottage, so I suggest we go back there for the night, have a good night's sleep and reconsider our options in the morning.'

Tom heard Izzy sniff and blow her nose. He guessed what she was thinking: she was blaming herself for Molly's arrest. He caught Jake's eye in the gloom and an unspoken understanding seemed to travel through the air between them.

Cautiously and silently, Tom and Jake lifted the mirror onto the sack truck, a metal frame on two wheels designed for carrying heavy objects, such as tall, magical mirrors with a thick wooden frame. They then draped an old curtain over the top of their load and manoeuvred it centimetre by agonising centimetre towards the front door, praying the wheels would not squeak and wake up Sam or Izzy.

Finally, they reached the front door, opened it and stepped out into the cold pre-dawn air. Tom glanced at his watch; it was just past five o'clock. Wrapped up in their coats, the two boys inched their load away from the cottage and into the darkness.

Tom looked over his shoulder at the slowly receding silhouette of the cottage behind them, dark and lifeless, and then whispered: 'Thanks, mate.'

Jake nodded. 'No worries. Still not sure I entirely agree with what you're doing, though.'

Tom frowned. 'I can't see I have a choice. I'm not going to abandon Molly.'

Pushing the sack truck in the dark along the mud path that circled the lake was hard going and progress was slow. But at least now that they were away from the cottage they could talk openly.

'I presume you have a plan,' continued Jake.

'Don't I always?' joked Tom. 'It's risky, but we still have the Iris. If we hand over the mirror in exchange for Molly, we then use the Iris to locate where Doomsday has hidden the mirror and get it back.'

'Sounds good. But I can see two huge problems with that. Firstly, you're still assuming that Doomsday is going to let you go. And as you know, I'm extremely sceptical about that one. Secondly, once she has the mirror, she'll keep it in the middle of the police station or some other highly secure building with armed guards and police dogs. How on earth do you propose getting into somewhere like that?'

'That's where you come in, Jake,' replied Tom, looking across and grinning at his friend. 'I need you on the other side of the mirror, back in your world.'

'No, no, Tom. My place is here with you. All of you.'

Tom put his spare hand on Jake's shoulder. 'I appreciate your support. But I need you on the other side. This plan won't work if you're not.'

'Jake sighed heavily. 'Fair enough. But how are you going to contact me?'

'Ah, well, that's what I haven't figured out yet. But at least if you're over there, you can keep an eye on things, see what Doomsday gets up to.'

'I guess so.' Jake looked thoughtful for a moment. 'But I don't want to leave you to sort this out on your own. And I want to help get Molly back.'

'I know you do, Jake. But it will definitely help if you stay in your world for now. And anyway, if this all goes horribly wrong, you'd be stranded here with no way of ever getting back home.'

'Aye, I suppose you're right,' conceded Jake.

For an hour or so more, they traipsed through the cold and dark countryside, taking it in turns to heave the mirror towards Porthgarrick. The closer they drew to the town, the more the lights from Porthgarrick could be seen casting an orange stain on the low-hanging cloud in the distance.

At last, the large silhouette of *Morladron House* loomed on the horizon. Once again, Tom had considered it to be the best place to carry out the exchange. When they reached the grounds of the house, he brought the sack truck to a halt. 'Right, Jake,' he said. 'Time to say goodbye.'

They hugged and slapped one another on the back. 'Are you sure about this hare-brained plan of yours?' asked Jake.

'No,' replied Tom with an anxious smile. 'Not at all. But it's all we've got. I don't know when we'll see one another again, so good luck. And keep an eye on that other mirror. Make sure it doesn't fall into the wrong hands.'

'Just make sure you get Molly back,' replied Jake. 'She'll

Guardians of the Mirror

know what to do next. She always does.'

After a quick thumbs-up, Jake hung the medallion around his neck, touched its reflection in the mirror and vanished from sight. Suddenly, Tom felt so alone. His two best friends in the world, Molly and Jake, were no longer with him, and that filled him with absolute terror.

He puffed out his cheeks, determined to press on, and wheeled the mirror towards the house. With a great deal of effort, he managed to haul it backwards through the front door. Inside the ruined house, the ground was still cluttered with fallen roof beams, bricks and tiles, signs of the destruction caused back in the summer, when a fire had ripped through the building. He found a suitable place to hide the mirror, then lifted some large pieces of wood to cover it up even more. He then went back outside, sat down on the cold stone step and took out his phone. After he had called Miss Doomsday to tell her where he was, he sat and waited.

A while later, the first signs of dawn began to creep across the sky, infusing the cloud with a pale glow. And then the flashing lights appeared. Three silent police cars hurried into the grounds of the house, their blinding headlights chasing away the shadows. Having been in the dark for so long, Tom had to shield his eyes from the glare. Immediately, several police officers leapt from the cars and stood facing Tom, who slowly rose to his feet. Was this it? Was he about to be arrested and thrown in prison?

The squat figure of Miss Doomsday emerged from the back of the middle car, the twilight rendering her harsh features even more severe.

'Well?' she said, striding towards him. 'Do you have it?'

'I do,' replied Tom flatly. 'Where's Molly?'

'Bring the mirror to me and you can see her.'

Tom laughed. 'Do you think I'm stupid? I've hidden it. You show me Molly and I'll tell you where it is.'

The deputy head glared at him. After a brief pause, she then barked an order behind her. One of the car doors opened and out stepped a police officer, dragging Molly behind him, her hands cuffed together in front of her. When she looked up, her eyes blazed with defiance.

Tom wanted to run over, throw his arms around her, to comfort her. Yet at the same time, the urge to rush over and punch Miss Doomsday for what she had done to his beloved Molly, was growing rapidly inside him. Fighting to restrain all these emotions, he said: 'Take those cuffs off and let her go. You get nothing till you do that.'

Miss Doomsday chuckled, an unnervingly calm laugh, which instantly made Tom feel like he was missing something. 'Let the girl go,' she ordered, her eyes holding Tom firmly in their grip.

The officer restraining Molly yanked hard on her arm as though she were a misbehaving dog, then lifted her hands and unlocked the handcuffs. With a slight movement of his chin, he indicated that she was free to go. Molly cast him a black look and then walked slowly forward, rubbing her wrists.

Tom felt a brief moment of joy well up inside him. He had to fight the compulsion to run towards her, grab her hand and run away as fast as they could. But instead, he continued to hold Miss Doomsday in his sights, expecting her or one of her officers to suddenly lunge forward and arrest them both. The moment he suspected something was wrong, they would have to run for their lives.

As Molly approached him slowly, he looked into her face,

where a mixture of anger and fear seemed to be jostling for supremacy. He held out a hand, touched hers and smiled. 'Are you all right?'

She smiled weakly back at him. 'Just about.'

'How very touching,' said Miss Doomsday. 'Now, where is it, Tom? Where's the mirror?'

Molly looked askance at Tom. 'The mirror? No, Tom, not that. You can't.'

'I don't have a choice,' he mumbled.

The deputy head chuckled once more. 'I don't think she approves, Tom. Shame. But a deal is a deal. Don't disappoint me now.'

Tom took Molly gently by the arm and began to slowly lead her away from the porch, shuffling backwards. Miss Doomsday took a pace forwards, and Tom could sense her impatience was growing.

'It's in the house,' he said, pointing. 'On the left, right in the corner, behind some planks of wood.'

'Tom, don't!' yelled Molly, glowering at him.

'Go and check,' Miss Doomsday ordered, and immediately a pair of police officers rushed into the house.

Tom continued leading Molly away, avoiding her disapproving glare. Every step they took was a step further away from the police. If it came to a chase, they would at least have a small head start. It was not much, but since dawn had barely begun, it might just be enough for them to escape into the shadows.

'It's here!' called out one of the police officers. Two more figures ran through the porch and into the house, and moments later, they all emerged, carrying the covered mirror between them like a corpse on a stretcher.

John D. Fennell

As Tom watched them manoeuvre it into the back of one of the cars, he felt a knot forming in his stomach, a painful lump in his throat. Was he doing the right thing?

Miss Doomsday broke her gaze and climbed into a car. All three vehicles turned and drove out of the driveway back onto the road, leaving Tom and Molly staring after them in the dark.

'What have you done, Tom?' gasped Molly.

'What I had to.'

Chapter Eight

The Man with the Crooked Nose

'Come on,' said Tom. 'We need to get out of here before she changes her mind.'

They had only gone a few paces when Molly grabbed his arm to stop him. 'I can't believe what you've just done,' she said, glaring at him wide-eyed through her small glasses.

'What? Saved you from a lifetime in prison, you mean? You're welcome.'

'You should not have swapped me for the mirror. That was irresponsible — stupid.' She put her hands on her head. 'You've just handed it to Doomsday on a plate. Heaven only knows what she's going to do with it now.'

Tom was exhausted. He had hardly slept all night, and looking at Molly's tousled hair and angry face, he guessed neither had she.

'Do you honestly think I was going to leave you in prison just to keep the mirror safe?' he said, fighting the urge to shout at her.

'Tom, don't you realise? She could arrest me again, at any time, just to get to you. Now she knows your weak spot. I didn't want to go to prison, of course I didn't. But if it meant stopping someone like her from getting her hands on something as dangerous as the mirror ... then so be it.'

'She doesn't have an Iris, only the mirror. Jake is back in his world, keeping an eye on things over there. I decided swapping the mirror for you was a price worth paying, while we work out what to do next.'

As dawn began to creep across the landscape, Tom could see that Molly's face was red with rage. 'Don't you see? You've put this whole town in danger,' she said. 'You've put my family in danger, by just handing over the most powerful object in the world to one of the most deranged people on the planet. What were you thinking?'

'I thought I was saving you,' replied Tom.

'It was selfish, Tom.'

'Selfish?' cried Tom. 'Selfish to want to rescue my girlfriend?'

Molly averted her gaze and looked at her feet for a moment. 'Tony was right: we have to get our loved ones out of prison by toppling this corrupt government, not by doing deals with the devil.'

Tom's frustration was growing. 'I couldn't wait that long!' he yelled, more forcefully than he had intended.

For a moment, Molly recoiled, staring at him as though she no longer knew who he was. Tears were rolling down her cheeks.

Tom reached out a hand to her. 'I'm sorry,' he said, almost in a whisper. But once again she recoiled, taking a step backwards.

'I — I don't think I can do this anymore,' she said.

'Do what, Molly?'

'Us.'

The word hung in the air, like a magic spell that had frozen them to the spot.

After several agonising seconds, while their eyes held one

another's without blinking, Molly said: 'I need to go. See my parents.' She turned and marched away, head hanging low.

Tom's throat was so dry, his mind so numb, he could not speak. Instead, he stood motionless, watching her silhouette walk away until it dissolved into the shadows and vanished.

Miss Doomsday ran a stubby finger over some of the unusual carvings in the frame around the mirror. There were ugly faces the size of apples, with leering eyes and tongues sticking out. Another had large, sharp-looking teeth and wide, manic eyes. There were also strange, unrecognisable animals peering out of carvings of foliage or from behind intricate, geometric shapes.

As she studied the peculiar frame, she caught the reflection of her own face in the mirror itself, a face with a faint, smug smile upon it. The first part of her plan was complete. It was now time for the second part.

There was a knock at her office door, and in walked a tall man dressed in jeans, a black bomber jacket and a plain baseball cap.

'Ah, Sergeant Smith, I presume,' said Miss Doomsday. 'Come in. The Prime Minister said you were coming.'

The man closed the door behind him, strode up to the desk, removed his cap and saluted. His cold, emotionless eyes stared over the top of the deputy head, who studied him carefully for a moment or two. Even with a thick jacket on, it was obvious he was powerfully built with broad shoulders. On one cheek there was a faint scar, which was a shade whiter than the rest of his skin, and his nose seemed to point slightly to the left, as though it had been broken sometime in the past and had never been properly fixed.

John D. Fennell

'At ease, Sergeant,' said Miss Doomsday. 'Now, before I begin, I must stress just how top secret this mission is. There are only three people who know the details: the Prime Minister, me and now you. No one else must *ever* learn about this. Is that clear?'

The man nodded.

'This will be the most secretive mission you will have ever undertaken.'

A wry smile crept into the corners of the man's mouth.

Miss Doomsday saw his reaction and chuckled. 'Oh, I'm sure you think you've been sent on some highly sensitive missions before. But you will have never done anything quite like this, trust me.

'Now, I have emailed you the details of the target. You are to locate and then bring the target straight back to me. It is, I believe, what you soldiers call an extraction. So far so simple. But this is where it gets interesting. The target is not from this world.'

She paused to see if there was any surprise in the man's face, but he just stood there watching and listening in complete silence.

'This,' resumed Miss Doomsday, pointing to the tall cheval mirror behind her in the corner of the room, 'may look just like a mirror to you. But it is not. It is actually a portal to another dimension, another world, much like our own.'

The soldier's eyebrows began to knit into a frown, but still he said nothing.

'You are to pass into this other world, find and bring this individual back with you. We know the target lives in the other Porthgarrick, but otherwise, we have little information on their exact whereabouts. We have the name and the appearance that I have emailed to your phone. Nothing else, I'm afraid. Any questions?'

'I take it you want the target brought back alive?' he inquired in a gruff voice.

'At all costs. You may use any means at all to bring the individual back, such as sedation, for example. But the target must be alive. Otherwise, the mission will be considered a complete failure. Is that clear?'

The soldier nodded once more. 'One last question, ma'am,' he said. 'How exactly do I get there and back again?'

After opening a drawer in her desk, Miss Doomsday pulled out a medallion and held it up with its thick chain hanging down. 'I will show you now,' she said.

'So, tell me again: what are we going to do?' asked Clare Goodman, as she and Jake walked up the hill towards *Morladron House*. 'I mean, it's a lovely sunny morning, and it's always nice to spend time with you. But it's still pretty cold and windy up here.' She smiled warmly at him, waiting for his response.

Jake smiled back. 'I have to keep an eye on our mirror, now that the other one has fallen into enemy hands, so to speak.'

'Why don't you just bury it again? Then no one could get through.'

'Exactly. No one could get through, including Tom. And I know he'll be fighting tooth and nail to get *his* mirror back. And when he does, I need to make sure the portal is still open, so he can come here when he needs to.'

'So, does that mean you're going to keep coming up here every day?'

'If I have to, yes. I thought about moving it into my house.

But my parents would ask too many questions. It's a wee bit too big to sneak it inside without them noticing. And besides, if Miss Doomsday decides to pay us a visit, having the mirror in our house would put my family in danger. So basically, coming up here is the only option.'

'I see.'

Jake looked across and saw that Clare looked rather crestfallen. 'It should only be for a short time,' he added quickly. 'Until Tom's got it all sorted out. I'm sorry, Clare, but he is my best mate. And I do owe him.'

Clare smiled at him again. 'Yeah, you're right — as usual,' she added, giving him a playful nudge with her arm.

Just then, they both looked up as a large figure approached them on the road. Marching briskly down the hill, he wore a baseball cap and a black bomber jacket over what was clearly a well-built torso. A small rucksack was slung over one shoulder.

'Morning,' said Jake, as the man drew close to them.

The man glanced up with a baleful look in his eyes, said nothing and marched past them down the hill.

'Urgh!' said Clare. 'Did you see his face? Not a nice-looking man. His nose was all bent to one side.'

'Now, now. We don't judge a book by its cover,' said Jake with a smirk.

'Well, I most certainly wouldn't want to read that particular book. It'd give me nightmares.'

They both laughed, but then Jake looked up at *Morladron House*, which was clearly visible through the bare trees just ahead, and stopped to think.

'What is it?' asked Clare.

He looked at her sweet, round face, encircled by the hood of her coat, and said: 'I think he just came from the house.'

Clare laughed. 'How can you be so sure? He could have come from anywhere.'

'Because beyond the house there is nothing but open countryside,' replied Jake, rubbing his chin. 'If he had come from the next village or a farm or somewhere else, he'd have driven or cycled or taken a bus. And besides, this is a small town, and I've never seen a man with a crooked nose before, have you?'

'Well, listen to Sherlock Holmes,' mocked Clare with a grin.

'Come on. I think we should follow him. See what he's up to.'

Feeling more dejected than ever, Tom trudged back to *Lynn Cottage*, taking extra care that he was not being followed. He felt so tired he just wanted to go straight to bed, but equally, he knew he would not be able to sleep. And then there was the inevitable dressing-down he was about to receive from his grandfather for secretly taking the mirror out of the cottage.

When he walked through the door, Sam was standing there, looking ready to erupt. 'You did it, didn't you?' he said, thrusting an admonishing finger towards his grandson.

'Yes, Grandpa, I did,' replied Tom wearily.

His grandfather then launched into a red-faced tirade about consequences and foolishness. Tom simply stared at the floor, too exhausted to argue. The words just washed over him, words like irresponsible and stupid and reckless. Eventually, Sam threw his hands in the air, roared like a lion and then stormed off, declaring he was going for a walk.

His head still hanging low, Tom dragged himself into the small lounge and collapsed onto the sofa.

John D. Fennell

Izzy walked into the room, smiled weakly at him and then sat in an armchair opposite. 'I thought it best to let Sam have his say first,' she said. 'He's been pacing up and down, chuntering away for ages.'

Tom looked up at her and guessed from her dishevelled hair, drawn face and red eyes that she had had as little sleep as him.

'I half expected to never see you again, Tom,' she said. 'And where's Molly?'

'She's free now. I swapped her for the mirror. Though I'm beginning to wonder why I bothered.'

'What on earth do you mean?'

Tom sighed. 'Molly agrees with grandpa. That I shouldn't have done it. We argued. I don't think she wants to see me anymore. It might be over between her and me.' He felt a lump form in his throat.

'Don't be daft!' scoffed Izzy with a smile. 'You're both just tired and emotional. It'll be fine, you'll see.'

Tom said nothing.

'Anyway,' she continued, perhaps sensing that Tom wanted to change the subject. 'I'm sorry about yesterday. I messed up, and then I wallowed in self-pity for too long. It can't have been nice to watch.'

'Oh, Izzy. My goodness, it was completely understandable.'

'Maybe. Anyway, I've cleaned out my laptop. There's not much left on it now. So we're going to have to start again. But I won't rest until that Doomsday cow is behind bars. She'll live to regret the day she crossed me, I can tell you.'

Tom chuckled. 'That's more like the Izzy I know.'

The moment morning breaktime began, Jake and Clare rushed

out into the playground. Trying not to look too conspicuous, they surreptitiously looked out of the school grounds and into the road running alongside the school.

'I can see him,' said Clare.

'Me too,' said Jake, smiling broadly at Clare as though he were discussing something completely different.

Earlier that morning, they had followed the man with the crooked nose down into Porthgarrick. After stopping briefly to get his bearings, the man had then headed straight for the school. While all the pupils had poured through the main gate, he had spent the whole time lurking outside the school grounds, sometimes standing, sometimes walking backwards and forwards past the entrance. Although he had made a show of looking into his phone a lot and generally trying to look preoccupied with something else, it was plain to Jake that he was looking for someone, though whether a pupil or a member of staff it was impossible to tell.

Jake had been tempted to skip school altogether so that he could watch the stranger, particularly as it was the last day of term before Christmas, so they were unlikely to be learning a great deal that day. But in the end, he had decided it would have been impossible to keep an eye on the man without being spotted. And besides, the stranger was clearly searching for someone in particular, and would presumably wait until the end of the school day before making his next move.

'Who do you suppose he's looking for?' asked Clare.

'I have absolutely no idea,' replied Jake, watching the man from the corner of his eye. Once again, the man seemed to be studying his phone with great interest. But to Jake, it appeared he was actually looking over the top and into the playground. 'But it doesn't seem to be me or you. He's hardly even looked in our direction. What is he doing?'

'I don't like this,' said Clare. 'I think we should call the police.'

The sun disappeared behind a cloud, causing Jake to look skyward. 'Oh, dear. I think we have other problems to worry about. Look up there.'

The pale blue winter sky was being rapidly devoured by ever-expanding clumps of black cloud. As the patches of blue diminished at an abnormally fast rate, Clare gave Jake a quizzical look. 'What do you mean? The threat of a storm means we shouldn't call the police about a possible stalker outside the school?'

'That's no ordinary storm, Clare. I've seen this many times before. Oh, crikey. We're in trouble now.'

A searing flash of lightning seemed to erupt from nowhere, causing Jake to flinch. Instinctively, he jammed his eyelids shut but could still see the imprint of the jagged fork. Moments later, thunder began growling in the gathering gloom.

'Time to go indoors,' said Jake, and grabbed Clare's hand.

As they, like so many others, headed for shelter, Jake glanced over his shoulder. The man was still there, standing motionless under a tree, staring into the playground, as though scanning each and every child in turn.

Giant drops of rain began to fall from the sky, leaving coin-sized circles of water on the ground. Since the sky was now nearly as black as night, the next crack of lightning was even more dazzling. It hung in the air over the school for several heartbeats, frozen like an enormous photograph.

For the next half an hour or so, Jake sat nervously in the classroom, looking out over the playground as torrents of rain lashed down, wave after wave driven by a tempestuous wind.

Guardians of the Mirror

Streetlights and car headlamps struggled to pierce the enveloping darkness. Only when one of the frequent bursts of lightning tore down from the sky could Jake see anything beyond a few metres.

His heart was pounding, his breathing shallow. He wanted to shout at the teacher at the front of the class, who just carried on as though nothing unusual were happening. Yet another terrible storm was about to descend on the town and no one but him seemed to fear the looming disaster. Should he just stand up in the class and scream at everyone to run?

The fire alarm sounded, urgent and ear-splitting.

Shouting above the noise, the teacher instructed the pupils to head out of the classroom in orderly fashion. Having seen the intensity of the rain, Jake made sure he grabbed his coat before he ventured outside. In no time at all, the whole school was assembling in the playground. Snakes of children stood in the driving rain while their teachers hurriedly ticked off their names.

It was only when Jake stepped outside and felt the full force of the pounding rain, that he realised why the alarm had been sounded. Maybe as few as two hundred metres away in the neighbouring farmer's field, a giant tornado was forming, barely visible in the gloom. It was growing and growing, sucking up pieces of rubbish, branches and leaves, making them spiral up into the sky at great speed. And it was on the move, slowly creeping towards the school.

'Oh, man!' he muttered to himself. 'I've really had enough of these things.'

With half an eye on the spinning twister, teachers were dismissing their pupils as fast as they could, ushering them towards the school gates and away from danger. In no time at all, hundreds of children were pouring out of the school, drenched, confused, frightened.

Lightning plunged into the field behind the tornado, momentarily revealing just how vast the vortex had grown in such a short space of time. At its base, the twister was now thicker than a large detached house, while it was impossible to see just how high it reached, because the top had disappeared into the black cloud above.

All that Jake could think about was ensuring that Clare was safe. With the increasing roar of the tornado in his ears and the rain pouring down his face, he searched frantically for her. At last, he spotted her, or rather he recognised her coat, since she had her hood pulled firmly over her head. After she had mouthed something inaudible to him, he grabbed her hand and pulled her through the crowd, using his strength and height to pull her along with him.

Despite the best efforts of several teachers, some of the children began to panic and run. In a matter of moments, pandemonium had broken out. Children were running in all directions, mostly through the school gates and into the road outside the school, causing cars to screech to a halt. However, some were now scrambling back towards the school buildings when they saw that the whirlwind appeared to be moving towards the road and away from the school.

A girl was jostled to the ground near to Jake's feet. Using his bear-like arms, he first held back the nearby children, then bent down to help the stricken girl to her feet, who mouthed her thanks before running away.

Once Jake and Clare were out of the gates and on the path, he coaxed her to one side so that he could look back at the tornado, which had now broken through the school perimeter and was ploughing a furrow through the school grounds. Pupils streamed past them, some of whom cast Jake puzzled looks, clearly astonished that he and Clare were just standing there, watching.

The whirlwind, writhing and massive, had reached the school car park. It picked up a car as though it were a toy, spinning it round and round inside its belly until it rose higher and higher and began to blur into the mass of other objects that had been drawn into its orbit. A few moments later, the vehicle came flying out like a small aircraft, spinning over the heads of the fleeing children, many of whom ducked instinctively. It crashed into a large tree trunk and then lay crumpled on the ground.

Clare pulled hard on Jake's arm, yanking his head closer so she could shout into his ear above the relentless roar of the rain and the tornado. 'What are you doing, Jake? We can't stay here. It's coming this way.'

Jake looked into her terrified eyes and then up at the tornado behind her, before turning back to face her. 'If I'm right,' he shouted, 'we're safe here. It's not after us.'

'What do you mean? How can you possibly know that?'

'That thing is here because of crooked-nose guy. He and his double must both be here in this world. So it's after him, not us.'

'You can't know that for sure. What if you're wrong?'

'I've seen enough of these storms by now to know how they work. Please, Clare, you need to trust me.'

With fear in her eyes, Clare looked deeply into Jake's face, then finally nodded, though she looked far from convinced.

Jake turned back to gaze at the twister, which by this time had veered away from the school buildings and was now tearing through the trees along the school perimeter next to the road. A large tree was uprooted and tossed aside as if it were nothing more than an unwanted weed in a giant's garden.

In no time at all, the panicked rush of children had eased. By now, most had fled to a safe distance and continued to flee out of sight, most of them too scared to even look back. Even the deluge of rain was easing, lessening the noise and improving visibility by a degree or two.

As the whirlwind burst out onto the road, no more than a hundred metres from where Jake and Clare were standing, Jake spotted the powerfully-built man on the other side of the road. After glancing up at the tornado, the man stooped down and picked up a slight figure, who was concealed behind a thick, hooded winter coat and who seemed to be unconscious. With remarkable ease, he hefted the limp person onto one shoulder and began striding away.

'That's him again,' cried Clare, pointing. 'And he's got someone.'

'Yeah, I know,' agreed Jake, squinting hard in an effort to see who the floppy person was. 'And I'd say that's a child he's got, too, looking at the size.'

Keeping a close eye on the tornado to their right, they set off in pursuit. The man with his captive slung over one shoulder moved with astonishing speed. Occasionally, he would glance over his other shoulder as if realising that the whirlwind was pursuing him, but somehow he kept moving almost at a jog, so that before long, Jake and Clare were breathing hard in their attempt to keep up.

The twister swallowed a pair of streetlights in quick succession, sucking even more light from the already dark road. The fleeing man was now no more than a shadow, trotting along the path with the body still over one shoulder.

Jake and Clare were on the other side of the road, one eye on the man ahead, the other on the tornado behind, which moved along the road, leaning over at an angle, drawing ever closer. They too were now having to jog along to keep up with the man as well as to keep ahead of the whirlwind.

A car sped along the road towards them, its blinding headlights illuminating the road. But then it skidded to an abrupt halt when the driver saw the towering giant of a whirlwind blocking his path. In his panic, the driver had slewed the car sideways across the road and stalled it. After several failed attempts to restart, he leapt from the vehicle into the pouring rain and ran for his life.

The man with the crooked nose darted up a side street and began the climb up the side of the valley. The sudden right-angle turn seemed to confuse the twister, which continued down the main road for several seconds, before slowing down.

Jake and Clare took shelter under a large tree and bent over, hands on knees, taking in great gulps of air.

'We can't go after him now,' said Clare, panting heavily.

'We don't need to,' gasped Jake. 'He's heading for *Morladron House* and this way is quicker,' he added, pointing down an adjacent road. 'He obviously doesn't know this town like we do.'

The tornado had come to an almost complete halt, looming over the area like the giant plume from a volcano, which was spewing great clouds of dark grey ash high into the sky. But then it began to move, teetering on its axis first one way then the other, until it too began moving up the side of the valley.

Jake and Clare were about to set off again when an almighty crash rent the air. The tornado had burst into a house on the corner of the street and was now carving a path through the building, demolishing it as easily as if it were made of nothing more than cardboard. Chunks of the house, large and small, spiralled up inside the twister.

Jake grabbed Clare once more and pulled her away from the deafening roar of destruction. Once they had turned down another street, Jake stopped again.

'Clare, go home,' he said. 'You don't need to be here. You'll be perfectly safe where you live.'

'Don't be daft, Jake. You might need my help.'

'Aye, but—'

'Come on,' said Clare with a coy smile. 'You're wasting time. Let's go.'

Up the side of the valley they zigzagged, stopping regularly to catch their breath and to check where the tornado was. It never seemed to be far away, clawing its way up the hill and leaving a terrible trail of destruction in its wake. At least, thought Jake, it was showing them exactly where the man with the crooked nose was heading.

At last, they had reached the edge of the town. Before them, only open countryside remained with the familiar sight of *Morladron House* on top of the hill just a few hundred metres away, nothing but a sinister silhouette in the dark.

The man burst out of a side path and onto the road a short distance ahead, the unconscious figure still over his shoulder like the corpse of a stricken deer he had just shot.

'Hey, you!' cried Jake, despite himself. 'Where are you going?'

The man spun sharply round, glaring at Jake. In the blink of an eye, he had lowered his load onto the narrow grass verge and was reaching into a pocket. Before Jake could react, a shot rang out. Instinctively, he dived to the muddy, wet ground, half expecting to find a large patch of blood forming on his coat where he had been shot. But he soon realised he had not been hit.

'Clear off!' yelled the man. 'Next time I won't miss.'

Having checked that Clare was all right, Jake watched from the ground as the man hauled the body back over his shoulder and jogged up the gentle slope towards the house. After only a few paces, he disappeared into the darkness.

Jake glanced over his shoulder and saw the enormous tornado continuing its inexorable climb up the hill. But for now, it was far enough away not to pose an immediate threat.

He scrambled to his feet, skidded a few steps back down towards Clare, who was cowering near a small tree beside the road. Crouching down, he put a comforting hand on the wet arm of her coat. 'Stay here. I need to try to stop him.'

He was about stand up when Clare grabbed his arm. 'Jake, no!' she yelled. 'Don't be stupid.' Her eyes glowed with a mixture of fear and fierce determination.

'But I have to,' insisted Jake.

'For goodness' sake, he's got a gun, Jake. There's nothing you can do.'

Jake bowed his head and closed his eyes. She was right, he knew it already. Even if he waited until the man had gone through the mirror before following him, he would, in all probability, be arrested the moment he set foot in the other world. He felt so useless, so helpless.

'Jake, what is it?' asked Clare softly.

'I saw who it was — who he was carrying.'

'Who was it?' asked Clare.

'It was Rachel Trump.'

Chapter Nine

An Impossible Choice

Tom woke with a start. For a moment or two, he had no idea where he was or how much of what was now flooding into his mind was real or had been a terrible dream. As he came round, he realised his phone was ringing on the small coffee table next to the sofa he was lying on. He snatched it up and looked at the screen.

Miss Doomsday was calling him again.

'What do you want this time?' he demanded gruffly.

'Good afternoon to you, too, Tom,' she replied in a voice that was as fake as it was chilling. 'We need to meet again. I have something to show you. Something that will interest you a great deal. Do you know the hill just outside Trevelyn Farm?'

'Of course I do.'

'Come and meet me there.'

'Why on earth should I? It's probably a trap of some sort.'

'Oh, this is no trap.' Her voice was so calm, so smug that Tom was feeling more and more anxious. 'Once again, as before, I promise you I have no interest in arresting you. I just want you to see something, that is all.'

'Stop playing games,' snapped Tom. 'Just tell me now what it is.'

'What and spoil all the fun? No, no. Come and see for yourself. You really, *really* do not want to miss this. Oh, and come now. Time really is of the essence. Lives could be lost.' She hung up.

With a thumping heart, Tom stared at his phone, an icy cold

dread running through his blood.

Izzy came into the room. 'What is it, Tom? You look like you've seen a ghost.'

'Doomsday wants to see me again. Whatever this is, it's not going to be good.'

It was a bright and crisp afternoon when Tom set off. Feeling the need to shake off the lethargy from his long daytime sleep, he decided to run, taking in large, pleasant lungfuls of cold air as he went. He tried not to second-guess what Miss Doomsday had in store for him, for that would have driven him mad. Instead, he tried simply to take in the countryside around him, focusing on the present moment and nothing else. He studied the lifeless trees all around him, the black crows that cawed as he ran past and the small, wispy clouds in the pale blue sky. It felt good to just clear his mind of all the unpleasant clutter for once.

At last, Trevelyn Farm came into view. It was a collection of large farm buildings next to a cottage, which nestled at the bottom of a bare and grassy hill in the background. The hill was not high, perhaps as little as four times the height of the cottage, but it did afford pleasant views across the countryside around Porthgarrick.

As Tom approached along a bridle path, which ran around the farm and led up the hill, he noticed there was a cluster of people close to the top of the hill, maybe a dozen tiny figures and a pair of parked vehicles. With increasing trepidation, he ran faster and faster until he had reached the foot of the hill. Halfway up the hill, he realised the vehicles were police cars, parked at an angle, and in front of them stood three or four police officers. Standing between them was the short and plump figure he knew instantly to be Miss Doomsday.

He ran up the hill until he stood, panting, in front of the deputy head, who stood with her arms folded.

'Hello again, Tom,' she said in that coldly superior voice of hers. She had a hint of a smile on her face, a thoroughly unpleasant and unsettling smile, which instantly made Tom feel he should prepare himself for something truly awful.

'What do you want?' he demanded, determined to sound defiant, even if inside he felt more scared than he could ever remember.

'Come with me,' Miss Doomsday replied, beckoning him to follow her up the last part of the hill.

The police officers, who all seemed to be wearing puzzled and uncertain expressions, parted to let Tom follow the teacher. As the scene opened up before him, Tom gasped. He thought he was going to faint or throw up — or both.

'No, no!' he murmured. 'What have you done?' He sank to his knees, all the energy draining from his body.

At the top of the hill, spaced roughly five metres apart, were two sturdy wooden stakes, which must have been driven firmly into the ground. Dressed in her favourite purple coat and tied to one of the stakes, her hands behind her back, was Molly, her wide, frightened eyes staring through her glasses, while her black ponytail swayed in the strong breeze. And tied to the other was Rachel, her long, flowing black hair dancing wildly in the wind. When her hair blew away from her face, Tom could see she looked just as scared and confused as her double.

Wiping the tears from his eyes, Tom, still on his knees, turned to Miss Doomsday who was standing next to him. 'Please let one of them go,' he pleaded. 'I beg you. Take me if you must. But don't do this.'

Miss Doomsday looked down at him with a smirk and patted him gently on the shoulder. 'Bring me the Iris, and then they can both go free.'

'I ... I can't do that,' replied Tom. He glanced up at the sky, desperately hoping there was no sign of any black cloud. For now, the sky was still clear.

'Then let me spell it out to you, Tom, shall I? Correct me if I get any of this wrong, but it is my understanding that sooner or later a storm will build caused by the presence of both these girls in the same world. The storm will then continue to rage until one of Molly or Rachel is killed. So, a fifty-fifty chance that it will be Molly. Not good odds, are they?'

'You can't do this,' said Tom, his voice cracking. 'This'll be murder.'

'Whoever it is who dies will not have done so at my hands, Tom. She will die at *your* hands. Your stubborn refusal to bring me the Iris will have killed her. I will have done nothing but let nature take its course. Bring me the Iris or let one of the girls die. The choice is yours.'

Without blinking, Tom stared into Molly's eyes, his mind simply unable to process what was happening. For several agonising seconds, their eyes were locked together, both pairs of eyes full of tears. Then, slowly, almost imperceptibly, Molly shook her head and seemed to mouth 'No.'

'I believe lightning usually comes first, doesn't it?' continued Miss Doomsday, matter-of-factly. 'That will most likely be the cause of death, don't you agree? Question is: whom will it strike first? Where's your money, Tom?'

Clenching his teeth, Tom looked back up at her. 'You are one evil cow,' he muttered.

She chuckled briefly and then turned on her heel and walked away. 'The clock is ticking, Tom,' she called out over her shoulder.

He turned back to Molly who was still shaking her head, telling him not to do it. But he had no choice. He could never let her die. Ever.

He jumped to his feet and ran, ran down the hill past the cars and the police officers, jumped over a style in one bound and sprinted along the bridle path. Every so often he would throw a glance up at the sky, relieved every time he saw no cloud, but then dreading the next time he felt compelled to look.

Sprinting so fast he thought he was going to be sick, yet not concerned one jot for his own wellbeing, he arrived back at *Lynn Cottage*. Izzy, who must have been watching his approach on the cameras, opened the front door before he had reached it. He ran into the house and immediately collapsed on the floor, breathing so hard he felt he was going to pass out.

'What is it?' asked Izzy, her face full of anguish.

'They've got Molly again,' gasped Tom, lying on his back.

Unable to speak further, he held out the miniature camera he had been wearing on his jacket to film what had just happened. Izzy took it and plugged it into her laptop, just as Sam appeared. The two of them then watched the recording of the events on the hill above Trevelyn Farm, while Tom caught his breath.

'No, Tom,' said his grandfather, when they had finished watching the short clip. 'Before you ask, it is out of the question.'

Tom was back on his feet. 'I am not after your permission, Grandpa. I am going to take the Iris, and that's that.'

Guardians of the Mirror

'You are not!' yelled Sam. 'There is too much at stake here. If Doomsday has an Iris, it will be Augustus Doomsday all over again. With the mirror and the Iris in her possession, who knows what ... what terrible things she will be capable of ...'

'Molly is going to die if I do not,' cried Tom.

'Doomsday could trigger a world war. How many will die then, eh? What is an acceptable number of casualties in exchange for saving Molly's life? A thousand, ten thousand? A million? Just to save one life. No, I cannot allow that to happen.'

'We stopped Harry,' said Tom through bared teeth. 'We can stop her. We'll find a way.'

'No, Tom. I'm sorry. I cannot let you do this.'

'This is Molly we're talking about!' roared Tom. 'I will not let her die. Are you really willing to sacrifice her? What about you, Izzy? She's your friend.'

'Oh, Tom,' sighed Izzy. 'I don't know what to think.'

Tom stared at them both, seething and incredulous. 'You know what, I don't care. You can either help me, or you can both get out of my way. I *am* getting the Iris.' He turned to leave.

Sam grabbed his arm. 'What would your father say, eh?' growled Sam. 'Would he—?'

'He would understand, Grandpa!' yelled Tom. He stared angrily into Sam's eyes. 'What if this was my mother — your daughter?'

'How dare you!' began Sam.

But Tom was in no mood to stop now. 'Would you have let her die like this? Would you? Because I know I wouldn't, not for one second. I love Molly.' The words stuck in his throat, made him swallow hard. 'I always have.' Tears were forming in his eyes once more. 'And I will not stand by and watch her die. Not for anything.'

Silence filled the room.

Izzy reached out and hugged Tom, tears in her own eyes. 'Of course I'll help you, Tom. Of course I will.'

Sam's shoulders slumped and he lowered himself onto the sofa, head in his hands. Tom reached out a hand and placed it on Sam's shoulder, but his grandfather showed no reaction.

'Right,' said Tom, wiping away a tear. 'We've wasted enough time.'

Before long, Tom was running again. He had grabbed Tony Singh's rucksack with the golden box containing the Iris, slung it over his shoulders and raced out the door. He knew that handing over the Iris to Miss Doomsday would be nothing short of a disaster. But what choice did he have? Not for one second had he even considered not saving Molly. Maybe it was not what she wanted. Maybe she would never forgive him. But, for him at least, letting Molly or Rachel die was simply not an option.

As he ran along, he looked up into the sky and saw the first smears of black cloud forming against the blue sky. They began to expand like blobs of black ink spreading rapidly across a sheet of paper. He found himself breathing deeply just to keep the panic at bay.

Briefly, the thought entered his head of putting the wristbands on himself and trying to control the lightning when it came. But he had no idea how it worked. In attempting to manipulate the weather he might easily end up inadvertently killing someone. So he quickly dismissed the idea.

Guardians of the Mirror

He reached into his pocket and took out his phone. He called Miss Doomsday, and before she could speak, he said firmly: 'Listen to me. This is what is going to happen.'

'I don't think you are in a position to make demands, young man,' she snapped. 'Time is running out.'

'If you want the Iris, you'll do as I say,' Tom yelled into the phone. 'Otherwise, believe me, I will use the Iris myself to hunt you down and make you pay for all this.' It might not have been true, but he hoped he sounded convincing.

A moment of silence followed, while the teacher took in what Tom had said. He prayed his gamble would pay off.

'Very well,' she said. 'I will humour you for now. Tell me what you want.'

'Make sure you have the mirror on the hill, close to the two girls. Once you have untied Rachel and handed her over to me, I will text you the location of the Iris. You will then allow me to take Rachel back to her world. Those are my conditions.'

'Well, well. You care more about Rachel than Molly. Interesting.'

'Listen, Rachel is not at all important to me. I only care about Molly. But if I can take Rachel home, that means Molly's life is no longer in danger. And in any case, I knew you would never allow me to take Molly through the mirror in case I never came back.'

'How do I know that you will come back, anyway? You might decide to stay in the other world and plot your return for another time.'

'Nothing would please me more than to stay there and never see you again. But my father and Molly are both still here. And my life is nothing without them. So, yes, I will be coming straight back.'

Again, there was a pause. 'Very well,' declared Miss Doomsday. 'I think those are agreeable terms. I accept. But do hurry up, Tom. The weather seems to be closing in.'

Tom hung up without further comment and then swore furiously at his phone. With a constant eye on the darkening sky, he sped up.

As he ran, he went over the events of the last couple of days. Miss Doomsday had been clever, very clever. She had simply outsmarted him. At first, she had coaxed him into handing over just the mirror, no doubt surmising that Tom and his friends would never have consented to giving her the Iris at the same time. But now, by putting Molly's life in immediate danger, she knew she had backed Tom into a corner. He had underestimated her. They had all badly underestimated her.

However, if she kept her side of the bargain there was still a good chance he could save Molly. But it was a big if.

After several more minutes of running, he rounded a corner, and there before him was the hill behind Trevelyn Farm. Even more vehicles had now turned up, one of which, he hoped, had brought along the mirror. If it had not, he had no idea what he was going to do. If only Jake were here, he thought, just to lend moral support and bounce ideas off.

Hanging over the hill, and growing by the second, was a giant anvil-shaped mass of writhing cloud. Tom knew the first bolt of lightning could only be seconds away. And there, perched on the summit, set apart from everyone else, were the two girls, still tied to their stakes.

Skidding to an abrupt halt, he tore the rucksack off his back and fumbled inside. After checking that he was still alone, he then bent down to conceal the Iris box under a bush by the side of the path, right next to a wooden post. Wasting no more time, he sprinted off towards the hill.

Almost all the blue sky had now vanished. The lights inside the nearby farmhouse shone more and more brightly as the late afternoon daylight faded by the second. It was as though night-time were falling at great speed.

In the heart of the swirling mass of blackness hanging over the hill, the first flashes began to light up parts of the bulging cloud. Tom knew he did not have long.

He raced up the hill towards the vehicles, which now numbered five: three cars and two vans, all parked haphazardly on the gently sloping side of the hill. At least a dozen people were milling about as if enjoying the view. Immediately, Tom felt furious at them. The lives of two innocent girls were in immediate and mortal danger, while a group of men and woman — police officers at that — stood around waiting to see the start of the show.

A sudden, blinding streak of lightning tore down from the black sky, its jagged tentacles plunging into the hill no more than fifty metres away. Instantly, many of the assembled police officers flinched and then began scurrying away. If they had not known before what they had come to witness, thought Tom with a degree of satisfaction, they did at least know now.

As the thunder roared around them, he burst through the line of vehicles, the police officers too shaken and distracted to challenge him. Two of the cars were facing forwards with their headlights on, bathing the summit of the hill in light. Ahead of him, in that pool of light, stood Molly and Rachel, arms behind their backs, the tops of the thick wooden stakes protruding above their heads. Tom felt the sudden urge to rush forwards in the confusion, untie Molly and just run.

John D. Fennell

'So where is it, then?' demanded a cold, impatient voice to his right.

Tom turned to see Miss Doomsday scowling at him through her thick-rimmed glasses. She then took a step sideways to reveal a tall object hidden behind a curtain, which was rippling constantly in the mounting wind.

'As you can see,' she continued, 'I have brought it, as agreed.'

In the growing darkness, Tom could not be sure what it was. He needed to be certain. 'That could be anything,' he replied.

Sighing her irritation, she grabbed a piece of the curtain and yanked it away like someone unveiling a statue.

Another fork of lightning erupted from the sky, its pure white branches reflected in the surface of the mirror. Feeling sick with fear, Tom shot his head to the left, dreading what he would see, but let out a huge sigh of relief when he saw the two girls still there, startled and afraid but alive.

'Hurry up, Tom,' urged an impatient Miss Doomsday. 'We don't have all day.'

'I told you,' snapped Tom. 'Untie Rachel, hand her over to me, then I'll text you the location.'

Miss Doomsday's eyes narrowed. She then clicked her fingers and barked an order. A police officer scurried over, looking less than pleased to be summoned like a common servant. Looking nervously up at the sky, the officer then jogged over to Rachel and began untying the bonds behind her. By now, Rachel's long black hair was being ruffled in every direction, looking like Medusa's head of snakes.

In the next instant, a jagged bolt of lightning shot down to the ground just behind the two wooden posts, followed almost immediately by a booming explosion of thunder. Instinctively, Tom jammed his eyes shut and covered his ears. The ground beneath him and the very air around him seemed to be shaking violently.

He forced himself to open his eyes, and even though his sight was still blurred from the burst of bright light, he could see that the police officer behind Rachel had been thrown to the ground. With his ears ringing painfully, Tom rushed forward and hastily freed her hands. When the rope fell away, she stared at him blankly, wide-eyed and stunned.

As Tom grabbed her arm and pulled her away, he looked across at Molly and caught her eyes in his. 'I'll come back for you. I promise.'

In the light from the headlights, Tom could see every line in her face, every emotion laid bare. There was anger, defiance but above all, fear, terrible fear that sent tears down her cheeks and made her tremble. He wanted to rush over, untie her and throw his arms around her. But in the same moment, he knew there was no time. He had to get Rachel back in order to save Molly. This was all for her. He would do anything for Molly, anything at all.

Molly simply nodded at him.

Then he ran the short distance from the stakes towards the mirror, still clutching Rachel's arm in one hand.

'Where do you think you're going?' barked Miss Doomsday, appearing out of the shadows like a ghost.

'Taking Rachel back home,' replied Tom through bared teeth. 'As we agreed.' He continued forwards until he and Rachel were standing opposite the mirror.

'Officers, here!' the deputy head ordered, and instantly two police officers joined her, standing either side of the mirror.

'Where's my Iris?' she demanded.

Fearing the next lightning strike was overdue, and with his heart pounding, Tom reached a hand into each pocket. In one he held his phone, in the other a medallion, which he hurriedly draped over his neck. After a few clicks of his phone, he looked up. 'I've sent you a text. The location of the Iris. Now let us go.'

'How do I know it really is there? You could be deceiving me.'

'Send someone there now, for goodness' sake!' said Tom, shouting in her face, all the anger of the past few hours welling up inside and erupting like a volcano. 'Before someone gets killed.'

Remaining icily calm, she showed the text to a police officer, who then scurried away down the hill. Miss Doomsday stood motionless, eyeing Tom with her arms folded across her chest.

More lightning exploded behind Tom and Rachel. Everyone flinched. Tom looked around to make sure that Molly was still there. Her head was hanging forwards, as if she had resigned herself to her fate. But she was at least still in one piece.

When he spun his head back round, the deputy head and the police officers guarding the mirror were still dazed and temporarily blinded. Without a second thought, he grabbed Rachel again and touched the medallion's reflection in the mirror.

If only he had known this opportunity to escape would arise, he thought, as they disappeared into the mirror, he could have hidden the Iris where Miss Doomsday would never have found it. But, instead, she now had it, quite possibly the most powerful object on the planet.

Chapter Ten

Into the Unknown

Compared to the noise of a few seconds earlier, when thunder had been crashing directly above them and the wind had been gusting in all directions, the darkened room in *Morladron House* was as quiet as a cave. A pale sun was setting outside, casting only weak shafts of light into the room.

For a short while, Rachel stood rooted to the spot, unable to speak or move. She then started for no apparent reason and turned sharply to face Tom. 'What just happened?' she demanded. 'What was that all about?'

Tom looked at her in the fading light. Apart from the long, tousled hair and the absence of glasses, she looked just like Molly: the same pretty face and the same lovely hazel eyes. He felt an instant pang of regret at having left Molly behind instead of this poor imitation of his girlfriend.

'I just saved your life,' he mumbled, and then reached into his jacket pocket for his second mobile phone, the one he used in Jake's world.

'What are you doing?' asked Rachel, still looking dazed and disorientated.

Tom just looked at her then spoke into his phone. 'Jake. Can you come to *Morladron House*?'

'Tom!' cried Jake in response. 'What's going on?'

'Please, just get here as soon as you can. I'll explain everything once you get here.'

'Okay, mate. I'm not far away. I'll be there in a few

minutes.'

They ended the call.

'You're Tom, aren't you?' said Rachel.

Tom nodded.

'Then why did you save me and not Molly?'

Tom smiled wryly. 'Oh, don't worry, I only saved you so I could save Molly. No other reason, I'm afraid.'

She smiled weakly in return. 'Well, thank you, anyway.'

Her unexpected gratitude surprised Tom and left him lost for words.

'Is Michael still around?' she asked.

'No. He was killed, I'm afraid. By all this ... supernatural stuff.'

Rachel frowned. 'Shame,' she said. 'We just never quite clicked, you know. He was always so angry.' There was an uncomfortable silence before she added: 'I always liked you, you know, Tom.'

Tom laughed, wondering what she was after. 'Is that so?'

'Yes, I really did,' she insisted, looking unusually sincere. 'It was just ... you were never really cool enough for my friends. I should have been more ... choosy with my friends, I suppose.' She smiled rather sadly. 'Molly's a lucky girl.'

'Not sure she sees it that way.'

Jake burst into the room. Even in the failing light, Tom could see the concern written right across his round face. There was a quick embrace, before Jake said: 'How did you get back? I thought Doomsday had the mirror.'

Tom then quickly recounted the events of the last few hours.

'But Tom,' said Jake, his demeanour dropping. 'They'll just arrest you when you go back.'

Guardians of the Mirror

'I know. But at least Molly is safe now. Anyway, that's why I called — to say goodbye and so you could take Rachel home.'

'But Tom,' gasped Jake, looking close to tears. 'There must be something else you can do.'

Shaking his head slowly, Tom found he could not speak. His shoulders slumped in despair.

'I wish I could somehow repay you for rescuing me, Tom,' said Rachel.

And then the idea came, lighting up his mind like a brilliant sun bursting over the horizon at dawn. Thoughts tumbled over one another in his brain at lightning speed. He puffed out his cheeks and tore the rucksack off his back. After rummaging around inside, he took out the cube that Tony had shown them.

'Yes!' he exclaimed.

'What is it?' asked Jake.

'Do you have your medallion on you, Jake. We're going to need two of them.'

'Er, well, aye, I do,' replied Jake, pulling out the medallion from his pocket. 'I've been carrying this thing around with me everywhere I go these last few days. You know, just in case ...'

'Great,' said Tom. 'Rachel, we're going to need your help, too. Jake, in a moment, we need to set the stopwatches on both our phones for a three-minute countdown. The moment I touch the mirror to go back, we set the timers going. Then after precisely three minutes, Rachel, you need to just touch the surface of the mirror with your hand, no medallions, just the main mirror. Jake, make sure you're holding onto her when she touches it. I'm going to need you there as well.'

For a moment, Jake looked thoroughly perplexed. But then his face lit up. 'Oh, I see. I know what you're planning to do.'

'Listen, it may not work. So if it doesn't, it's been nice seeing you both for one last time.'

'Is one of you two going to tell me what on earth you're talking about?' demanded Rachel, looking much more like her usual sassy self.

'Jake can fill you in,' replied Tom. 'We need to move now. Jake, you ready?'

Jake fiddled with his phone, while Tom moved in front of the mirror, his own medallion still dangling in front of his chest. After a quick countdown, the two friends pressed their timers just at the moment when Tom touched the medallion's reflection in the mirror.

In a heartbeat, Tom was back in his own world. He took a few seconds to take in his surroundings. Already, the mass of black cloud above was beginning to disperse as rapidly as it had formed. However, since the sun had already sunk below the horizon, the surrounding landscape looked almost as dark as it had during the storm that had been raging only a few minutes earlier.

To his left, the two police cars still had their headlights on, casting a pool of light across the summit of the hill. One wooden stake stood empty, while in front of the other, a police officer had just finished untying Molly.

Tom quickly spun his head around. In the distance, halfway down the hill behind him, he could just about make out the familiar squat figure of Miss Doomsday. The light from a torch glinted briefly off the surface of a shiny, golden object in her hands. With a pang of regret, Tom instantly knew what it was.

He glanced at his stopwatch: 2:51 became 2:50.

Wasting no further time, he ran towards Molly and the police officer, who was attaching handcuffs to her prisoner. As

Guardians of the Mirror

Tom approached, Molly looked up, and her face froze in surprise. But Tom ignored her and went straight for the police officer. Sparkling in the light from the headlights, he could see the keys to the handcuffs attached to her belt. With her back still to him, he grabbed the key fob and immediately began wrestling frantically with the latch. The police officer tried to pull herself free, but as the keys came away in Tom's hands, she twisted around, lost her balance and fell to the ground.

With only a cursory glance at Molly, Tom ran over the summit of the hill, leaving her behind, perplexed. Pumping his arms and legs as fast as he could, he sprinted away, the weight of the medallion, which was still around his neck, beating him painfully in the chest. In no time, he was running down the other side of the hill, out of the pool of light and into the gathering darkness, not daring to look back. Behind him, he heard frantic shouting.

Once he was halfway down the hill, he turned sharply to his right, straining to keep his balance on the slope, and kept on running hard. He chanced a look back up the hill and saw three black silhouettes cresting the hill and moving down into the shadows. With any luck, they would be looking down the slope, not expecting him to be doubling back and about to come back up.

After a few more seconds, he turned sharply once more and began sprinting back up the hill, leaving the police officers away to his right running out of sight. His lungs were bursting, his heart ready to explode, his legs like jelly. Yet he refused to ease up. He shouted at himself in his head to keep going. He would rest only when he and Molly were finally safe.

He was back in the pool of light, closing in on Molly, who

stood alone bewildered, hands clasped behind her back. He made her jump when he appeared behind her and began fumbling with the keys to unlock her handcuffs.

'Tom,' was all she could say.

Breathing so hard and fighting the urge to be sick, he focused on the keys, trying to steady his hands, which were trembling uncontrollably. At last, the handcuffs fell away.

'What are we going to do?' she asked.

Tom stared at her, elation filling him from head to toe like a sudden burst of invigorating energy. 'Do you trust me?'

She looked up at him uncertainly.

'I'll take that as a yes,' he said, grabbed her hand and tugged her away with him.

He looked at the stopwatch on his phone: 1:43 changed to 1:42.

He cursed his bad luck. So far things had gone much better than he had dared hoped. But that now meant he still had a minute and a half before they could get back. They were close to the mirror, but where on earth could they hide for ninety seconds?

'Hey, you!' cried out a voice. 'What are you doing?'

When Tom turned his head to the right, he saw a police officer pointing at them. As they ran further away from the mirror, he looked around, desperate to find somewhere to hide. Those last few seconds were going to seem like an eternity.

With more and more shouting rising into the night air, torch beams flashing in all directions and heavy boots closing in, Tom pulled Molly around the side of a police van. 'Quick! Under here,' he whispered, diving onto his stomach and crawling under the vehicle.

Guardians of the Mirror

As Molly joined him, she gave him a quizzical look.

'They'll be expecting us to run away down the hill,' he mouthed to her, as several black boots hurried right past them.

He pulled out his phone again. 1:07 ticked down to 1:06.

'Why do you keep looking at your phone?' whispered Molly.

'Because in one minute's time, you need to touch the mirror. Rachel is on the other side with Jake. If you two touch it at the same time, I'm pretty sure you'll go straight into the void.'

Molly shot him an anxious look. 'What are *you* going to do?'

'As long as I'm touching you when you touch the mirror, I'll go through as well. Remember in Michael's house last summer?' he added with a grin, recalling when Molly had followed him into Michael's house and touched him on the shoulder just as he was about to pass into the void, and had thus travelled through with him.

Molly gave him a half-smile. 'What did you do to get Rachel released?'

'I'll tell you later. We don't have much time.'

There were thirty seconds left.

Tom looked out from under the van and sighed: 'Oh, great. There's a policeman standing right next to the mirror.'

He crawled across the damp grass towards the other side of the van. Then something small caught his eye on the ground. The miniature camera that Izzy had given him had fallen out of his jacket. He realised there was at least a way to let her know what had happened.

'What's that?' asked Molly.

'Something for Izzy to find.' He pressed it into the ground, then twisted the top to activate it.

John D. Fennell

Twenty seconds to go.

'I'm going to cause a distraction,' he said hurriedly. 'When you hear me shout, just run straight to the mirror. Do not look for me. Just go and touch it. I will make it, I promise you.' She opened her mouth to speak, but Tom said simply: 'No time.'

He crawled out from under the van and ran into the open.

Ten seconds left.

'Hey, you morons!' he yelled. 'Over here.'

He started running backwards, with one eye on the two police officers who had turned sharply to see who had called out, the other checking for Molly, willing her to appear in the shadows. At last, he saw her running across the grass towards the mirror. The policeman who had been standing guard in front of the mirror was now heading his way. At least Molly would get away, he thought with grim satisfaction.

Five seconds to go.

Molly was poised in front of the mirror. The odds were against his getting to her in time, but he had no intention of conceding defeat just yet. As two police officers closed on him, arms spread wide, faces set, he slowed right down, as though ready to hand himself in.

Time was almost up. He took a deep breath ... then sprinted as fast as he could, straight for the narrow gap between the two officers. He ducked at the last minute when he burst through their waving arms, as they sought to seize him. In front of him, Molly was reaching out a hand.

The last few seconds, even fractions of seconds, seemed to pass agonisingly slowly, his legs not moving as fast as he wanted, as if he were running in a dream. Urgent voices called out behind him, closing fast. Figures seemed to be emerging from the shadows all around him, like phantoms rising from the ground.

Molly's hand was touching the dark surface of the mirror. At the same time, she was turning around, searching anxiously for him. Her other hand reached out towards him. He still had several metres to go. He was not going to make it. He could see those tiny maggots of electricity creeping over Molly's hand on the mirror, riding up her forearm. Any second now, she would disappear in front of his eyes.

Even Miss Doomsday had appeared from nowhere, barely three metres from the mirror. 'Stop him!' she roared.

He ran with one arm extended, willing it to get longer, to reach Molly's own outstretched hand before she disappeared. Surely, she was beginning fade before his very eyes.

His hand touched her splayed fingers.

And then they both vanished.

After the mayhem of just moments before, the silence of the void was almost overwhelming, like being under water. Breathing hard and feeling faint, Tom stood close to Molly's slight frame, their arms stretched out in a line, touching at the fingertips, as though frozen in the middle of a dance. For a moment, he thought he was going to pass out. But slowly his breathing returned to normal.

'Tom, you made it!' said Jake, rushing forward, his large frame emerging from behind a small flock of drifting Irises.

As Molly stared at him, her face unreadable, Tom just burst out laughing for no reason and dropped to his knees. 'Oh, my goodness!' he said. 'How on earth did I manage that?'

He wanted to hug Molly, but something about her demeanour told him she would not reciprocate. He guessed she was still angry at him for having exchanged her for the mirror.

'Well, however you did it,' said Jake with a grin, 'it's great to have you back — both of you.'

'What is this place?' asked a bemused Rachel. 'Where am I?' She was standing at the other end of the rainbow pathway, her back to the other portal, gazing wide-eyed at the sight all around her.

'I never thought I'd be so pleased to see her again,' chuckled Tom, as he stood back up.

'She came good,' smiled Jake. 'Perhaps a cow can change its spots.'

Both boys laughed, while Rachel remained hypnotised and Molly stood with a faint frown developing on her face.

'What's the plan now?' asked Jake.

'First we need to take Rachel back. Come on, let's do it now.'

They walked over to Molly's double, who was transfixed by a floating Iris that glided in front of her.

'Rachel,' said Tom. But she did not respond. Tom smiled and clicked his fingers in front of her frozen face. 'Rachel. Hello.'

She blinked and then jerked her head as though waking up suddenly from a daydream. For a moment, a fierce scowl flashed across her face as if the usual Rachel were rising to the surface once more. But then it was gone, replaced by a sad little smile. 'Hi, Tom,' she said.

'Listen, Rachel,' began Tom. 'I can't begin to thank you for what you did just then. You saved my bacon. And Molly's.' He then removed the medallion from around his neck and handed it to her. 'Now I just need you to do one last thing. Take this and press it against the back of the mirror back there. As soon as you do, you'll go straight back to your world. And, this is really, really important, once you're back there, go home and hide this medallion. If you or anyone else touches its reflection in the big mirror, you will be transported directly into the other world, bypassing this place. And I'm guessing you don't ever want to go back there.'

She smiled sweetly back at him, and he was immediately reminded of Molly. 'Okay,' she said. 'I understand.' She paused and looked at him wistfully. 'Are you ever coming back, Tom?'

'One day, I hope.'

'Good. Well, goodbye, Tom.' Rachel turned around, pressed the face of the medallion into the shimmering oblong and then vanished from the void.

Jake chuckled. 'I think she finally likes you, Tom.' Molly shot him a filthy look, which instantly made him change the subject. 'What now, mate?' he asked. 'Should we go back and bury the mirror? Stop Doomsday coming through again.'

'We can't. Molly's with us, don't forget. She can't stay in our world for long.'

'So, Tom,' said Molly, moving closer to him. 'Did you do a deal with Miss Doomsday? Did you give her the Iris?'

'Yes, I did.'

She closed her eyes for moment and sighed heavily. 'Oh, Tom, you fool. What have you done?'

'I saved your life, Molly. And I would do it again without a second thought.'

'I know I should be grateful to you,' said Molly, her face going red, 'but you should not have done that. You should have found another way. Heaven knows what that evil witch is going to do with that much power.'

Tom could feel himself getting as angry as she now looked. 'I don't want another lecture about what I've done. I've heard it all from Grandpa Sam. Am I really the only one who thinks that what I did was the right thing?'

'It was reckless, Tom. As usual you've come up with a stupid plan without thinking it through. How many innocent people is Doomsday going to kill now, thanks to you?'

'Guys!' said Jake calmly, stepping forward. 'This is not helping. Please don't do this. Stop now, before one of you says something you regret.' He moved his eyes back and forth between the two of them, while they just stood glaring at one another. He then put a hand on Tom's arm. 'Come on, mate. What should we do next, eh? Let's just focus on that.'

Tom's heart was pounding. Molly was infuriating him. Why was she behaving like this when everything he had done was for her? 'We need to get hold of another Iris,' he said, still looking into Molly's fiery eyes. 'I've got Tony's cube with me. If we travel to another world, I'm hoping we can find another Iris box and Iris.'

'Is that really your plan?' asked Molly, folding her arms. 'Travel the universe in the hope that one day we'll find another Iris?'

'Yes!' snapped Tom. 'Do you have a better plan? Because I'm sure we'd both like to hear it.'

'That is enough, you two,' said Jake, more forcefully this time. 'Let's just calm down and try to work together, shall we? I don't know about you two, but I've had enough of being in here.'

'Yeah, you're right, mate,' conceded Tom.

'Look,' continued Jake. 'Should I go back with Rachel and bury the mirror, to stop Doomsday sending someone through to my world again?'

'No, Jake,' said Tom. 'I really want you with me, if you'll come. If you do, we would need to leave your portal open for now, because there's no chance of going back to my world just yet.'

'I think Jake should bury the mirror,' said Molly. 'Otherwise, Doomsday can just repeat what she did with Rachel, whenever she wants. We can't allow that to keep happening.'

'So you'd rather spend an eternity with me, travelling to other worlds, than go home one day?' asked Tom, half joking.

Molly gave him a fierce look. 'If it meant saving lives at home, then yes, I would.'

Feeling his irritation rising, Tom said: 'If Jake buries that mirror, we have a stark choice between life imprisonment back in our world, or going to another world where a storm will almost certainly try to kill us sooner or later. I'm not ready for either of those options just yet. While there is still a chance that I can make this right again, I want to take it. Are you with me, Jake?'

Deep in thought, Jake puffed out his cheeks, shook his head slightly, glanced uneasily at Molly. 'Yes, Tom. Of course I am.'

Molly rolled her eyes. 'You're as bad as one another,' she mumbled.

Fearing tiredness and frustration would indeed make him say something he would later regret, Tom finally averted his gaze from Molly and reached into a pocket. He took out Tony's small cube and placed it onto his open palm. 'Let's see if I can remember how this works,' he said, and then began moving it towards an Iris. When it was close enough, he pressed the circle on top of the cube. As before, there was a pause where nothing happened, before the cube then erupted, shooting out straight lines of dazzling light in all directions. In a matter of seconds, all the Irises had been transformed into a vast network of rainbow pathways, linking all the distant portals.

'I guess we start with the nearest pair,' suggested Tom.

He expected Molly to have something helpful to say, but instead she just stood brooding in silence.

Trying not to show just how much it hurt to see Molly treat him like this, he focused solely on trying to identify the closest pair of portals. When he and Jake had agreed which path to take, they set off along the shimmering rainbow.

After only a few minutes, they arrived at a crossroads. Straight ahead led off to a distant point, which seemed impossibly far away, while to the left and to the right a short path led straight to a rectangular portal at each end, both identical to the ones that accessed their own two worlds.

'Left or right?' asked Tom.

'I guess it hardly matters,' replied Jake.

'Well, I'm left-handed,' said Tom. 'So let's go left.'

They turned onto the path and made for the thin oblong at the end. Jake took out his medallion and was about to press it against the back of the mirror when he stopped.

'Wait!' he said. 'Once we leave this place, there's no way back in here, is there? Not without an Iris.'

Tom shrugged. 'Nope.'

Jake and Molly both looked at him with shocked faces.

'Hey,' said Tom with another shrug. 'I never said it was a perfect plan. But it was all I could come up with in the circumstances.'

'Oh, well,' said Jake. 'Here goes.'

Guardians of the Mirror

Tom and Molly placed a hand on each of his shoulders, and then Jake pushed the medallion against the portal.

In the next moment, they were standing in a dark and eerily quiet room, unable to see or hear anything. Tom assumed it must be *Morladron House* and was about to say as much when, in the blink of an eye, the darkness and the silence were gone. White light filled the room, so blinding they had to screw their eyes tightly shut. And, at the same time, klaxons assaulted their ears, ringing painfully in their heads.

Despite the discomfort, Tom was desperate to see what was happening. He forced open one eye, shielding it as best he could with his hands. Two massive spotlights stood facing them in each corner of the room, blazing down on them like mini suns, whilst a pair of doors directly in front of them was opening out towards them.

'Stay where you are!' boomed a voice, somehow cutting across the blaring klaxons. 'Put your hands on your heads.'

Into the room shuffled dozens of feet, until facing them was a line of figures. Straining to see through the glare, Tom noticed all of them held a gun. And every single one was pointing directly at the three of them.

Chapter Eleven

Utopia

'Get down on the floor,' boomed the voice once more. 'Lie face down. Do it now!'

While the three friends did as instructed, the klaxons stopped sounding, and several of the armed guards rushed forwards, seizing the teenagers' wrists and locking them in handcuffs behind their backs. The three of them were hauled to their feet and then ordered, still at gunpoint, to head towards the doors.

With guards in front and behind, they were marched out into a brightly-lit corridor. Tom's ears were still ringing from the sound of the klaxons as though they were still blaring out somewhere nearby. And his eyes were still half closed as they struggled to adjust to such bright lights, having spent so long in the void.

While his mind tried to make sense of what was happening, a large photograph on the wall caught his eye. It was the portrait of a bearded man in his thirties or forties with a faint smile on his face. Tom's heart leapt. He would know those eyes anywhere. Underneath the photo it read "Director of Operations, Professor Padgett". The man may have had a beard and his surname may have been spelt differently, but Tom would recognise his own father's face anywhere.

Having stopped for a second or two to study the photo, Tom was suddenly shoved in the back by a guard and told to keep moving. Now that his curiosity had been piqued, he started scanning the walls of the corridor, looking for anything else that might help.

There were signs and notices everywhere, all written from left to right. Although he had spent the last six months learning to read from right to left, the first fourteen years of his life had been spent in a world where everything was written the other way round, so for him reading the signs was easy.

They went past a door with a sign which read "Archive Room. Level 3 access". Then another door which said "RA Room. Level 5 access only. No unauthorised personnel". The more snatched glimpses of writing he saw, the more Tom began to realise they had to be in some sort of high security building. But at least, it seemed, the man in charge was the equivalent of his father. Surely that had to be a good thing.

After turning sharply to the right, they were led down another corridor and then into a small room. All three of them were ordered to sit down behind a desk, their hands still manacled behind them. A few seconds later, the door was closed, and they were left alone in silence.

Tom, who was on one end, turned to Molly next to him. 'You all right?'

'I'll live,' she said without looking at him.

Jake, who was on the other side of Molly, leaned forward. 'Where do you suppose we are?'

Tom looked around the empty room. Although three of the walls were grey and blank, he guessed the large mirror immediately to his left was being used to spy on them. They always were in these kind of interrogation rooms, he thought.

'I reckon we're about to be asked a few questions,' he mumbled as quietly as he could. 'I've got an idea. Leave this to me.'

'Is this all part of your plan?' muttered Molly sarcastically.

But before Tom could respond, the door burst open and in walked a man and a woman. They were both wearing dark blue uniforms and blank, disconcerting expressions. Pulling out the empty chairs, they sat down opposite the three friends. Tom noticed they both had a small logo on their breast pockets which read MIRRA.

The woman was holding some sort of electronic tablet, which she placed on the table. 'We have some questions for you three ...' she said, eyeing them coldly.

'I want to speak to my father,' demanded Tom, leaning forward.

The two officials looked momentarily taken aback, while both Molly and Jake shot him startled looks.

Before the two interrogators could speak, Tom pressed on. 'My father, you know — Professor Padgett. Where is he? I want to speak to him — now.' He was trying hard to sound and look as fierce as possible, hoping it would conceal his nerves.

'The Professor is currently not here,' replied the man. 'You will have to wait—'

'I'm not waiting,' Tom cut in, trying but failing to rise to his feet. 'When he hears about this, boy, are you guys going to be in trouble!'

'Please calm down,' said the woman, her own voice the very definition of calm. 'Now, kindly tell us what you were doing in the Mirror Room?'

'We are not saying anything until I see my father,' insisted Tom, leaning back and staring to his left at the reflection of his sullen face in the large mirror.

He watched with satisfaction as the two officials exchanged a look and then stood up to leave. So far so good, although what he was going to say to the man who looked like his father was still racing through his mind.

When the door to the room opened again, the two officials stood to one side and in came three tall, burly men. It was not what Tom had been expecting. Each of the men was holding what looked like a very small handgun. Moving quickly, they positioned themselves behind the three captives.

Tom noticed the woman standing in the doorway give a slight nod to the men behind them, and in the next moment, he felt something cold and metallic press against his neck. There was a sharp pinprick of pain, which lasted only a split second.

'Ow!' exclaimed Tom, forcing himself to sound indignant. 'What are you doing?'

But then the room began to spin, and he passed out.

Izzy was pacing up and down the room. Not knowing what was going on with Tom and Molly was killing her. She kept going over in her mind what she could have done differently. If only she had enabled the transmitter on the miniature camera she had given Tom; then she and Sam could have followed events live as they unfolded. But then again, she knew she had been right not to turn it on. Thus far, Miss Doomsday had outwitted them at every turn, so she would almost certainly have had devices searching for any unauthorised signals being transmitted nearby. She would therefore have found the transmitter and destroyed it.

Her laptop beeped, breaking the awful silence as violently as if a firework had just gone off in the lounge. She leapt across to her laptop like a cat jumping on a mouse. On a map of the area, a small dot was flashing.

No doubt stirred by the noise, Sam hurried into the room.

John D. Fennell

'What is it?' he asked.

Izzy was tapping her fingers across the keyboard. 'It's the camera I gave Tom. It has a one-hour delay on it, meaning Tom activated it an hour ago. I did that so it would start transmitting a signal long after everyone has left. Or that was the plan, anyway. Let's go and find it.' She closed the laptop, called up an identical map on her phone and then headed for the front door.

Wrapped in their thick winter coats, the two of them headed out into the chilly darkness. Using her phone to guide them, Izzy went up the hill behind Trevelyn Farm, where there was no sign of any life, just an empty, windswept hill. Numerous pairs of tyre tracks crisscrossed the muddy slopes of the hill.

Izzy turned on the torch on her phone and began scanning the ground, still following the pulsing flash on the screen. Sam joined in the search with his phone.

'There it is,' whispered Izzy, dropping to her knees. Buried in the mud, with only the top showing, was the tiny miniature camera.

They hurried back to *Lynn Cottage*. Once back in the lounge, Izzy opened her laptop and plugged in the miniature camera, with Sam poised eagerly over her shoulder.

'Even if they ended up being taken prisoner,' said Izzy, as she waited for the file to load, 'I'm hoping there is something here we can use. Something against that awful Doomsday.'

They then sat and watched the footage on the laptop screen. The camera had recorded everything: the shocking sight of Molly and Rachel tied to stakes on top of the hill; Tom taking Rachel back to her world and meeting with Jake; and Tom's rescue of Molly. It ended when Tom pressed the camera into the ground and activated the one-hour timer.

Izzy sat back, a tear in her eye. 'Poor Molly.' She wiped her cheeks. 'What we don't yet know is whether they got away. But I don't understand what Tom was trying to do.'

Sam then explained to her that if Molly and Rachel touched the two mirrors at the same time, they would be transported into the void. 'An ingenious plan,' he added.

'But did it work?'

'We won't know for a while. Not until Tom makes another appearance, or we hear that he's been arrested.' Sam then sat back and stared up at the ceiling, breathing deeply. 'I think, maybe, I was too harsh on the lad.' He swallowed hard. 'I do hope I get to see him again.'

Izzy patted him on the knee. 'We will, Sam. He's resourceful. And, if he's got Molly and Jake with him, those three have got the brains to sort this mess out if anyone can.' They shared a brief smile. 'But for now, it's just you and me left. Let's see what mayhem we can cause.'

Slowly, Tom came round. At first, he had no idea where he was or even how long he had been asleep. But, as his head began to clear, he felt an annoying itch in the side of his neck. And then he remembered.

Sitting bolt upright, he quickly looked about. He was lying on a single bed, tucked lengthways up against a wall in a small, square and windowless room. It was hard to make out much in the dim light, but he could see two other beds, one each against two of the other walls. The large figure on one bed he guessed to be Jake, whilst the slender figure on the other he presumed was Molly.

He swung his legs off the bed and gently shook the other

two awake.

'Where are we?' asked Jake, rubbing his eyes, then running a hand through his thatch of blond hair.

'No idea,' whispered Tom. 'But I reckon it's some kind of cell. And they're probably listening to us, so mind what you say.'

As if to demonstrate his assumption was correct, a light in the ceiling burst into life, blinding the three teenagers. The door opened and someone walked in. Straining to see through his fingers, as his eyes adjusted to the brightness, Tom could only see a pair of shiny black shoes approaching.

'Tim? Milly? Jack?' said a puzzled voice. 'What on earth are you all doing here?'

With some effort, Tom took away one hand and managed to look through one eye. A tall, bearded man was standing, looking down at them, his face full of confusion but with no obvious malice. It was clearly Professor Padgett. He too wore a jacket with the MIRRA logo on one side.

'Dad!' said Tom. 'Thank goodness you came. They've locked us up in here for ages for no reason.'

'Well, they tell me you were in the Mirror Room yesterday evening. That you came through the mirror and set the alarm off.'

Tom swallowed hard, trying to hide his nerves and to sound confident. 'What? How likely is that? Honestly. We just wandered in there by mistake, that's all. We were looking around. I know we shouldn't have, but it's kind of fascinating this place.'

'Well, come on, Tim,' said the man with a kindly smile. 'You all need to come and have some breakfast.'

They were escorted out of the room and along yet another

long corridor, Tom at the front next to the professor.

'I know it's the start of the school holidays,' said Mr Padgett, 'but you shouldn't be playing around in here. How did you get in, anyway? This is meant to be a highly secure facility.'

'Ah, I can't tell you that, Dad,' replied Tom with a grin. 'That's our little secret.'

'Well, maybe I need to employ you as our security consultant. You could help us find vulnerable spots in our security. Anyway, I've got work to do. One of these guards can take you to the canteen.' Still smiling, the professor stopped and looked down at the three teenagers.

Tom smiled back, still trying to look relaxed, even though inside his heart was pumping fast. 'Dad, would it be all right if we didn't stay and went straight home? It's been a long night and none of us slept particularly well.'

The professor appeared to cast a furtive glance up at one of the guards, before smiling back at the trio. 'Sure. Why not. See you later. And don't go trying to break into any more top-secret facilities,' he added with a wink.

As they were being escorted outside through the car park, Tom looked back at the building. It was a large, warehouse-size structure, with no windows or signage outside to indicate what was inside. All he could see was a large sign with that same MIRRA logo on one wall. In front of the building, there was a car park with around fifty cars parked, whilst all around the site ran a double fence, which was at least three metres high with barbed wire coiled along the top. Between the two fences, armed guards patrolled with large dogs beside them.

Once they had been led through the main entrance, their armed guard left them and went back into the compound. As the three of them walked away, Tom peered over his shoulder and saw a group of five or six guards standing with their machine guns, eyeing them suspiciously.

Jake turned to Tom and sniggered. 'Well, Tim, that was easy.'

'Yes, Jack, it was,' laughed Tom.

'A bit too easy if you ask me,' added Jake.

'Yeah,' replied Tom thoughtfully. 'I don't suppose you still have the medallion on you?'

Jake patted his pockets. 'Er, no. They must have taken it. And my phone. Do you still have that cube thing?'

Tom felt his own pockets and then shook his head.

'Great!' said Molly. 'So now we have no way of getting back.'

'Well, as long as that professor thinks I'm his son we should be able to get back in there,' said Tom.

'Oh, come on. It won't take him long to work out you're not his real son,' suggested Molly, still looking rather irritated. 'And anyway, we've got worse things to worry about. What if our presence here sets off a storm?'

'We'd better hurry up then, hadn't we?' said Tom.

'And do what exactly?' asked Molly. 'Aren't we supposed to be looking for an Iris? Because if we are, it's going to be back there, if anywhere, with the mirror, isn't it?'

'Yes,' agreed Tom. 'But for the moment, I don't think we can get back in there. I think we should just go and have a look around this world first. Then, maybe if a storm does come, we can use that to try to get back in that building.'

Molly rolled her eyes but said nothing more.

As they began walking along the road, Tom could not help laughing at the irony of it. After years of open hostility, Rachel seemed to be finally warming to him, whilst Molly was now apparently growing tired of him. He had always found girls to be unfathomable creatures and guessed he always would.

A loud humming sound caught their attention. When they looked up, they saw a small plane flying towards them. As it drew near, getting lower and lower, Tom realised it was actually a cross between a car and a small aircraft, with the body of a car but with small wings protruding from its sides. It touched down in the road, close to the entrance to the site they had just left.

'Oh, cool!' gasped Jake. 'Flying cars. I like this place already.'

A young couple stepped out of the vehicle. From behind, they looked to be a similar age to the three of them. The boy was slim with light brown, well-kept hair, while the girl was slightly smaller than him and had a long black ponytail.

At that moment, the couple turned around, just as the flying car took off again. They were no more than ten paces away, but immediately, Tom gasped. He was staring at the mirror-image of himself and Molly. Equally mesmerised by what they were seeing, the couple stood frozen to the spot, mouths open.

'Oh, crikey!' said Jake, while none of them quite knew whether to run or say hello.

Eventually, the other Tom and Molly took the first steps forwards. They were holding hands, and very quickly their shock turned into warm smiles.

'Hi,' said the boy. 'I'm Tim. And this is my gorgeous girlfriend Milly.'

The girl leant in closer to Tim to place her head against his shoulder and smiled coyly at them. Like Molly, she was wearing a small pair of stylish glasses. 'Nice to meet you,' she said, and then giggled.

Tom, Molly and Jake all smiled rather nervously.

'We were just going to see my dad,' said Tim. 'He works in there. But I think we've just found something a little more interesting.' He then leant forward and whispered. 'By the look of you, I'm guessing you've come through from the other world.'

'Er ... yeah. That's right,' said Tom. 'We ... we are just visiting.'

'And my dad just let you go?' asked Tim, looking puzzled.

'Er, well, I kind of ... pretended to be you, actually.'

Molly let out a disapproving sigh.

'Oh, I see,' said Tim.

'How very naughty,' giggled Milly.

'Sorry,' said Tom and pulled an anxious face.

'Would you like us to show you around?' asked Tim.

Momentarily taken aback, Tom was not sure what to say. He had not expected his lookalike to suggest that. 'Er, yeah,' he said eventually. 'Why not.'

Tim and Milly smiled again, while Tim took out his smart phone. 'I'll just call us another cab,' he said, tapping into his phone.

Within minutes, another flying vehicle glided down from the sky and landed in the road next to them. They all climbed inside the vehicle, which had no pilot and looked just like the interior of a normal, spacious car. Before long, they were climbing steeply into the air, and when Tom looked out of the window, he recognised various landmarks and realised that the building they had just been escorted out of, had been built in a field just outside Porthgarrick.

Guardians of the Mirror

'Oh, my goodness!' said an anxious Jake. 'There's no one flying this thing.'

Tim and Milly, who were sitting at the front, glanced back and laughed. 'I guess you don't have these where you come from,' said Tim.

Tom looked across at his two companions in the back. Jake looked scared out of his wits, while Molly sat in the middle, arms folded, looking rather disinterested.

Tom knew he needed to keep one eye on the sky in case a storm did break, but he found it hard not to get swept along in the excitement of what was happening. For now, they were flying towards what looked like Porthgarrick. Tom recognised it as his hometown because of the steep-sided valley, which headed towards the sea, as well as the familiar sweep of the coastline. However, the town itself was nothing like the two versions of Porthgarrick he knew already. As they flew in low ready to land, he could see several glittering glass buildings reaching high into the sky, all sleek lines and sharp edges. In between them, every house and shop was immaculate: freshly painted and spotlessly clean on the outside. All the roads were smooth and perfect. All the vehicles, some of which were flying about whilst others glided gracefully along the roads, were gleaming and desirable. It was how he could imagine his Porthgarrick might look in a hundred years' time.

When he glanced up, he could at least see the familiar and somehow comforting sight of *Morladron House*, perched on the highest point overlooking the town and the sea. Yet even that building looked well cared for and was certainly not derelict, as could be seen by the sun glinting off its many windows and the collection of cars parked out front.

'You look impressed,' said Tim grinning, as they all stepped out of the car.

Tom realised his jaw had almost fallen to the floor, so he quickly closed his mouth. When he glanced at Jake and Molly, he noticed they too were astonished by what they were seeing.

'Wow!' said Tom. 'This is nothing like where we come from.'

'Yeah, I've heard it's a bit different there,' said Tim, suddenly averting his gaze and looking a little uneasy.

'Now, now, babe,' said Milly. 'No gloating about our little paradise here.' She moved next to Tim, gave him a quick peck on the lips and rested her head on his shoulder. 'So are you two an item?' she asked, looking at Tom and Molly.

Tom opened his mouth to speak but could not think what to say. Looking at Molly, he could see she was just as uncomfortable.

'Oh, dear, sorry,' giggled Milly. 'Have I put my foot in it?'

'Oh, babe,' said Tim, staring longingly into his girlfriend's eyes. 'That's you all over, isn't it? Always putting your foot in it. That's why I love you so.' He leant across and gave her a kiss.

Tom and Jake exchanged a quick smirk, while Molly too looked to be straining not to smile.

'Anyway,' said Milly. 'We've been ever so naughty. Should we tell them, babe?'

Tim feigned exaggerated shock but then burst into a grin. 'I don't see why not, sweetheart.' He reached into a pocket and took out something the size of a credit card. 'We've stolen two of these passes. They can get you into anything. And I mean anything. Swipe this and any door will unlock. My dad's department has been working on them. Come on, let's go and have some fun.'

'Where shall we go?' asked Milly, looking expectantly at the three of them, who in turn looked at one another, bemused.

'I've no idea,' said Tom. 'Surprise us.'

'What about Porthgarrick Museum?' suggested Tim with obvious delight. 'We could get in there for free. Come on.'

And so up the hill they walked, the two lovebirds arm in arm leading the way, as they chatted to Molly, while Tom and Jake trailed behind.

'Hey, babe,' whispered Jake in a mocking voice. 'Why aren't you and Molly more like those two, eh?'

'Oh, shut up!' replied Tom, trying not to laugh.

'Seriously though,' mumbled Jake. 'They've got a pass that gets them into anywhere and they've chosen to take us to a museum?'

'Might be a really good museum,' said Tom with a snigger.

'Still, it'd be good to get hold of one of those passes. That might come in dead handy later on.'

The further they trudged up the hill, the more Tom suspected they were heading for *Morladron House*. With less and less of the town in front of them, there was surely nowhere else for a museum to be.

'So, if Rachel is now a goodie, does that mean Molly is not as nice as we thought?' asked Jake.

'Yeah, I'm beginning to wonder that, too?' replied Tom, looking up at Molly's back a short distance ahead.

'I was joking, Tom,' said Jake. 'Seriously, you two need to patch things up before I bash your stubborn heads together.'

'Yeah, you're probably right. But for now, we need to focus on finding a way home. Maybe this museum will have something that will help us.'

After a few more minutes of puffing up the hill, they finally arrived at the entrance to *Morladron House*, which as Tom had suspected was indeed the home to Porthgarrick Museum. Tim gave them his extra card, which allowed them all to get in without paying.

'Well, this is weird,' mumbled Jake, as they began wandering around the exhibits inside the house. Everything looked so different to what they were used to seeing. Some of the walls were covered in polished wood panelling, while others were freshly painted. And everywhere they walked, there was a pristine red carpet under their feet.

'Remember, keep your eyes peeled,' said Tom. 'You never know: there might be an Iris box in a glass case.'

'Oh, wouldn't that be great,' replied Jake with a chuckle.

'I tell you what, Jake. We should try to get into the cavern under here. With any luck, all the stuff we need will be down there.'

'Hey, you're right,' agreed Jake, his face brightening.

However, as they turned into the large room where he knew the giant fireplace was normally situated, Tom's heart sank. Where the fireplace should have been, a large door now stood ajar with a sign nearby stating that downstairs was the natural history section of the museum. A quick peek through the doorway showed Tom a vast underground chamber, brightly lit and full of glass cabinets as well as a few full-size dinosaur skeletons. The place was clearly too neat and orderly to contain any hidden artefacts relating to the mirror.

'What are you two up to?' asked Molly, appearing next to them. She still refused to smile at Tom, which was hurting him more and more, though he was determined not to show it.

'I was hoping we'd find something down there,' replied Tom. 'But no luck.'

'We've got another problem,' mumbled Molly. 'We're being followed.'

'Are you sure?' asked Tom.

'Of course I'm sure,' snapped Molly. 'I got used to recognising when I was being tailed whenever I visited *Lynn Cottage*. And I'm telling you, someone is following us.'

'I knew they let us out of that place far too easily,' said Jake. He then looked around the room, where twenty or so people were wandering about studying the exhibits and reading the information on display. 'This place gives me the creeps.'

'You never did like this house, did you?' said Tom.

'No, I mean this whole world. Everyone is smiling and happy. They've got flying cars and impossibly clean streets. It's all so perfect. Which makes me think there's something sinister lurking behind it all.'

'What are you three plotting?' asked Tim, grinning. He was still arm in arm with Milly, who wore her permanently sweet but rather vacuous smile.

Tom felt the pressure of time. They needed to get back before Miss Doomsday caused too much trouble, and also before they triggered a storm. There was nothing for it. He had to be bold.

'Tim,' he said, gently coaxing the couple to one side of the room, away from other visitors. 'I need to ask you something. The reason we came here was to find something to take back to our world, to help us fight someone very evil. It's called an Iris box. About this size and made of gold. Have you ever seen anything like that?'

Tim and Milly stared blankly at him. There were no furtive glances over their shoulders or urgent demands to keep his voice down. Nothing.

John D. Fennell

'Sorry, I have no idea what you're talking about,' said Tim.

Tom was disappointed and frustrated. 'But you didn't seem that surprised that we came from another world,' continued Tom. 'So, you must know about the mirror and all that stuff.'

'Well, yeah. We get taught about all that at school. Plus, my dad tells me stuff.' Tom stared intently at him, making it obvious he wanted to learn more. 'Look. We know there is a mirror to a parallel world, kept in my dad's institute. People used to travel back and forth many years ago. But then the other world became greedy, envious of our progress here. They tried to steal our technology. So to stop them, the mirror had to be locked away and guarded by the army. But that's all I know, I'm afraid — honestly.'

'Tom,' said Molly pulling his sleeve. 'We've got company.'

Tom spun round and saw a tall man in a black suit with broad shoulders and a dark look, clearly striding straight towards them. Tom turned to look for another way out, but saw another two, virtually identical men, closing in on them.

He turned sharply back round and glowered at his double. 'What have you done, Tim?' he snarled.

Tim wore an apologetic smile and shrugged his shoulders. 'Sorry, Tom, I really am. But my dad said I had to. He said it was a matter of national security.'

Chapter Twelve

The Audacious Plan

The impeccably dressed, red-haired Prime Minister Sheeran was sitting once again across the table from Miss Doomsday, a supercilious smile stretched across his face. 'I understand you have now acquired all the objects you required,' he said.

'Yes, Prime Minister,' replied Miss Doomsday, no less smugly. 'It all went rather smoothly. And didn't take me long in the end. We're only dealing with children, after all.'

'Well done,' said the Prime Minister, rubbing his hands together with obvious glee. 'I knew I could count on you. So what happens now?'

'Well, I need some hostages from the other world. Once they are here, the storm clouds will build. And, well, you know the rest.'

'Perfect. Perfect. Now, you realise I can't be associated with any of this. If it all goes wrong, I will have no choice but to deny all knowledge of these events.'

'Understood.'

'And what will happen to these hostages?'

'No harm should come to them. They will be kept somewhere safe. They will be a precious commodity to us, after all. We don't want to keep travelling back and forth to the other world. That would eventually raise suspicions, in both worlds.'

The Prime Minister screwed his face with confusion. 'So, this storm cloud you're going to create when you have some

John D. Fennell

hostages — we can't really have it hanging permanently over Porthgarrick, can we? That would raise some awkward questions, wouldn't you agree?'

'Yes, I had considered that. I plan to keep it somewhere off the coast, where few will be able to see it.'

'I see. You believe you can do something like that?'

'With some practice, yes. Then, when we need it, I should be able to move the storm back over the land, unleash what we need, then move it back out to sea again until the next time. Most people will just see a series of severe storms, nothing more.'

'You seem to have thought of everything.'

Miss Doomsday smiled haughtily. 'I like to think so, yes.'

Prime Minister Sheeran then stood up. 'Well, I'd best leave you to it then.' He turned to leave but then stopped. 'I understand the boy who's mixed up in all this got away.'

'A minor detail, Prime Minister,' said Miss Doomsday with a dismissive wave of the hand. 'We control the mirror at this end now. There's nothing of any consequence that Paget boy can do, I assure you.'

'Come on, Izzy,' said Sam, standing over her shoulder. 'You've been working on that laptop for hours now. Take a rest.'

She was sitting at the table in the lounge, her back perfectly upright and her head still. In fact, the only things moving were her fingers and her eyes. For several seconds more, she continued typing feverishly without saying a word. Finally, she paused, sat back and looked up at Sam. 'I'll rest when this is all over,' she said. 'There's too much to do.'

'What exactly are you trying to do?'

'I'm trying to find out where Tony is being held. If we could somehow break him out, he should be able to help us defeat that evil Doomsday witch.'

Sam chuckled. 'Even if you do find where he is, how would you ever break into the prison, let alone break him out?'

'I will find a way, Sam. Even if it takes me years.' Izzy grimaced and then began typing again.

'I'll go and make us a cuppa,' said Sam, heading for the kitchen.

A few minutes later, he came back in holding a steaming mug of tea in each hand and placed one down on the table next to Izzy. Ignoring him completely, she continued typing, utterly absorbed in her work. Sam moved away and sat on the sofa.

A short while later, Izzy sat back and declared: 'Right. There we are. I've found him. He's being held in some maximum-security prison on Bodmin Moor. It's not on a map, but I'm sure I can find it.'

'If it will help, I'll allow myself to get arrested,' said Sam. 'I could smuggle something in, hand it to Tony.'

'Nice idea, Sam,' said Izzy. 'But there's no guarantee you'd be sent to the same place as him. And besides, it says here he's in isolation, so you'd never get anywhere near him.'

They both sat in silence, staring into space, trying to come up with a plan.

At length, Izzy's face broke into a mischievous smile. 'I know what I need to do,' she said.

Once again, Tom, Molly and Jake were sitting behind a desk in a small room, staring at four windowless walls. They had been arrested in Porthgarrick Museum and brought straight back to the top-secret facility where the mirror was housed. And they sat waiting to be interrogated once more.

At last, the door burst open, and in walked Tim's father, Professor Padgett. He closed the door behind him and stood opposite the trio, his hands on the back of an empty chair in front of them. This time his bearded face was less pleasant than before, as he eyed them suspiciously.

'Before you say a word,' he said evenly, 'don't call me dad or anything daft like that.' He glowered at Tom. 'Did you really think I would not know my own son? How stupid do you think I am?'

'I can explain ...' began Tom.

But the Professor cut him off with a raised hand. 'I'm sure you can. But the fact is we saw you on camera coming through the mirror. So I know exactly where you have come from. The only thing I didn't yet understand is why you have come here in the first place. You see, we haven't had visitors from the other world in years. So I decided to let you go, to have my son — my real son — stay with you, to follow you around, see what you would get up to. But he tells me you didn't do anything of any significance. So, talk. What exactly are you doing here? No lies. Just the truth.'

Tom glanced across at his two friends, who sat looking uncertainly at him. He thought about lying, about making something up, but quickly decided he would be better off telling the truth.

'We were hoping to find an Iris and an Iris box,' he said. 'Someone back in our world has stolen ours.' Out of the corner of his eye he could see Molly rolling her eyes, but he pressed on regardless. 'And the person who stole them is set on using them for her own ends, to cause mayhem in our world. I just thought if we could find another Iris here, we could take it back with us to help defeat this evil person.'

Professor Padgett gave Tom a quizzical look. 'An Iris? I have absolutely no idea what you are talking about.'

Looking deeply into the man's eyes, eyes that were identical to his own father's, Tom knew immediately he was lying. 'But you must know,' he insisted. 'You have a mirror. You know all about travelling between worlds, so you must know about medallions and Irises. How else were you able to travel between worlds?'

'That's classified.'

Tom puffed out his cheeks. 'Look. We only want to borrow an Iris, to help get our one back. If you could lend us yours, you have my word I would bring it back.'

The man stood up to his full imposing height and began slowly pacing the room. Finally, he stopped and looked down at them. 'Listen. I have a lot of sympathy for the plight of your world. Many wrongs were committed against you many years ago. But my job is to protect this world from any threat posed by that mirror. So, I'm afraid I cannot help you. And now it's time for you to return to your world.'

'But—'

'I will give you your medallion back, so that you may return. But understand this: if ever you come back to this world, you will be arrested and then imprisoned for the rest of your lives. Now, come. Let's go.' With a wave of his hand, he indicated they should stand and follow him.

As they headed out into the corridor, Tom said: 'Just one thing, Professor. We have been here nearly twenty-four hours and yet there has been no sign of a storm. Why is that?'

The professor turned around and gave Tom a wry smile. 'I assume from what you have told me you know about the pendant you can wear around your neck to protect you from storms?' Tom nodded. 'Well, years ago, we managed to make a compound from the stone in those pendants. We injected a tiny amount into your necks, together with a sedative, when you arrived. That has been protecting you — and us for that matter — the whole time.' He then turned away and began walking back down the corridor.

'Blimey!' whispered Jake in his ear. 'They sure are more advanced than we are.'

'Yeah,' agreed Tom. 'And I guarantee they have an Iris somewhere, too.'

Under armed guard, they were marched back to the Mirror Room. As they were escorted up to the dais on which the mirror stood, Tim's father handed Tom the medallion they had used to get there.

'There you go. And you might as well have these back, too,' he said, handing over their mobile phones. 'These are real antiques. Not much use in this world. And good luck. Sorry, we couldn't help you. And of course, I hope to never see you again.'

'Just one more thing,' said Tom, looking at the man's jacket. 'Out of interest: what does MIRRA stand for? It's everywhere around here.'

'It's the name of this place — the Ministry for Investigation and Research into Rare Artefacts. Clever, eh?' And with that, the Professor indicated the mirror, implying it was time for them to leave.

As the three of them approached the mirror, Molly said: 'You realise without an Iris we're going straight through to the other world?'

'Yeah,' agreed Jake. 'And what did he mean by "I have a lot

Guardians of the Mirror

of sympathy for the plight of your world"?'

'I don't know,' replied Tom, placing the chain around his neck. 'But I have a feeling we're about to find out.'

The taxi driver kept glancing at her in his rearview mirror. 'So you're a doctor, are you?' he asked.

It was hard for Izzy to tell whether he was just making conversation or whether something about her appearance was suspicious.

'Yes, I am,' she replied simply. She gave a brief smile and continued looking out of the window at the countryside speeding past.

Was it possible he could tell she was a fake? Her first few attempts at disguise at looked laughable in the mirror. Even for seventeen, she looked young. So, a pair of fake glasses and smart but rather drab clothes had simply made her look like a schoolgirl going to a fancy-dress party. She had therefore had to spend ages studying pictures of older women and then applying makeup to age her face. Eventually, she and Sam had agreed that her attempt at a disguise was passable. But now that the taxi driver kept looking at her, she was beginning to doubt herself again.

'What sort of doctor are you?' pressed the driver.

Izzy quickly held up a finger and took out her phone. 'Sorry,' she said. 'I've got to take this.' For the next ten minutes, she pretended to be in deep conversation with someone on her mobile, letting her imaginary colleague do most of the talking while she threw in her occasional agreement. To add to the effect, she also opened her laptop and made herself look completely preoccupied with work.

However, what she was in fact doing on her laptop was

double-checking all the fake documents she had created. After managing to hack into the prison where Tony was being held, she had inserted a fictitious appointment into the prison calendar. She had then created a fake identity and added it to the prison's database, so that if anyone cared to check, they would see that Doctor Audrey Lloyd, psychiatrist, appeared to be a real person, who was due to visit the place that day.

After checking their location on the map on her laptop, she asked the driver to pull over.

'This is the middle of nowhere,' he said, looking puzzled.

'I'm sure you know what's at the end of this road, don't you?' she replied with a knowing smile, then put a finger to her lips. 'I'm not supposed to take a taxi here, and you're not supposed to know about this place. So let's just both pretend this journey never happened, shall we?' She then handed him twice the fare that was due, which he accepted with surprise.

'Right you are, madam,' he said with a grin and a pretend tug of his forelock. 'Sorry, Doctor, I should say.'

She stepped out of the cab and walked the last mile to the maximum-security prison, carrying her laptop in one hand and a small bag full of papers in the other.

When the prison finally came into view, she raised her eyebrows at the imposing sight. The collection of large, anonymous buildings was situated in a hollow in the surrounding rolling countryside. Around the perimeter was a massive brick wall with barbed wire running along the top, and four watch towers, one in each corner. As long as her fake identity held up to scrutiny, she was confident of getting inside. However, getting out again was clearly going to be a challenge.

Outside the giant walls was a car park encircled by a sturdy chain-link fence and guarded by a security hut and barrier. Trying to look confident, Izzy walked up to the security guards and handed them her fake pass.

'Doctor Lloyd,' she said haughtily. 'I have an appointment.'

A sullen and suspicious guard with a cap pulled low over his eyes, examined her pass and glanced at her face. 'Where's your vehicle?'

Izzy frowned. 'I believe your job is to guard this place,' she said. 'Mine is to check on the wellbeing of those here. Might I suggest we stick to our respective roles?'

The man scowled at her, before marching off to his hut, muttering something inaudible under his breath. A few moments later, he returned, handed back the pass and instructed Izzy to follow him. She was led to the main gates of the prison, which were large steel doors set into the massive brick walls, which towered over her like those of a castle. A single door, which was set into one of the much larger main doors, opened and another grim-faced guard greeted them.

'This is highly irregular,' said the guard, looking at her pass and screwing his face into a frown. 'We don't normally get visits like this.'

Izzy rolled her eyes and pretended to be straining to keep her temper in check. 'I'm sure you don't,' she sighed impatiently. 'But shall I phone Commissioner Doomsday to say you won't let me in, or do you want to do it yourself?' She stood staring at him with a sweet smile. She may have looked self-assured on the outside, but inside, her stomach was doing somersaults and her heart was thumping.

The guard took one last wary look at her before indicating with a quick tilt of his head that she should follow him inside. He then made her wait outside his small office while he studied his computer, no doubt, she thought, looking through the list of appointments for that day.

She took a few deep breaths, trying to calm her nerves. If her fake appointment failed to look genuine, she was about to be arrested and then thrown into a cell in the very prison she was now standing in.

A few minutes later, he reappeared and said: 'That all checks out. I'll get someone to escort you to him.'

Izzy strained hard not to let out a huge sigh of relief.

Yet another guard appeared, a burly woman, who seemed intent on making sure that Izzy noticed the gun in its holster on her hip. With a rather manly swagger, the guard led Izzy through a maze of windowless corridors. Whilst trying to look relaxed and in control, Izzy was in fact concentrating furiously, attempting to memorise the route they were taking.

Eventually, they turned into yet another corridor with dozens of doors on either side stretching into the distance like an infinity mirror. The guard stopped at the door with 067 written on it and used an electronic pass to open the lock. An automated voice blared out "Stand back" twice, while the guard poked her head into the room. She then stood by the open door and declared it was safe for Izzy to enter.

Izzy took a deep breath, telling herself to show no emotion, and then stepped into the small room. There was a single bed against one wall, a basic toilet in the corner and sitting on the only chair at a small desk was Tony Singh, haggard and looking like he had not slept for days. The faintest flicker of recognition seemed to flash across his face.

'Please now leave us and close the door behind you,' demanded Izzy.

'Sorry, that's not prison policy,' sniffed the guard.

'I don't care,' replied Izzy indignantly. 'Just close the door, before I have to phone the governor. I will take full responsibility for anything that happens.'

For a moment, the guard stood staring back, before finally relenting. 'All right. Just knock when you need to come out. And don't try anything, you,' she snarled at Tony.

As soon as the thick steel door had closed, Izzy sat on the bed and whispered: 'How are you?'

Tony smiled wearily. 'Just about all right, I suppose. Didn't expect to see you again quite so soon. A lovely surprise.'

Izzy smiled back. 'Right, we don't have much time.'

Tony furrowed his brow. 'You can't surely be hoping to break me out?'

'Watch me,' grinned Izzy. 'Now, in a minute, I'm going to call that gorilla back in,' she added, nodding towards the door.

'Izzy, I really think you should leave while you still can. There is zero chance of us both getting out of here.'

'We need you, Tony. Doomsday has got her hands on the mirror and the Iris. Tom and Molly have disappeared into the void to do, well, who knows what.'

'But you won't be able to help me get out if you're stuck in here as well.'

'I'm not leaving without you, Tony,' she muttered, then thumped a fist on the cell door.

The prison guard opened the door and moved her large frame into the doorway.

'I need to give this man an injection,' said Izzy in her most superior voice. 'Kindly help me to restrain him.'

The guard's face broke into a wicked smile. 'It would be my pleasure.'

As the large woman stepped into the room, Izzy fumbled

about in her bag, until the guard had walked past her and was leaning towards Tony, who sat paralysed on his chair, eyes wide and unsure what was about to happen. Izzy then took out a small square of cloth, reached forward and jammed it against the guard's mouth and nose. For a few terrifying seconds, the stocky woman struggled, lashing out with her arms and legs. But by the time Tony had leapt to his feet to help restrain her, the sedative was taking effect and the strength was rapidly draining from her. Finally, her limbs went limp and suddenly, she became a dead weight and had to be lowered to the floor with considerable effort.

'Well,' said Tony, still looking uncertain. 'That's one guard down. Now just another two hundred or so to go.'

Izzy grinned at him and opened her laptop. 'That was only part one. Now for part two. While you're waiting, take the uniform off the nice pretty lady, there's a good boy.'

'You have got to be joking.'

'No,' said Izzy as she began typing. 'Chop, chop! We haven't got all day.'

'But it'll never fit me,' protested Tony, as he began wrestling with the guard's huge, dark shirt.

'No one will even notice. Trust me.'

'Oh, well,' shrugged Tony. 'What have I got to lose?'

'Exactly!'

A few minutes later, Tony stood in front of her, the shirt and trousers hanging loosely on his slender frame. Next to him lay the unconscious guard, now dressed only in her white underwear. Izzy sniggered at Tony's appearance.

'I look ridiculous, don't I?' he said.

'Yes. But it'll have to do. Now put that cap on, low over your eyes and try to act with authority. If you walk around

Guardians of the Mirror

like a wet rag, you'll stand out like a sore thumb.'

'Yes, ma'am,' replied Tony and gave her an exaggerated salute.

Smiling and returning to her laptop, Izzy then pressed a button. In the next moment, the prevailing silence was shattered. The fire alarm went off, echoing painfully down the corridor, while all the cell doors sprang open at once.

'Come on!' yelled Izzy. 'Escort me out of the prison.'

They rushed out into the corridor, where the sirens were wailing, and lights were flashing. Izzy directed Tony to the left, just as the first inmates began to poke their heads out of their doors, clearly bemused by what was happening. A guard rushed past them in the opposite direction but cast both of them only the most cursory of glances.

On they hurried, twisting left and right along the labyrinth of corridors, Izzy, concentrating furiously, frantically trying to picture the route in her mind. More guards rushed back and forth. Angry shouting could be heard rising above the ear-splitting alarm.

By now, the two of them were striding along so fast they were almost jogging. But with all the chaos around them, Izzy hoped their haste to get out would not look out of place.

Just when Izzy was starting to fear she had made a wrong turning and that they were going around in circles, there before her was the main exit, with the glass-walled security office right next to the large metal doors. Two nervous-looking guards stood either side of the doors, machine guns pointing at them as they approached. Izzy flashed her pass at them.

'I'll make sure she gets out okay,' yelled Tony to one of the guards, all the time trying to keep his cap low over his face.

Izzy was almost holding her breath, so anxious was she.

After a moment's hesitation, the guards opened the small door and let the two of them walk out into the cold December air. Trying not to rush, Izzy walked through the car park towards the exit with Tony right beside her. For every deep breath she inhaled through her nose, she could feel her heart beating at least ten times.

The fire alarms stopped sounding; an eerie silence descended on the scene.

Once again, Izzy showed her pass as they approached the exit barrier. The guard glanced at it, remembered having let her in earlier and raised the barrier to let them through.

They were almost out. She was on the verge of achieving the impossible.

'Just a minute,' said the guard. 'Where are you going, pal?'

Izzy spun round. The guards were staring at Tony, who suddenly looked conspicuous with his baggy uniform. Before he or Izzy could react, four guards had surrounded Tony, had drawn their guns, were pointing them at him and at her.

'Down on the ground!' yelled one of them.

'How dare you ...?' protested Izzy.

But before she could say anything further the guard thrust his gun at her and barked: 'Just do it!'

Izzy felt sick, despondent beyond words. She and Tony had no choice but to comply. They lay down side by side on the cold tarmac, exchanged an anxious look.

One of the guards crouched over Tony, patted him down, and then rolled him over onto his back. He tore the cap off Tony's head, then grabbed him by the scruff. 'Where did you get this uniform, eh?' he roared. 'Answer me.'

'I found it,' said Tony through bared teeth.

'A likely story,' said the guard. He then released the front of

Tony's loose-fitting shirt, the top of which fell open. The guard was about to stand up when he looked closely at Tony. 'What's that?' he demanded, and reached for something around Tony's neck. He pulled out the pendant with the faintly glowing almond-shaped stone, then yanked it off him. 'I think I'd better look after that,' he added and stuffed it into his pocket.

Tony flashed a horrified look at Izzy, who muttered simply: 'Oh, no!'

Chapter Thirteen

Dystopia

In the blink of an eye, they had left behind the bright lights of the Mirror Room and now stood in a different room, which was dark and cold. For a few moments, the three of them waited while their eyes adjusted to the dim light.

'Well, this is creepy,' said Jake.

'I was just waiting for more flashing lights and blaring alarms,' said Tom.

But nothing happened. All he could hear was the faint whistling of the wind, seeping its way through an unseen crack into the room.

When he was satisfied that nothing untoward was going to happen, Tom moved forward into the room and looked around. The three of them, like the mirror behind them, were on a low dais at one end of the room, which seemed almost identical in size and shape to the Mirror Room they had just left. Yet this place was apparently lifeless.

A thin, vertical line of bright light appeared momentarily in front of them, followed by a rumble of thunder overhead.

'I think there's a door over there,' said Tom, straining his eyes. He jumped down off the low platform and trotted a few paces across a concrete floor. At the end of the room, a thick metal door was ajar, more closed than open, but with enough of a gap that he caught a clear glimpse of the next jagged bolt of lightning as it briefly planted itself into a nearby field, lighting up dead-looking trees and hedgerows.

'Please tell me that is just a normal storm,' said Jake,

moving beside Tom. 'I'm not sure I can take another of those killer ones.'

'Well, whatever it is, it hasn't been caused by us,' said Tom. 'It's too soon since we arrived. And don't forget, we've still got those things in our necks.'

'Oh, good,' said Jake. 'Perhaps it is just an ordinary storm. I miss a good old-fashioned thunderstorm, don't you? I used to love watching them as a kid. But I've kind of grown tired of them in the last year.'

'I know what you mean,' laughed Tom, as he peered outside again. It was as dark as night, until one of the frequent bursts of lightning lit up the open countryside once more.

He turned back to face Jake with a wry smile on his face. 'I just saw a tornado in the distance.' He chuckled and shook his head in disbelief. 'It's just not our day, is it?'

'Oh, great!' sighed Jake.

'On the plus side, this place looks sturdy enough,' said Tom, looking up at what appeared to be a solid concrete roof. 'And I suppose it shouldn't be heading towards us, either.'

'I hope you're right ... for once,' mumbled Molly, who had been unusually quiet until then.

Tom was going to respond, but then thought better of it. He wanted to take her to one side, shake her and scream that he was not the baddie in all this. But he knew he would have to save that argument for another time when this was all over. For now, they just had to find a way home.

Meanwhile, Jake had taken his phone out and was sweeping the weak torch around the room. But everywhere they looked, there were just plain concrete walls.

When the next flash of lightning sent light flooding through the crack in the door, Tom looked out once more. 'It's moving away,' he said. 'Looks like the storm is clearing.'

'Begs the question, what caused it?' mused Jake. 'Your dad, I mean your professor dad in that other world, seemed to imply they hadn't used the mirror in years.'

'Yeah, he did,' agreed Tom. 'But I'm not sure we can trust anything that man said. Anyway, come on. Let's take a look outside.' He pressed his shoulder against the heavy door, but it refused to move. 'Give me a hand, you two.'

The three of them pushed hard against the cold metal door, until eventually, it began to creek and opened just enough for them to pass through the gap one at a time.

Once outside, there were only a few paces before a small set of steps lead up to higher ground. When he was at the top, Tom turned around and looked back. The mirror was housed in a bunker built into a small hill. Apart from the steps leading down to the door, through which they had just come, there was no outward sign that anything lay there at all, just a small grassy knoll.

'It's a bit different to *Morladron House*,' said Jake.

'Yeah,' said Tom. 'Makes you wonder if that even exists here.'

It was getting late in the day, and even though the storm was now clearing, the landscape looked grey and devoid of life. A keen wind was blowing across the rolling hills, carrying occasional icy raindrops into their faces.

'Hey!' called out a voice. 'What are you guys doing out in this?'

Tom spun round and saw a man waving at them from a dozen paces away. He was dressed from head to toe in waterproof clothing, the kind Tom had seen fishermen wear in the winter when they ventured out on stormy seas. The man pulled back his oversized hood to reveal a thickly bearded face.

'Come on. Back to the shelter,' he insisted with a wave of a hand.

'Might as well,' shrugged Tom, looking at Molly and Jake.

They walked down the gentle, wet slope towards the bedraggled figure, who smiled warmly as they approached.

'Were you sheltering in that old bunker?' he asked, as they all began walking away. When Tom said they had been, the man's jolly face darkened. 'You want to keep away from that place, trust me. Nothing good ever came out of there.'

Tom was about to ask the man some questions, but after glancing at Jake and Molly's wary faces, he decided against it. Until they knew what sort of world they were in, caution was perhaps the better approach.

The landscape around them was desolate. In the far distance, they could see the recent storm receding over a hill, flashes of lightning continuing to illuminate patches of the low, forbidding cloud. In the frequent bursts of white light, Tom was certain he could see at least three mighty tornadoes, swaying like giant spinning tops.

In the dim light, the rest of the land all around was barren. The few trees dotted about in fields looked dead, not just the usual winter trees without their leaves but twisted, lifeless skeletons of black wood. Indeed, the more his eyes scoured the landscape, the more fallen trees he saw, lying on their sides or uprooted completely, as though a giant had plucked them from the soil and then abandoned them.

'You're not from around here, are you?' asked the bearded man.

'Er, no,' replied Tom. 'We're from a long way away.' He

gave a quick, knowing smirk to his two friends.

'Although, you two look familiar, come to think of it,' the man continued, staring at Molly and Tom in particular.

Tom laughed nervously and looked away.

After a few minutes' walking, they crested a hill, and before them, a short distance away, was what appeared to be a campsite of some sort. Several small fires were blazing amongst the crumbling stone ruins of what had been at one time a large building, whilst many silhouetted figures moved about in the shadows.

As they approached the site, Tom gasped. 'Oh, my ...!' Even in the encroaching darkness, he recognised the landscape, the hills, the road, the cliffs nearby, the downward slope into the valley just beyond the ruins. 'That's *Morladron House.*'

The bearded man sniffed. 'Yes, of course it is. At least, what's left of it.'

All that now remained were piles of rubble here and there and sections of stone wall still standing, the tallest of which were no higher than an average person. It looked like nothing more than the remnants of some ancient Roman building. Amongst the ruins, a few dozen people meandered about or stood warming themselves around the numerous makeshift fires.

Gaunt, sad faces turned towards the trio as they walked into the remains of the house. Some even eyed them suspiciously, their haggard features rendered even more sinister by the shadows cast from the crackling fires.

'Who've we got here, then?' asked someone out of the darkness.

Their bearded escort was about to respond, when a woman sprang forward, her face lined and snarling like an angry witch. 'I know him,' she yelled, pointing a finger at Tom. 'That's Tom Paget. Except ... it can't be ... because Tom died a few days ago.'

'What?' cried someone else.

'You know what that means?' shouted another. 'They've come through the mirror!'

A man's angry face appeared in front of Tom's. 'Is it true? Did you come here from that other place?'

'Well, yes. But ...'

'What have you come here to do?' roared someone.

People were gathering quickly around them, appearing out of the shadows, moving ever closer, their faces angry and menacing.

'What are you going to steal this time?' screamed someone right behind Tom, making him jump.

'String 'em up!' cried another.

His eyes flitting back and forth, Tom moved in close to Jake and Molly, who both looked as terrified and confused as he was. A small crowd had now gathered all around them, teeth bared and eyes glowering, like a pack of hungry, angry wolves.

'What's going on here?' called out a man above the rising clamour.

Some muttering continued, but then the crowd fell silent, while a tall, thin man walked through the throng of people and eyed the three teenagers intently. He wore a long, shabby coat and his face was lined and unshaven.

'They've come through the mirror,' said someone in a tone that made it sound like the worst crime anyone could possibly commit.

'Is this true?' asked the man.

'Y-yes,' said Tom. 'But we haven't come to cause any trouble, I swear. To be honest, we're confused. We have no idea what is going on here.'

Once again, many of the assembled people began jeering and shaking their fists.

'He's wearing a medallion,' said someone. 'Let's use it to go through the mirror and storm their world.'

A great roar of approval rose up into the dark sky, until their tall leader calmed them down with his hands.

'That won't work,' said Tom hurriedly. 'It's guarded by soldiers. They'd arrest you straightaway. Or worse — shoot you on the spot.'

The tall man studied Tom closely for a few seconds, then said: 'Take them below. Before the next storm arrives.'

Back in Jake's world, a school minibus was being driven cautiously along the winding country lanes. Inside, Miss Butterworth was not having a good morning. The schools had just broken up for the Christmas holidays, so she was meant to be at home with her feet up, enjoying a much-needed two-week break. But then she had received a phone call from the headteacher at the school where she taught, informing her that Mrs Crawley, who was meant to be taking the children on their trip to the Porthgarrick Christmas market, had gone down with the flu. So, rather reluctantly, she had agreed to step in at the last minute and take the small group of year 3 children on their special trip. There might have only been eight children in the bus, but the excitement of the adventure was causing them to make more noise and mischief than Miss Butterworth would have imagined possible from so small a group.

Guardians of the Mirror

Sitting at the front near the driver, she was having to constantly turn round to ask them to settle down. Perhaps if she had been more in the mood, she would have initiated a sing-along or a game of I spy to distract them, but she was struggling to find the motivation.

As the minibus filled with shrieking once more, she twisted around and was about to berate the children, when, without warning, the bus driver slammed on the brakes.

'What's that fool doing?' he said.

Having been jolted in her seat, Miss Butterworth turned back round and looked out of the windscreen. There, sitting cross-legged in the middle of the road, was a man, head down under a baseball cap.

'Looks like he's asleep,' said the driver. He then wound down his window, leant out and shouted. 'Oi, mate! Time to wake up.'

When the man did not respond, the driver climbed out of the minibus and walked towards the seated figure. In a flash, the man sprang to his feet. He was tall with broad, powerful shoulders and looked down on the diminutive bus driver, pointing a handgun straight into his face.

Miss Butterworth gasped. The inside of the minibus was now silent, as everyone watched the gunman force the driver to the side of the road, hands behind his head. Once the driver, visibly shaking all over, was lying prone on the grass verge, the man marched towards the bus.

'Get everyone out — now!' he demanded, looking menacingly through the open driver's door.

For a few seconds, Miss Butterworth was paralysed with fear and simply stared back at the man. Under his cap, his face looked cold and hard, devoid of any emotion. And his nose seemed to be twisted to one side, somehow adding to the man's threatening appearance.

One of the children began to whimper. Miss Butterworth swallowed hard and tried to compose herself. 'What do you want?' she asked, her voice cracking. 'These are only small children.'

The man with the crooked nose waved his gun over the driver's seat. 'I said get out,' he roared. 'All of you.'

While another child began to cry, the teacher hurriedly climbed out of her seat, slid open the side door and directed the children out onto the side of the road. Three of them were clinging to her and attempting to bury their faces in her clothing.

'Now get moving,' ordered the man. 'And quickly. Over there, towards the old house.'

Miss Butterworth spread her arms wide, trying to corral the children forward, smiling and talking to them in a soothing voice as she went, whilst inside she felt sick.

The trembling bus driver was ordered to his feet and joined the group as they covered the short distance down the lane towards a derelict-looking old mansion with boarded up windows. Still at gunpoint, they were marshalled inside the dark and lifeless house.

All sorts of terrible thoughts and fears were now racing through Miss Butterworth's mind. But she kept forcing herself to stay calm, for the sake of the children. She began to feel bad at having been cross with them earlier.

They ended up inside a large but mostly empty room. The man with the crooked nose had by now turned on a small torch and was directing everyone into the corner of the room where a tall mirror stood angled slightly upwards on a

Guardians of the Mirror

wooden stand.

'Now listen carefully,' the sinister man snarled. 'Everyone is to hold hands with the person next to them.' He then marched round the group, sweeping his torch across all the hands, making sure everyone was linked together.

'What are you going to do with us?' asked the bus driver.

The gunman shone his torch right into the driver's face and poked him painfully in the chest with the muzzle of his gun. 'Just make sure you're holding hands. That's all you have to do, understood?'

The driver nodded silently.

'Good!' cried the man. He then put the torch down on a table such that its beam shone onto the mirror. With his freed hand, he reached inside his jacket and pulled out some sort of large medallion, which glinted in the torchlight reflecting off the surface of the mirror. He then grabbed Miss Butterworth's wrist, took one last cursory look around his assembled group of hostages and touched the surface of the mirror with the hand holding the gun.

Miss Butterworth blinked and in the next moment, they were all standing in a room full of bright sunlight. After a few seconds of complete silence, some of the children began to chatter excitedly.

Completely disorientated, the teacher just stood still, trying to fathom what had just happened and where they were. All ten of them, as well as the man with the crooked nose, were standing in an empty room, which had a line of windows along one wall. They were high up, overlooking rolling countryside in the distance. Behind them stood a mirror, identical to the one they had just seen in the old, dark house.

Miss Butterworth watched as their kidnapper began talking

into his phone. However, while he was still casually waving his gun in the air, neither she nor the bus driver felt inclined to move or to say anything. Instead, the teacher tried to gather the children around her and to whisper comforting words to them.

A door opened and in walked a short, dumpy woman with black hair tied back into a bun and a pair of black-framed glasses on her nose. Her cold eyes darted around the room and looked at the group of children with apparent dissatisfaction as though an unpleasant smell had just entered her nostrils. She strode over to the gunman, looking far from pleased.

'What on earth have you done?' she demanded, her voice a seething murmur.

Continuing to calm her pupils, Miss Butterworth tried to edge closer so she could overhear the conversation.

'You wanted a group of people,' muttered the man. 'That's what I have brought you.'

'But children, for goodness' sake!' the woman snapped.

The man shrugged, rather indifferently. 'You never specified.'

The stocky woman sighed dramatically. 'Well, I suppose they will have to do for now.'

At that moment, the door opened again, and this time a slender, middle-aged woman entered the room, wearing a smart, black police uniform. She, too, looked across at the children, but her eyes widened, and her jaw slackened with surprise and then horror.

'What's going on here?' asked the police officer. 'Who are these people and how did they get in here?'

'This does not concern you, DCI Prideaux,' replied the short woman.

Guardians of the Mirror

'It concerns me, Miss Doomsday, when they are in my police station.'

Frowning and looking up at the taller woman, Miss Doomsday said: 'Kindly arrange to have a vehicle ready to transport these people.' She was well spoken, but her voice was dripping with menace. 'And quickly, if you would be so kind.'

One of the children tugged at Miss Butterworth's dress. 'I want to go home now,' the little girl murmured with tears in her eyes, but loud enough that the whole room fell silent.

The policewoman looked across with, Miss Butterworth thought, the concern of a mother in her face.

The teacher crouched down to look into the girl's face, whilst also glancing up to briefly catch DCI Prideaux's eyes. 'Don't worry, Beth,' she said. 'There's a nice police lady here to sort it all out for us.' She then shot a brief smile at the police officer.

DCI Prideaux turned sharply back to face Miss Doomsday. 'You need to tell me what is going on here.'

Miss Doomsday had a face of thunder, ready to explode. Instead, she pointed an aggressive finger at the police officer, whilst muttering in hushed tones. 'These are matters of national security. You have seen the Prime Minister visit me on a number of occasions recently, have you not? So do not ask questions that do not concern you. Now, kindly arrange that transport I asked for. If not, you will be replaced.'

For a moment or two, DCI Prideaux glared down at the other woman, before storming out of the room, unable to meet Miss Butterworth's anguished gaze.

Miss Doomsday glowered at the retreating figure and then turned to the man with the crooked nose. 'Make sure they are

John D. Fennell

taken to the agreed location. We need to move fast on this. Before the storms break. And make sure you move this mirror. I don't like it being here. It's too exposed.'

With every deafening explosion of thunder, the pillars under what remained of *Morladron House* trembled in ever more disconcerting fashion. Or was it simply that the numerous guttering candles were quivering in such a way that made it look like the giant stone pillars were shaking? Either way, Tom found he was staring up at the distant, black ceiling the whole time, worried the cavern was about to collapse at any moment.

He, Jake and Molly were being held captive in a dank corner of the underground chamber. Though they were not shackled in any way, it was plain they were not free to move about, as witnessed by the stationing of two surly-looking men who sat nearby, casting them frequent, disapproving looks.

Out of the shadows, a slender figure approached their two guards. When the figure's face appeared in the nearby, weak candlelight, Tom smiled wryly. 'Well, look who it is,' he muttered to his two friends.

Standing before them was yet another spitting image of Molly. She had the same dark hair, swept back into a ponytail and wore glasses, but hers looked rather battered with one of the arms patched up with tape.

She approached the trio and sat down on the floor in front of them. 'Hi,' she said. 'I'm Molly.'

'What?' said Jake. 'The same name?' When she gave him a puzzled look, he added: 'This is also Molly.'

'So you must also be Tom,' said the girl, staring intently at him with a terrible sadness in her eyes that made Tom uncomfortable.

'Er, yes. I am. And this is Jake.'

A flicker of a smile appeared on her face but was gone in an instant. 'We lost our Jake months ago,' she said, not taking her eyes off Tom. 'And then ... I lost my Tom a couple of weeks ago.'

As she wiped away a tear, another rumble of thunder exploded overhead. 'I'm sorry,' said Tom.

After what seemed like several minutes of awkward silence during which none of them knew quite what to say, the Molly in front of them said: 'They tell me you came through the mirror. From the other world.'

Tom sighed. 'Look, I think there has been a misunderstanding here. We did travel here through the mirror from the other world. But that's not where we come from. There are actually loads of other worlds out there, thousands of them, all linked by those mirrors. We travelled from our own world to what you call the other world the other day, if that makes sense. We weren't welcomed there, and they kicked us out at gunpoint, forcing us to come here, to this world ...'

'A likely story,' muttered one of the nearby guards.

'Why would we lie about something like that?' spat the Molly beside Tom. 'If we were from the other world, as you call it, why in heaven's name would we choose to come to this god-forsaken place?'

The man snorted and turned away.

'It's true,' said Tom, looking at the Molly in front of him. 'But I don't understand. What has happened here? Why is your world like this?'

She continued staring at him, perhaps trying to decide whether she could trust him or not. Finally, she broke the silence. 'You really don't know, do you?' Tom shook his head. 'Years and years ago, when the portal between our two worlds was first opened, the people from the other world began immediately to exploit us. They have always been much more advanced than we are, in everything. They invaded us, stole what useful technology and resources they could find, and even began taking slaves back with them. But then of course, they quickly realised that those slaves were causing terrible storms in their world. So they stopped that and started using our world as a prison instead, for all their dangerous criminals. They controlled both ends of the gateway between our two worlds with armed guards, you see. So they could send through whoever they wanted, whenever they wanted.'

'Oh, my goodness!' gasped Jake, instantly realising the implications.

Molly nodded sadly. 'Yes. Not only did all these horrible criminals come through, but their presence here quickly began to cause terrible storms, over and over again. But the other world didn't care; they just kept sending more and more people. In the end, the climate began to change, permanently. Storms just kept on occurring, regardless of whether there were two identical people here or not.

'They no longer send prisoners these days. Perhaps they feel ashamed of what they've done. But it's too late now. Our planet has been ruined. It is dying. The storms are more and more frequent. Even when I was a little girl, it wasn't too bad. But now the gaps between storms grow shorter and shorter. Nothing grows anymore. We're starving. And the other world has pulled up their drawbridge and lives its happy life in paradise.'

'That is awful,' said the other Molly.

Guardians of the Mirror

'Maybe there is a way we can help one another,' said Tom. 'A friend of ours can, with the right items, control the weather. He could come here, teach you what to do.'

'Really?' said the girl.

'Yes. But it's kind of the reason we came here in the first place. We're looking for something called an Iris and an Iris box. With those things, he can control the weather. But the ones in our world were taken by someone, so she can use their powers for herself.'

A tall figure emerged out of the shadows. It was the thin man who appeared to be the group's leader. 'I'm afraid we haven't seen anything like that here for years,' he said. 'Anything to do with the mirror is controlled by them. Many years ago, some from here tried to rebel against them. But they were brutally crushed in order to preserve their paradise. Then anything of value was taken and they closed the portal for good. Until you came through, that is.' He then laughed, rather bitterly. 'For what's it's worth, I think I believe your story. If you can come up with a decent plan, I might just be able to persuade the others to let you leave.' He then wandered away again, shaking his head.

'I've heard their world is wonderful,' said the Molly in front of them. 'But they built it on the back of us.' She stood up to leave. 'If you can find a way to help us, I'll make sure they listen to you. That man is my uncle.' With one last sad smile at Tom, she turned and left.

'Wow!' said Tom. 'Makes our problems seem pretty small, doesn't it?'

'Maybe this is an indication of what Doomsday is going to do to our planet, now that *someone* gave her an Iris,' said Molly.

John D. Fennell

Tom sighed. 'Jake, will you ask Molly to keep her thoughts to herself unless she has something more constructive to add?'

'And will you tell Tom–' began Molly, before Jake cut her off.

'Guys!' he said with uncharacteristic irritation. 'Are you really doing this? Seriously? We've been halfway across the universe, or several universes or however this all works — it makes my head hurt. Anyway, the point is: you two are meant to be together. Wherever we go, you are an item. You two, Rachel and Michael, Milly and Tim, the Molly and Tom in this world. So, don't you think it's about time you put your petty differences to one side and started working together to get us out of this mess. Because I for one can't stand being here a moment longer. And especially not with you two bickering away like this. And to make matters worse, they don't have any chocolate here either.' He folded his arms and turned away from them.

Tom looked at Molly who simply averted her gaze. He then patted Jake's thick shoulder. 'You're right, mate, sorry.' He rubbed his chin. 'Look, it seems what we need is not here. And we have no way back into the void. So, the only option left is to go back to that other world and try to get hold of their Iris. That's what we need to do. We just need to work out how to do it.'

Chapter Fourteen

The Pendant

Even though she had been anticipating it for hours, the first clap of thunder still made Izzy nearly jump out of her skin. She had been sitting on the bed, hugging her knees, for what seemed like hours, but which was probably much less. It was hard to judge the passage of time in a tiny prison cell.

Immediately, she jumped off the bed and looked up to the small, square window. Through the bars, she could see black clouds gathering in the sky, moving as fast as thick smoke belching from a terrible fire. Unable to close her eyes, let alone sleep, she had been dreading this moment for ages. As if being in prison was not bad enough, knowing that Tony was now unprotected without the pendant around his neck made her tremble with abject fear.

A flash of lightning lit up the small square of sky she could see. Barely had she blinked when the thunder crashed, shaking the building. She felt so helpless. And if only she had not turned up in the first place, trying to rescue Tony, he would probably still have his pendant.

Before she had time to blame herself anymore, there was an almighty explosion directly overhead, or so it felt. The single light in the ceiling flickered a few times, before going out altogether. In the dark, she stared up at the light, willing it to come back on. A few seconds later, much to her relief, it burst back into life.

Following another streak of lightning, the heavy rain came.

Blotting out all other noise, it pounded the building like the roar of a great engine.

Izzy was pacing the tiny room, her heart racing, not knowing what to do.

Another terrifying crash shook the building, followed by yet another even louder explosion. The light went out again, this time with a terrible finality.

The roar of the rain was easing, but in its place a different yet equally frightening sound was growing by the second. It sounded as if a gale-force wind were buffeting the prison, and as it grew louder and louder, she could hear the building begin to creak and groan in protest.

With little light to see by, she tried to open her cell door, hoping the loss of power would mean the locks no longer worked. But the door was still bolted firmly shut. If only she had her laptop, she thought.

A terrible wrenching sound rose up from somewhere outside. A deafening boom quickly followed, then a great clatter of masonry and shattering of glass, as though a wrecking ball had just demolished a part of the prison.

By now, Izzy was as frustrated at not being able to see what was occurring outside as she was terrified at the thought of what was about to happen next.

Without warning, another mighty explosion rocked the prison. The walls shook; even the floor seemed to tilt a fraction to one side. Out in the corridor, she could hear frantic voices, running footsteps.

Then the floor lurched once again. A giant crack ran across one of her walls. A chunk of plaster fell from the ceiling and thumped onto her bed.

The thick metal door creaked and groaned, protesting at the

forces being exerted on it, while the frame around it began to twist alarmingly. Izzy rushed at the door with her shoulder, while more plaster fell from the ceiling and more cracks shot across the walls. Tears welled in her eyes, whilst panic rose inside her. She was desperate to get out.

The building shook violently once more, as though from an earthquake. She was thrown sideways and only just managed to keep her balance against a wall. The roar of the wind, the sound of destruction were mounting by the second.

The door was ajar.

Without the slightest hesitation, she leapt towards the thin gap and managed to squeeze through, out into the dark corridor. She looked right and saw that a section of the roof had collapsed, blocking the exit. With the bangs and screeches and moans of devastation still ringing in her ears, she turned left and ran.

After skidding around a corner, she came to a stairwell. Needing to know what was happening, to assess the danger, she tore up the stairs two at a time, even when common sense was telling her to go down and to get out of the building as fast as she could. After only a few flights of steps, she came to a door that led onto the roof of the building. She burst through the door and onto the flat roof.

The sight that met her forced the air from her lungs, made her blood run cold. From atop the building, she could see the entire prison complex, with its collection of large cellblocks surrounded by the massive brick wall and four watchtowers. But much of her view of the surrounding, empty moorland was now obscured by three enormous, swirling tornadoes, which rose up massively into the black cloud above. Inexorably, they were closing in on the prison from different directions, like three giants converging on the same inviting meal. Indeed, one of them had already cut a wide path through the perimeter wall, and was now devouring the corner of Izzy's building, sending unnerving tremors rippling through the structure.

She had seen enough. Despite having experienced little of this phenomenon at first hand, she nevertheless knew enough to realise that the twisters would not stop until either Tony or his double, Harry Singh, were dead. And since she already knew that Harry was not in this particular prison, the realisation that these tornadoes existed solely to pursue Tony was utterly terrifying. The idea of trying to save Tony filled rapidly inside her like an inflating balloon until it was all that she could think about.

As she hurtled back down the stairs, forcing herself to breathe deeply, to suppress the panic that was straining to break out, she tried to picture in her mind the layout of the prison. She knew where the entrance was, willed herself to remember the route she had taken to get from there to Tony's cell. He was in a different part of the prison, she was sure of it.

Still the building was shaking, the air full of unusual creaks and groans and booms and smashes, all rising above the constant roar of the wind.

A guard appeared on the stairs, having just run out of a corridor. He glanced up at Izzy, a few steps above him, but his face was full of fear and he simply rushed down the stairs. She followed him down to the bottom of the stairwell and then out of the door into the central courtyard. In a flash, he was gone, running for his life.

To her left, one of the vast twisters was looming high above the prison, roaring like a beast. As it tore a slow path through the building, pieces of rubble were being drawn inside its massive belly, swirling around, being carried ever higher. But then some smaller pieces of brick or wood were ejected, crashing at speed into the ground like the falling fragments of a meteor.

She ran across the courtyard as more and more people emerged into the gloom. Some were guards with their dark uniforms and caps, whilst others were clearly escaped inmates like her. One or two guards were shouting, trying to maintain order, but their cries could not be heard above the roar of destruction. But most were simply running away with everyone else.

Racing past a red-faced guard, Izzy sprinted across the courtyard and went straight into the opposite building, praying it was the one in which Tony was housed. Once inside, the noise seemed to lessen a fraction, such that Izzy could now hear her own pulse pounding in her ears. She looked down the first corridor she saw. The lights were still on and no one was about. She stopped for a second or two, steadying herself against the narrow corridor walls, and closed her eyes, trying to picture the route she needed to take.

Certain she now knew where she needed to go, she then set off at speed, her feet echoing down the corridor. The place was a confusing warren of passageways. She made a sharp left turn, then moments later, a right turn. She found herself in yet another long corridor, but this one seemed familiar. Sprinting along, glancing at the numbers on the doors, she felt a sudden surge of excitement. She skidded to a halt in front of door number 067.

'Tony!' she yelled, thumping on the metal door. 'It's me. Are you in there?'

Moments later, there was a tapping coming from the other side. She then noticed a small viewing hole in the door, through which, when she put her eye to it, she could see a tiny image of Tony in his room. The door was locked and the only way in was with the swipe of an electronic card.

A loud crash filled the corridor. All the lights in the ceiling began flickering and the walls started to shake. Izzy thumped the door in frustration.

'Oi!' bellowed a guard. 'What are you doing there?'

She turned her head and saw a guard striding towards her, patting his truncheon in one hand in a threatening manner.

'Get back to your cell,' he roared as he approached.

Again, the ground shook, the lights flickered. The sound of a window shattering nearby filled the air.

'Do you have any idea what is going on out there?' spat Izzy, shouting above the growing noise and glaring incredulously at the man. 'This whole place is about to be destroyed and you're seriously worried about what I'm doing.'

'Get back in your cell, before I make you.'

'For goodness' sake, tell me how to open this door,' demanded Izzy.

It was getting hard to make herself understood over the approaching roar of wind and destruction. A dizzying mix of panic and anger at the man's stupidity was rising inside her.

Then he lunged at her with his baton, trying to strike her on the arm. But Izzy was too nimble, too well practised at kendo to be taken by surprise. In the blink of an eye, she had dodged to one side, grabbed his thrusting forearm and twisted it behind his back. Before he could react, he was lying face down on the floor, Izzy kneeling on his back. Seeing the handcuffs attached to his belt, she unclipped them and snapped them shut around his wrists.

Yelling into his ear so there was no chance he could not hear her above the growing crescendo, she then demanded: 'Tell me how to unlock that door. Or I'm going to leave you here.'

At first, he glared at her with hatred in his eyes. But then, when the lights went out and the roof at the far end of the corridor collapsed, fear spread across his face. Slowly, the long, dark corridor began to become shorter and shorter as the building collapsed in the face of the assault by one of the whirlwinds.

The guard wriggled frantically on the floor while he watched the approaching cloud of swirling debris. 'All right!' he yelled. 'The card. Take my card, for goodness' sake. It's in my top pocket.'

'It won't work, you fool,' she screamed back at him. 'There's no power.'

'The key! The key on my belt. Quickly, quickly.'

Izzy rolled him over onto his back, fumbled along his belt until she found a bunch of keys and yanked them off. One by one, she held them up in front of his terrified face until he nodded rapidly, eyes wide with panic.

A large section of the roof came crashing down, filling the corridor with smoke and dust. Instinctively, Izzy buried her head in her hands. Moments later, when she looked up, she saw a large wooden beam angled down at forty-five degrees only three metres away from where they were.

She leapt to her feet, thrust the master key in the lock and opened the heavy metal door. Almost immediately, Tony appeared in the doorway, eyes wild with confusion and fear. She seized his wrist and pulled him out, and was about to run when she stopped, knelt down and unlocked the guard's handcuffs. Not bothering to check whether he had got safely to his feet, she turned and ran with Tony down the corridor.

Jake fumbled in his jacket pocket. 'Do you think we could somehow use this?' he asked, holding up what looked like a credit card in the firelight.

'What is it?' asked Tom.

'It's that card Tim gave us at the museum. The one he said could get us into anything.'

Tom looked at it then turned back to gaze into the crackling fire. Since the last storm had passed, many of the small community living under the remains of *Morladron House* had climbed back outside to enjoy a few moments gathered around small fires, before the next storm arrived. A few fleeting rays of sunshine lit up the ruins of the old house as everyone sat around chatting in hushed, subdued tones. Many were still throwing regular unpleasant looks at Tom, Jake and Molly, but now that the other Molly and her uncle were with them there seemed thankfully little chance of a lynching.

'It'll be tricky going back,' said Tom at length. 'They'll want to arrest us as soon as we appear out of the mirror. But if we go after dark, it might be quieter. And with Jake's card, we might just be able to escape and find the Iris. It's a long shot, but I can't think of any other way.'

The earnest, gaunt face of Molly's uncle studied him for a moment. 'There are many here who want to lock you up or even worse. But you haven't done anything wrong while you've been here, so I see no reason not to let you go.'

'Thank you,' said Tom. 'I give you my word, if we make it, I'll come back as soon as I can and do what I can to help save your world.'

The man smiled thinly, perhaps sceptical that he would ever see Tom again. 'Probably best if you go now, before too many people round here object,' he said. 'You can wait in the old bunker till nightfall. We can give you plenty of water but nothing else, I'm afraid.'

Tom thanked him again, before the man trudged away to another group huddled around a fire.

'This is hard enough for me, saying goodbye,' said the other Molly, looking close to tears. 'So, I'll just go now and wish you good luck.'

Tom briefly touched her proffered hand and felt an unpleasant lump growing in his throat. He just wanted to hug her and tell her everything would be all right, but he knew that was not true. And besides, despite the obvious likeness, she was not the Molly he loved.

As she turned and walked away, his Molly stood up and hurried after her. Looking back over her shoulder, she said: 'I'll go with her and fetch our water.'

Tom watched them walk away, chatting like twin sisters. It was good of Molly, he thought; if anyone would know how the girl was feeling, it was Molly.

A few minutes later, with a cold breeze blowing in off the sea and with dusk descending fast, the three friends set off back towards the concrete bunker. For a while, hardly a word was spoken.

'Well, that was pretty grim,' said Jake eventually.

'Yeah, makes you appreciate what you've got, doesn't it?' agreed Tom, glancing across at Molly.

'Yes, it does, babe,' she mumbled in response.

They carried on walking in silence for a few more paces.

But then Tom came to an abrupt halt and turned to face Molly. 'What did you just call me?'

For a moment, Molly looked startled before her recent disapproving frown returned. 'What do you mean? I didn't call you anything.'

'Show me the pendant I bought you for your birthday.'

Molly could only hold his gaze for a moment before looking down at her feet.

'Guys,' said Jake. 'We don't have time for this. There could be a storm at any moment.'

But Tom had not taken his eyes from Molly. 'You've never called me babe before. And now you can't show me the pendant.'

'I lost it, all right!' snapped Molly. 'I'm really sorry. I've been through a lot these last few days and I really don't need you having a go at me.' Although her face was red with anger, a tear was rolling down her cheek. She glared back at him before walking away.

'Well done, mate,' said Jake evenly. 'You can be an idiot sometimes, do you know that?' He then hurried after Molly.

Tom bit his lip, then rushed after them. He put a gentle hand on Molly's shoulder. 'I'm sorry.'

She threw him the briefest of glances before sighing crossly.

Tom chuckled. 'It kind of reminds me of when we first met,' he said. 'We didn't get off to the best of starts then, did we?'

A hint of a smile played on her lips.

'When I saw you in that school disco ... I knew then. And I walked over to you and said something daft. I can't remember what you said back to me exactly.'

Molly smiled again. 'It was probably something rude or aggressive.'

Tom's smile dropped in a flash. With both hands, he grabbed the sleeves of Molly's purple coat and twisted her round to face him. 'What have you done with her? Tell me now?'

'Ow, you're hurting me,' protested Molly, shaking herself free.

Jake stepped in, his large frame looming before Tom. 'That's enough, Tom. For heaven's sake, what has got into you?'

Tom glanced up at his friend before returning his gaze to Molly. 'We never met in a disco. We met in the playground when Sean was teasing you with one of your books, remember? But no, you can't, can you? Because you weren't there,' he yelled.

Jake looked ready to thump Tom. But then when Molly burst into tears and slumped onto the sodden grass, he turned round and looked uncertain, eyes flitting between the two of them. 'You'd better be right about this, mate,' he scowled.

'He is,' sobbed Molly. 'I'm sorry, I really am. I didn't plan this. It just sort of happened.'

Tom crouched down opposite her. 'Where is she?'

'In the cavern. I'll show you.'

Tom helped her to her feet, and they all hurried back to the ruined house. Just as yet another storm was breaking overhead, they rushed down the steps into the gloomy cavern where hundreds of tiny candles flickered in the sea of darkness.

For once, Tom did not even notice the peals of thunder booming overhead or the pillars shaking. He only cared about one thing and that was finding Molly.

The other Molly led them deep into the dark cavern and

then pulled back a thick curtain. There, sitting on the floor, hands tied behind her back and a gag in her mouth, was Molly, wearing the patched-up glasses of her namesake. Tom removed the gag and untied her bonds. She immediately stood up, looking ready to attack her double. 'Why, you little cow ...' she hissed.

Her lookalike gave her back her glasses and her purple coat, then buried her face in her hands. 'I'm sorry. It was a moment of madness. It wasn't because I wanted to escape this place. It's just ... I miss my Tom so very much. And, well, your Molly just doesn't seem to love you as much as I loved my Tom.'

Ignoring her sobbing doppelgänger, Molly put her glasses back on, then stared at Tom. 'How could you tell it wasn't me?'

Tom smiled. 'Just little things. I could tell pretty quickly, actually.'

'But she's the same as me. Identical in fact. You could have just left and you would still have had a version of me with you. She really loves you, you know.'

Tom sighed. 'Oh, for goodness' sake, Molly,' he said taking hold of one of her hands. 'Yes, she looks like you, even has all your mannerisms. But she is not *you*, is she? She never will be.'

'Oh, Tom,' she replied, her lips quivering, and then threw her arms around Tom's neck. 'I'm so sorry. I've been a real cow recently, haven't I?'

'I'm sorry, too,' said Tom. Hugging her just as tightly, he smiled but said nothing more.

'That's enough, you two,' laughed Jake, as their embrace lingered on and on. 'I think I preferred it when you two hated one another.'

Guardians of the Mirror

Izzy and Tony were running for their lives. All around them, people were dashing about in blind panic while the three gigantic tornadoes drew ever closer, like giant chess pieces moving relentlessly towards a king that was both isolated and ultimately doomed. Izzy realised an identical attack had to be taking place at that very moment wherever Harry Singh was currently being held and, for a brief, terrible moment, she wished that storm would hurry up and kill him quickly, thereby saving Tony's life. Immediately, she hated herself for thinking such a thing.

To their left, part of a building collapsed with a sickening crash of steel and bricks. Great clouds of dust billowed into the air, until some of the debris was drawn into the nearest twister, which rose high into the dark sky like a giant cobra rearing up. Pieces of the building spiralled round and round caught in the whirlwind's orbit, whilst regular flashes of lightning erupted inside the beast.

Izzy and Tony skidded to a halt in the middle of the central courtyard, their eyes flitting from one tornado to the next. Quickly, they changed direction, heading for the one remaining building that was still largely intact, even though one of the twisters was looming high over the back of the block, poised to strike. The whirlwind that had almost broken through to the courtyard was the immediate threat. For now, escaping it was all Izzy could think about.

Unable to speak above the cacophony of noise, Tony waved to Izzy to try a side door. Together with several others, they raced through the door, almost stumbling in their haste to escape. Izzy pointed down a corridor, urging Tony to follow her. Running after a pair of guards who, Izzy guessed, must have known the quickest way out of the prison, they arrived at the main exit. Even though one of the twisters was gyrating dangerously close to the large doors, several guards ran straight out and disappeared into the darkness of the car park.

Without a second thought, Izzy, too, sprinted through the doorway and out into the cold air. The wind from the nearby tornado was tearing at her hair and her clothes, as though a multitude of invisible hands were clawing at her limbs, trying to pull her in.

Tony ran beside her, throwing fearful glances over his shoulder at the vortex that swayed barely twenty metres from where they were. It seemed poised to assault the massive brick wall running around the prison complex. But then, as though under the control of someone, it paused, altered course and began heading towards the two of them.

Ejected at speed by the twister, a car flew low over Izzy's head and crashed dangerously close to where she was. She stumbled and fell awkwardly on her side. When she quickly rolled over, she gasped. Tony was lying close by with a crumpled car across his legs. Behind him, twenty metres away, reared the tornado.

Frantically, she scrambled towards him. He was at least still conscious.

'Are you all right?' she yelled.

'I think so,' he cried back, grimacing. 'But I'm stuck.'

Together they tried to move the vehicle but to no avail.

Tony grabbed her arm. 'It's no good,' he shouted. 'Find the pendant. And, Izzy, promise me if you can't find it in a few seconds, just run.'

'But where is it?'

'The guard may have kept it in his hut. Go!'

Izzy was back on her feet in a flash. Not daring to even look at the tornado spinning in the background, she tore across the car park. Another car was cast through the air and crashed into two other parked vehicles nearby.

She was in the guard's small office near the exit barrier. Her eyes scanned the room, but all she could see were dark shapes everywhere: a coat was hanging on a peg; paperwork was strewn across a small desk; a chair was overturned. Desperately, she pulled open drawers, casting the contents on the floor. She yanked open a filing cabinet, burrowing through the contents with her hands.

Something unseen and heavy crashed into the hut, shattering one of the panes of glass, rocking the walls.

Time was running out. Tony was about to be consumed by the insatiable whirlwind and there was nothing she could do. In a terrible panic, she ransacked the room, as much to vent her frustration as to look for the pendant.

In the dark of the now cluttered hut, something was glowing brightly on the floor. She dived to the ground, brushed aside some folders and saw it, shining with the intensity of a tiny torch. Snatching the pendant up, she raced outside, kicking aside dark pieces of debris as she went.

The tornado had all but reached Tony. It towered over him and the crumpled car like a giant poised to stamp on an ant. Several cars were now circling around the frequent bursts of lightning, which were flashing inside the belly of the tornado. To that collection of vehicles, it then added the one lying across Tony's legs, lifting it slowly at first then gobbling it up with ease.

Izzy ran towards him. The whirlwind lifted him briefly off the ground, but somehow, he managed to break away from its pull just long enough to scramble awkwardly on all fours a metre or two away.

When Izzy was still a few metres away from him, she hurled the pendant at Tony, who caught it with an outstretched hand. In one swift motion, he pulled the thin cord over his head.

It was as though the tornado had suddenly lost its sight. It veered one way then the next, moving away from the direct line towards Tony that it had been on. One by one the cars crashed back down to earth. The flashes of lightning ceased. And gradually, the tornado lost some of its height and thickness.

Izzy threw her arms around Tony as he sat on the ground, breathing heavily.

'I think you just saved my life,' he said, hugging her back.

They separated, looked at one another and then burst out laughing, an uncontrollable laugh of sheer relief. If Izzy had not laughed, she knew she would have cried.

Tony looked at the pendant around his neck. 'Goodness!' he said. 'I've never seen it glow this brightly before.'

'What does that mean?'

'It means there are a lot of people in this world who shouldn't be here.'

Chapter Fifteen

The Ministry

With her eyes hardly blinking, DCI Prideaux stared across her office, whilst tapping a pen on her desk. After puffing out her cheeks, she then leant back in her chair, staring up at the ceiling. Her mind was so full of confused and contradictory thoughts.

Unable to resolve anything, she stood up and began pacing the room, replaying the arguments over and over in her head. She had been a police officer all her life; it was all she had ever wanted to be since she had been a schoolgirl. She had spent the past thirty years obeying every order she had been given, even when it had meant occasionally turning a blind eye to some of the more unpleasant actions of the local secret police. By doing as she was told and looking away at the right moments, she had gained promotion every few years. And with several years still to go before retirement, she could expect more promotions to come if she continued to do the same.

However, now her conscience was screaming at her, refusing to give her a moment's peace. She kept asking herself why she had become a police officer in the first place. The same answer kept coming up: to catch wrongdoers and to help people. Yet the more she thought about it, the more she realised that what Miss Doomsday was increasingly doing these days had very little to do with catching criminals and helping people. And just when her doubts had started multiplying, along had come a group of schoolchildren, frightened and crying. Their teacher, though clearly terrified herself, had been an example to them all: apparently not concerned for her own wellbeing, she had ended up shouting at her captors, demanding to know what was happening, then pleading with them to let the innocent children go.

Miss Doomsday had said it was a matter of national security. But they were just a small group of English schoolchildren. What possible threat could they have posed? Even the jittery bus driver with them seemed to present a danger to no one and was clearly not a terrorist.

No, something was very, very wrong about all this. And she could not sit by and do nothing. There had to be something she could do — but what?

Suddenly resolved to act, she hurried back behind her desk and began composing an email.

'Right, are we ready?' asked Tom.

He, Molly and Jake were standing hand in hand in front of the mirror in the dark of the bunker. Tom's pulse was racing and despite the cold, his palms were clammy. Even without looking at them, he could tell his friends were as scared and as full of adrenaline as he was.

'As ready as we'll ever be,' replied Jake.

'Remember,' said Tom. 'The moment we appear on the other side, we have to act fast.'

The other two nodded.

'Here goes,' he said, swallowing hard, and reached out a hand to touch the mirror.

In the next moment, the cool draught had gone, and they were standing with their backs to the mirror in the other world, the room almost as dark as where they had come from.

Without hesitation, they leapt off the dais and raced across the room to the double doors. The first time they had come here, there had been several seconds before anything had happened. So, this time they were determined to use every one of those precious seconds.

With the access card already in his hand, Jake pressed it against the reader next to the doors. Almost as if his actions had set them off, the bright lights burst into life and the klaxons began blaring at that precise moment.

The tiny green light on the reader appeared and the doors began to open. Having been unintentionally holding his breath, Tom let out a huge sigh of relief. If the card had not worked, their plan would have been dead in the water before they had even started. They would have been arrested immediately and, if the Professor was true to his word, they would have spent the rest of their lives in prison.

They scrambled through the doorway into the corridor, where red lights were flashing all along the ceiling. The sound of heavy boots was pounding on the polished floor, drawing closer, rising above the piercing screams of the klaxon. Without stopping to think, they ran in the opposite direction.

Just as they began hurtling along the corridor, three or four guards appeared behind them, guns at the ready. A shot rang out down the corridor, the bullet flying over the heads of the children and exploding with a puff in the wall in front of them. As they turned the corner and ran for their lives, a booming voice rang out. 'Stop shooting, you fool! We need them alive.'

'In here, quick!' said Tom, pointing to a door.

Jake touched his card on the pad and in they rushed, closing the door behind them. Not daring to turn on the light, they stood panting in the dark, listening anxiously to the approaching footfalls. Someone rattled the door handle, but for now the door remained locked.

'They won't be in there,' cried one of the guards. 'They won't have a pass.'

Seconds later, the heavy boots were pounding away into the distance.

'We need to move,' said Tom. 'It won't take them long to realise we do have a pass.'

'Wait!' said Molly. 'We should at least check where we are.' She flicked on the light to reveal a room full of electronic equipment reaching from the floor to the ceiling. 'Okay. Nothing here,' she said. 'Let's go.'

Cautiously, they eased open the door and crept back into the corridor. Abruptly, the klaxon stopped, although the red lights continued to pulse on and off.

'Come on,' said Tom, leading them back along the way they had just come. He had an idea where the Iris might be. He only hoped he was right and that they would have enough time to take it back with them.

Now that the klaxons had stopped, they could hear footsteps everywhere, or so it seemed. They raced along the corridors and every time they came to a right-angle turn they had to skid to a halt, peer round the corner before setting off again once they saw the way ahead was clear.

Footsteps were getting louder behind them. In front, just around a corner, more steps and agitated voices could be heard echoing through the building. But then at last, they were standing in front of the door Tom had noticed on the day they had been arrested. "RA Room. Level 5 access only. No unauthorised personnel" it said. Jake tapped his card and once more they flung themselves through the doorway.

'We need to barricade the door,' said Tom. 'Quick!'

This time they turned the light on. Tom and Jake raced over to a table, picked it up and hurriedly placed it across the door. With Molly's help, they added a pair of chairs and a small filing cabinet, too.

'It won't hold them for long,' admitted Tom. 'But it might give us some time.'

'But how on earth are we going to get out?' asked Jake.

Tom smiled. 'I haven't thought that far ahead.'

'And why this room, anyway?' asked Jake, starting to look around.

'After what the professor said about MIRRA, I'm hoping the RA stands for Rare Artefacts.'

'Guys, look!' said Molly.

They turned around to face Molly, who was bending over, looking into a glass cabinet.

'There's a medallion in there,' she said.

Sure enough, the small display case housed a spotlessly clean medallion as though on display in a museum. It was of no particular use to them, but it did make them rush around the room excitedly to see what else they could find. The room was a jumbled collection of glass cases, filing cabinets, bookshelves and a small number of cluttered desks.

'Hey, look what I found,' announced Jake triumphantly.

Tom spun round to see his friend standing over a desk and holding aloft the small cube they had used to open the network of pathways to the other worlds.

'Brilliant!' said Tom, rushing over to take it from Jake. 'We're going to need that.' After it had been confiscated the previous day, Tom had wondered whether he would ever see it again.

'Guys!' called out Molly. 'Over here!'

They rushed over to Molly who was standing over a different glass display case, which stood right at the back of the room. Inside, gleaming and pristine, lay an Iris box, the lid closed. Tom punched the air. At the side of the cabinet was a digital keypad. Trying to think fast, Tom put his fingers against his temples.

'Gosh, it could be anything,' said Molly, wracking her brains, too.

Tom punched in his father's birthday. The pad flashed red.

He then typed in his own birthday. Again, it flashed red.

He ran his fingers through his hair. 'Think, think!' he urged himself.

He entered his mother's birthday. It had to be.

The keypad went red again, but this time it stayed red and a message saying "error" appeared on the small screen and remained there.

'No, no!' he cursed and thumped the glass top. Three attempts and now they were locked out.

Someone outside the room rattled the door handle. The three of them froze for a moment, before Jake ran towards the door. 'I'll hold it,' he whispered. 'You guys get the Iris.'

Tom looked around, then saw a fire extinguisher standing in the corner. He picked it up while Molly stood back and then brought it down heavily onto the cabinet. Instead of the glass shattering as Tom had fully expected, the heavy fire extinguisher bounced off the surface of the glass and nearly hit him in the face.

Urgent voices were chattering outside in the corridor. Tom thought he could hear the sound of someone tapping a card against the reader. Jake had shoved yet another filing cabinet and a chair against the door and was now pressing with all his might against the makeshift barricade. But the door was starting to inch open.

Tom threw the fire extinguisher as hard as he could against the glass of the cabinet and ducked out of the way. Once again, it rebounded up into the air and then clattered onto the floor, leaving not a scratch on the glass.

Jake was straining manfully to hold back the guards, yet slowly but surely, he was losing ground.

Tom looked at Molly, whose face had a sad and resigned air about it. She placed a hand on his arm, as if to say they had tried everything, but now it was time to concede defeat and accept their fate.

But then he remembered. One last throw of the dice. An almighty risk, but they now had nothing to lose. He took the cube out of his pocket and rotated it so that the circle was on top.

'No!' said Molly. 'Not that. Tony said we should never do that outside of the void.'

'I know,' replied Tom, a grin spreading across his face. 'He did, didn't he.'

Under Molly's horrified gaze, and before she could stop him, he pressed the circle on top of the cube.

Nothing happened.

Jake was finally flung backwards and landed heavily on his back. A snarling guard had forced his way through the doorway and was now wrestling with the makeshift barricade.

And then there was an explosion. Without even thinking, Tom dived on top of Molly, forcing both of them onto the floor, as hundreds of tiny pieces of shattered glass flew into the air and then tumbled down around them like hailstones.

John D. Fennell

Tom rolled over and looked up. Coming out of where the glass display case had been only moments earlier was a huge, multi-coloured beam. Over a metre thick, it shimmered in a straight, horizontal line, roaring like a great furnace. The spectrum of colours inside revolved, round and round, the horizontal bands of colour constantly changing places with one another.

Tom instantly knew the Iris inside the box had been transformed into a pathway such as they had seen inside the void. But, whereas in the void, the pathways were silent, graceful things of beauty, this one seemed to burn with anger and menace. It had punched a great hole in the far wall and was now flickering and crackling, arrow-straight, obliquely across the room. He guessed it had made an instant beeline for the mirror in the Mirror Room.

'Can you turn it off?' Molly yelled in his ear, trying to make herself heard above the roar.

'I think so,' he shouted back. 'But when I do, we may only have a short while to get to the mirror.'

He looked around the room, waved at Jake, who was lying on the floor looking shocked, and beckoned him to join them urgently. Close by, the guard who had managed to get through the doorway, but was still tangled in the barricade, was frozen to the spot, mesmerised by the giant fiery beam.

When Jake darted over to them, Molly and Tom stood up. Then Tom pointed at the small cube in his hand. 'When I press this, get ready to run through that hole. If I'm right, it should lead straight to the mirror. Don't hesitate or look back — just go straight into the mirror. We won't have long.'

Molly and Jake both nodded. After one last deep breath, Tom pressed the circle on the cube. A second or two later, the multi-coloured beam vanished, leaving nothing but a loud ringing in their ears. And a large, circular hole in the far side of the room.

While Tom reached into the remnants of the display case and picked up the now empty Iris box, Molly and Jake ran straight for the gaping hole. With the golden box tucked under his arm, Tom ran after them. The hole was so large he barely had to duck to pass through it. Into another, darkened room it led. On either side were signs of the beam's destruction: mangled and charred pieces of furniture lay scattered on the floor, together with upturned computer screens and other pieces of electrical equipment, which sparked intermittently in the dim light.

Behind him, Tom heard shouting, then scurrying feet. He had left the second room behind and was now bounding across a corridor and into another hole on the other side. Ahead of him, Molly and Jake were now in the Mirror Room, heading straight for the mirror, which stood alone on the dais.

With footsteps echoing ever closer behind him, Tom willed the portal to remain open for just a few seconds more. The mirror's shimmering surface, rippling like a vertical rectangle of oil, swallowed Molly's slender figure. A moment later, Jake's stocky frame disappeared into the mirror.

'Stop!' bellowed a voice. 'Or I'll shoot.'

But Tom had no intention of stopping, not now. The mirror was getting closer and closer. If he had not passed through it so many times before, he would have hesitated, worried that it was too small, that he would collide into the thick wooden frame.

He reached out his free hand and felt himself being sucked into the void.

A moment later, he was standing on a rainbow path and all

seemed serene and peaceful. He walked forward and accepted the hug from Molly and Jake.

'Stop right there!' a voice bellowed.

Tom spun round. Standing half a dozen paces away, with his body obscuring the portal, was one of the guards. At the end of his outstretched arms, he held a handgun and was pointing it right at the three of them.

'Move slowly back towards me,' he ordered. Although his attention was mostly on the three teenagers, his eyes kept flitting to either side, glancing at the peculiar sight around him.

Tom eased towards him, holding out one arm. 'Listen to me,' he said calmly, though, with the barrel of a gun pointing at his head, he felt anything but calm. 'That portal behind you is going to close any second. If you don't go back now, you'll be stuck here, unable to return to your world.'

'Come-back-here!' snarled the man.

'Go now, while you still can,' urged Tom. 'We're going home to our world. Go back to yours.'

The man's eyes moved from Tom, to Jake and Molly behind him on the rainbow path, to the Irises floating about aimlessly all around them. He lowered his gun, turned back and disappeared through the back of the mirror. Barely a second later, the rippling surface of the mirror hardened once more into a solid, impenetrable rectangle.

Tom emitted a long sigh, turned around and hugged his friends once more.

'Come on,' said Molly. 'Let's go home.'

'Right,' said Tom, as he took the cube out of his pocket. 'This is where the real fun starts.'

Guardians of the Mirror

Bodmin Moor was no place to be in the middle of December, and certainly not after dark. A biting, unrelenting wind was blowing across the slopes as Izzy and Tony trudged across the moorland, trying to avoid rocky outcrops one minute, boggy marshland the next. The progress in the dark was slow, not least because Tony was badly injured. Not that he was complaining, thought Izzy with no little admiration, but he was limping badly and needed her constant support.

However, stopping to rest was not an option. Since the secret prison had been attacked by the storm, they knew the police would be out hunting for escaped prisoners very soon, if they were not already. So, on they pressed across the treacherous countryside. They had at least stolen a pair of warm coats from the security guard's hut before they had left.

At last, after what had seemed like an interminable walk, they arrived at the silhouette of a derelict farmhouse. Although largely still intact with a tiled roof, the stone building had no windows or doors. But it would at least afford them some shelter from the chilly wind.

Izzy led Tony into a corner of the house away from any windows and helped him down onto the cold floor. She then scurried away in the dark, before returning a few minutes later, carrying a duffle bag.

'What have you got in there?' asked Tony, his face barely discernible in the shadows. 'An inflatable tent?'

'Not quite,' laughed Izzy. 'But here, there's a blanket.' She took it out of the bag and then sat down next to him, spreading the blanket across his legs. 'Don't protest. You need it more than I do. I've even got some food and drink in here.'

When she handed him some biscuits and a bottle of water, he said: 'That bag was a lucky find.'

John D. Fennell

'Nope,' she said, then took a mobile phone out of the bag. 'I planned all this. When I found this house yesterday, I hid a bag of provisions here, knowing we might need somewhere to escape to.'

'Wow! But I bet you lost your precious laptop back there in the prison, didn't you?'

'Don't be daft. That was just an old spare one I had lying around.' She then pulled out a laptop from the bag. 'This is my real baby here.'

Tony chuckled. 'You've thought of everything, haven't you? I'm certainly glad you're on our side.'

Izzy frowned. 'Mmm. Don't forget I'm the one who got us into this mess in the first place. Anyway, I'm just going to phone Sam.'

After a brief conversation, Izzy put the phone down.

'How on earth did you get a signal out here?' asked Tony.

Izzy laughed. 'I take it you're not into technology?'

'Not really my thing,' he said. Then when he saw her smirk, he added: 'Hey, I've grown up in Marazion. We've only just stopped using a horse and cart.'

Izzy laughed and fired up her laptop.

'Where is Sam, anyway?' asked Tony.

'He's a few miles away, waiting in his car. But he says the area is crawling with police and soldiers. There's no chance we can move any time soon. How's the leg?'

'Probably broken somewhere. But there's no bleeding that I can see. I'll live.'

Izzy smiled and then began reading her emails. 'Oh, that's funny,' she said, her face now bathed in a faint glow from the laptop screen.

'What is it?'

Guardians of the Mirror

'I've got an email from an old school friend of mine, Amelia Prideaux. We drifted apart when her mum became the head of Porthgarrick police. She says: *Hi Izzy. I hope you're well and that you still use this email address. My mum wanted me to pass this info on to you and hopes it will be of some use.* There's an attachment as well.'

'Be careful of that. You don't want another virus.'

She looked at him askance. 'That won't happen again, trust me. Anyway, her mum's email says:

Hi Isabelle,

I hope this email finds you well, wherever you're currently holed up. I learned recently that you have been the mysterious hacker who has been causing all the trouble around here for the past few months. Well done. You certainly had us fooled for a long time.

Anyway, it is time for you to put your considerable skills to good use once again. It is now my view that our beloved head of secret police has finally taken a step too far. The attached files contain video footage and stills of a group of what I believe are entirely innocent schoolchildren, kidnapped and held prisoner for some unfathomable reason on the orders of Commissioner Doomsday. There is even a firm connection with Prime Minister Sheeran, who has been regularly visiting our station in recent days. I can't pretend to have any idea what is going on here, but something just doesn't feel right about all this.

Do with these files as you wish. I have also enclosed details on how to bypass the encryption currently blocking access to the nationwide Internet and beyond. They will be able to shut you down pretty quickly, but hopefully not before you have broadcast these files to the world.

There is a very real chance that this leak will be traced back to me. But I no longer feel able to sit idly by while crimes such as this are

John D. Fennell

committed in the name of law and order.
I wish you good luck.
Regards,
DCI Prideaux.'

'Is that genuine?' asked Tony.

Izzy scanned the attachments then opened one of the files. A group of clearly very frightened young children was being marched across a car park and into a bus. A woman was remonstrating with the police officers around them, demanding to know what was happening and where they were going.

'That looks real to me,' said Izzy when the clip had ended. 'Wow! I need to get this stuff out there as soon as I can.'

Chapter Sixteen

Practice makes Perfect

Having trapped an Iris in the golden box, Tom and his two friends moved to the end of the rainbow path and stood in front of the portal that led back into Tom and Molly's world.

'Can you see anything?' asked Jake, peering into the tall oblong in front of them.

It was like trying to look through a window that was under water. The image was distorted and grey. They were clearly looking into a room, but beyond that they could make out very little.

'No, it's too dark in there, wherever it is,' replied Tom.

'I can't see anything moving, though,' said Molly. 'It must be getting late, so maybe the room is empty.'

'I think we're just going to have to go for it,' said Tom. 'If there's someone in there, we'll have to be ready to come straight back in here.'

They held hands, then Tom pressed the medallion against the portal. In the next moment, they were standing in a darkened room, straining eyes and ears to discern where they were.

'Can you hear anything?' whispered Jake.

Concentrating hard, Tom held his breath while he listened. 'No, nothing.'

'Try your card over there, Jake,' said Molly, pointing to the only door in the room.

Next to the doorframe there was a keypad with a reader.

John D. Fennell

Jake tapped his access card several times, but no lights flashed. He tried the door handle. 'No good. And the door's locked.'

'Oh, great!' sighed Tom. He then began laughing. 'We've come all this way and now we're locked inside a room.'

His eyes were slowly adjusting to the dark. They were inside a small room, no bigger than about four metres by three. Aside from the mirror standing in the corner next to a two-wheeled sack truck, there was a small table and nothing else. High up in the opposite wall were two small windows, through which almost no light was now showing.

Then Jake discovered a light switch near the door and flicked it on, flooding the small room with a cold, white light.

'Well, we can't just stay here all night,' said Molly, covering her eyes from the glare. 'We might suffocate for one thing.'

'Hey, Tom,' said Jake. 'Why don't you use your new powers to break us out of here? You've got an Iris and those wristband things now.'

'Yes, maybe,' said Tom, looking down at the golden box in his hand.

'Guys, no!' said Molly. 'We've never practised like Tony has. Who knows what could happen. Plus, we don't know where we are. We might kill someone by mistake.'

'Ah, good point,' conceded Tom.

'Look, Doomsday's left her medallion here,' said Jake, moving towards the table and picking it up. 'We should take it back with us to my world. At least that would be one less way for her to travel through the mirror.'

'Sounds like you have a plan, Jake,' said Tom hopefully.

'Well, maybe. Look, why don't we just go through to the other world? My world. Molly's got one of those things in her neck, so she'll be safe there. I don't know about you two, but I really need to eat and to sleep. So why don't we go and get some rest and come back in the morning with a plan.'

It was true: Tom felt so desperately tired and hungry that it was hard to think straight. 'Of course, Jake,' he agreed. 'That's exactly what we should do.'

'Crikey,' chuckled Jake. 'I think I'm finally getting to grips with all this stuff now.'

'You'll be a Guardian of the Mirror before you know it,' laughed Tom.

'Izzy! Izzy, wake up!' urged Tony, gently shaking her shoulder. 'I think I heard a drone or something.'

Izzy came round and for a few seconds, she had no idea where she was. She had been working on her laptop all night and must have fallen asleep, for the lid was still open in front of her. Hurriedly, she switched it back on and scanned the screen. 'Yes, there's one about fifty metres away.'

'Will it have seen us?' asked Tony.

'It may not have picked up our heat through these stone walls. But I bet they'll send someone to check the building out, anyway. We need to move once it's gone.'

Tony looked across at her laptop. 'How did you get on last night?'

'Well, I posted all that stuff, together with some of the footage of Molly and the other girl tied to stakes. People will be waking up all over the world to see those images on the Internet. Let's hope enough people see them before they shut us down.'

'How can we tell if it worked?'

'Let's stick the news on,' said Izzy. 'All we can do now is wait. And hope.'

John D. Fennell

Despite having a head crammed full of thoughts and worries, Tom had fallen asleep the moment he had put his head down. In the cold and draughty *Morladron House* in Jake's world they might have been, but the physical and emotional exertions of the previous few days had taken their toll. After Jake had returned with food and blankets, they had eaten and then lay down to sleep for hours.

However, the moment Tom had awoken, he had been keen to return to his world, even though it had meant returning to the small, locked room where that mirror was being stored. Although dawn had now broken, sending some weak light through the high windows, the room still felt more like a prison cell than anything else.

'Well, there's still no one here,' said Jake. 'What now?'

Tom took out his phone and began a video call. Before he had a chance to speak, Izzy's startled face filled his screen.

'Tom!' she cried. 'Where are you? Are you all right?'

'We're fine,' he said, as Molly and Jake moved into the screen beside him to wave at Izzy. 'Listen, I'll explain everything later. But for now, we've just come back through the mirror and we're stuck in a locked room. Any chance you can tell where we are?'

'Hang on, I'll have a look. It'll take me longer than before after they hacked me the other day. Have a chat with Tony while I work on it.'

'Tony!' cried Tom. 'I thought we'd lost you.'

Tony smiled warmly. 'Izzy got me out. She's pretty amazing your cousin.'

'Shh! Don't tell her that. We'll never hear the end of it. Listen, Tony, we've got hold of an Iris and an Iris box. Any chance you can come over here and help us fight Miss Doomsday? She's got her own Iris now, you see.'

'Yes, so I heard. I'm afraid we're in hiding at the moment. And I think my leg might be broken. So it could be a while before I can get to you.'

Tom winced. 'In that case, you'll have to teach me how to use this thing,' he said, holding up the golden box.

At that moment, Izzy reappeared on the screen. 'Right, Tom. I can see you're in some warehouse about two miles outside Porthgarrick.'

'Is there anyone around?'

'I can't tell that, I'm afraid. I can see your signal on a map, but I've got no live cameras to look at. It looks pretty isolated though. So, unless you can hear anyone, I doubt there'll be many people about, if anyone.'

'So how do we get out of here? The door's firmly locked. Should I use the wristbands?'

Izzy and Tony looked at each other uncertainly, before Tony said: 'Without any practice it would be very dangerous.'

'I'm not sure we have any choice,' sighed Tom.

'All right. Stick to lightning, though. Don't even try to form a tornado just yet.'

'Fine. So what do I have to do?'

'Once you've put the wristbands on, clear your mind. You need to concentrate really hard. Firstly, you'll need to bring the storm to you ...'

'Just a thought,' said Tom. 'Do we know if there are any people here from Jake's world? Otherwise, I won't be able to do anything.'

Tony pulled out the pendant around his neck and showed it to the camera. 'There are several people here,' he said grimly, as the stone glowed a dazzling yellow. 'I have never seen it this bright before.'

'Oh, right.'

'Anyway,' continued Tony. 'Concentrate on bringing a storm to you, on seeing all that black cloud move over the top of you. Move your hands towards you over and over again, as though you're dragging the cloud towards you. Once you've done that, picture in your mind a bolt of lightning. Then raise your hands to the sky and bring them down sharply. As you do so, it's important to focus intently on where you want that lightning to land, otherwise it could just land anywhere, including on top of you.'

Tom smiled nervously. 'I'll bear that in mind.'

'Just try to aim your bolts at the walls near you. They should eventually break open. If not, call us back. We'll have to think of something else.'

Once they had ended the call, Tom turned to Molly and Jake. 'I think you two should go back to Jake's world and wait for me to fetch you.' Molly opened her mouth to speak, but Tom cut in quickly. 'This is going to be dangerous. I'll stand right next to the mirror with this medallion at the ready. If the building starts to collapse, I'll dive into the mirror.'

Jake grinned at his friend. 'Good luck, mate. And, well, what could possibly go wrong, eh?'

'I think we might need to stay here a while longer,' said Izzy walking back into the derelict farmhouse. 'I've just seen another drone buzzing about.'

'Never mind about that,' said Tony with a grin. 'Come and look at this.' He pointed excitedly at the laptop which lay across his outstretched legs.

Guardians of the Mirror

Izzy rushed over to join him just as a news bulletin was starting.

'I've just seen the headlines,' whispered Tony, as the newsreader began.

'Footage has emerged today from Cornwall, allegedly showing a local police force engaged in the kidnap of young schoolchildren. The images, which have been broadcast across the Internet since the early hours of this morning, are of a group of children aged around seven to eight, being herded, apparently against their will, into a minibus, while a woman who appears to be their teacher is protesting at their treatment.' While the newsreader was speaking the video footage she was describing was being shown on the screen. 'Other images have also been broadcast, which appear to show two teenage girls tied to stakes on top of a hill during an electrical storm and being threatened by the local Police Commissioner. In a statement accompanying these images, the anonymous individual responsible for releasing this footage, states that, and I quote: "These innocent children have been kidnapped by the Porthgarrick Police under orders from Commissioner Doomsday who is working directly with Prime Minister Sheeran."

'The Prime Minister, who has been visiting a school in Manchester today, was asked about these images by journalists.' The picture then changed to one of Christopher Sheeran surrounded by at least a dozen journalists outside a school.

'Prime Minister! Prime Minister!' they were shouting.

He turned around to glare at them, before quickly adopting a fake smile.

'Prime Minister. Have you seen these images on the

John D. Fennell

Internet?'

He held up both hands to calm the journalists in a rather condescending manner. 'I have indeed seen these images. On the face of it, they are very, very disturbing. However, we need to be careful not to jump to premature conclusions until we have verified the authenticity of these pictures. There is a saying: the camera never lies. However, in these days of unprecedented technological advances, I'm not so sure that the saying holds true anymore. It has become all too easy to doctor images such as these. So, we must all be very careful before we draw any conclusions from what we have seen this morning.'

'And what about Commissioner Doomsday?' asked one of the journalists, thrusting a microphone in front of the Prime Minister, who was beginning to look decidedly uncomfortable.

'Well,' he replied, somehow managing to maintain his false smile. 'These are indeed very troubling accusations. So, I think it prudent that the Commissioner be suspended, for the time being, while a full enquiry is carried out.'

He turned and walked away, while the journalists continued firing questions at his back.

Tony turned the volume down while the newsreader began discussing with a studio guest the implications for the Prime Minister and what was likely to happen next.

'Well, Izzy,' he said. 'My goodness! I think you might have finally done it.'

A wry smile creased Izzy's lips. 'It's only the beginning, Tony. He's a politician. He'll do everything to wriggle out of this and pin the blame on someone else. But let's see if I can't stoke the flames some more, now they've started burning.' She took the laptop from Tony and began typing once more, a smug little grin creeping across her face.

Guardians of the Mirror

With a thick mass of swirling dark cloud hanging over her, Miss Doomsday stood alone in a field. In the distance, beyond the edge of the cloud, the sky was clear and bright. But for a wide area over the large field and beyond, the grim twilight had sucked nearly all light and colour from the landscape.

In the centre of the field stood an old, disused barn with crumbling stone walls and a partly collapsed wooden roof. As Miss Doomsday clamped the golden cuffs around her wrists, she stared intently at the building, which stood perhaps one hundred metres away. She had spent weeks poring over the green translation of the Book of Mysteries and the red diary until whole sections were stored in her memory. Now it was finally time to put it all into practice.

She summoned a bolt of lightning from the seething cloud. Thinner jagged tentacles radiated from a much thicker, zigzagging trunk. It pierced the ground close to the barn. Without the slightest delay, she pictured another vivid tangle of lightning in her mind, then flung her arms in the direction she wanted it to land. Again, it crashed to earth mere metres from the decaying building, illuminating the crumbling walls for a second or two.

Again and again, she practised, each time feeling the euphoria rise inside her. Being able to control such forces with nothing but the power of her mind was intoxicating, thrilling beyond words.

Finally, after several failed attempts, lightning tore down right into the middle of the barn. The wooden beams of the roof exploded with white-hot electricity and then fire, before creaking and collapsing.

Bolt after bolt of lightning assaulted the remnants of the

barn, until even its stone walls began to break apart under the onslaught.

Just when she contemplated turning her attention to the creation of a tornado, her phone rang. At first, she ignored it and let the call go to voicemail. But then it rang again, immediately afterwards. With a mighty huff of frustration, she took out her mobile and looked at the screen. It was DCI Prideaux.

'What?' she demanded loudly.

'Sorry to disturb you, ma'am. But could you come back to the station?'

'What is this all about? Tell me now.'

'I think it would be better if you were to return to your car first.'

Miss Doomsday turned around to look back at her car, which was parked a short distance away in a narrow lane next to the field. Behind her vehicle were the flashing lights of a police car, in front of which stood DCI Prideaux, her phone pressed to her ear.

The Commissioner ended the call and began striding towards the DCI, jaw clenched. 'What exactly is the meaning of this?' she barked as she drew near. 'I gave strict instructions that I was not to be disturbed.'

'Sorry, ma'am,' said DCI Prideaux, who was now standing between two other police officers. 'But we have orders from above to escort you back to the station.'

'What do you mean? What orders?' bellowed Miss Doomsday.

'From the Chief Constable, ma'am. Something to do with those children.'

The deputy head thought she spotted a spark of glee in the

Guardians of the Mirror

DCI's face. 'What have you done?'

'Not me, ma'am. It's all over the Internet. Video footage and everything.'

'That's not possible!' she roared, her eyes gazing directly up into the police officer's face, looking for signs of smugness or even betrayal.

But DCI Prideaux remained impassive. 'I think it best you come with us and then I'm sure you and the Chief Constable can sort this all out.'

Miss Doomsday glared up at the taller woman for several seconds more, before turning away. She walked towards her car, then turned back. 'I shan't be coming with you today.' She then glanced at the two other officers, who stood with their hands poised over their holsters. 'I wouldn't do anything stupid if I were you. Now get back in your car and just drive away.'

'I'm afraid we can't do that, ma'am,' said DCI Prideaux.

'Yes, you can. And you will.' And with that, Miss Doomsday summoned a streak of lightning, which struck a tree directly behind the three police officers, who all flinched. As the tree began to burn, casting long shadows across the small group, she added: 'I am leaving now. I have no intention of hurting any of you. Unless I have to.'

Her gaping eyes flitting back and forth between the flaming tree and the Commissioner, DCI Prideaux at last looked disconcerted, uncertain what to do. The other officers, too, looked paralysed with indecision.

Miss Doomsday climbed into her car and drove off.

Standing alone with his back to the mirror, Tom looked up at the two small windows opposite him. Large grey clouds were scudding across the winter sky. Yet as cold and windy as it appeared to be outside, there was no sign of a storm, and for once, a storm was exactly what he needed if he was going to make anything happen.

Recalling what Tony had shown him before, Tom removed the golden cuffs from the lid of the Iris box and snapped them shut around his wrists. No doubt designed to be worn by an adult, they were loose and moved about freely on his forearms, so thin were his wrists. He had also expected to feel something, some tangible increase in energy or a growing sense of power. But rather disappointingly, there was nothing.

He placed the golden box containing the Iris into a small rucksack, which he then hung on his back, in case he needed to beat a hasty retreat back to Jake's world.

He forced himself to clear his mind, to breathe deeply, to expel all thoughts on each outward breath until his mind was a blank. Closing his eyes, he imagined the arrival of a storm, pictured the growing black clouds, the gusting wind, the rapidly failing light. Over the past few months, he had seen such storms on more occasions than he cared to remember, so conjuring up the images in his mind was easy. Then, slowly, he moved his hands out and back in, as though pulling on invisible, horizontal ropes.

For what seemed like ages, he repeated these movements over and over again, replaying the pictures in his head again and again, imagining himself dragging the storm towards him with nothing more than his hands and his thoughts. As the minutes ticked by and nothing seemed to be happening, he found it increasingly hard to maintain his concentration, his mind wandering off every now and then until he chided himself to regain his focus.

Guardians of the Mirror

A mighty crash of thunder shook him from his trance. When his eyes shot open, the two high-up windows were full of black cloud, and the small room was now almost devoid of any light. Suddenly, his heart was pounding with a peculiar mix of excitement and fear.

Breathing deeply once more, he tried to calm himself. But now it was hard to focus his mind. It kept jumping ahead to what might happen next, to what he needed to do, to what he might get wrong. There was nothing for it: he needed to just make an attempt and see how it went.

Using nothing but his hands and his jumbled mind, he commanded a bolt of lightning to land just outside the window. Almost instantly, the two windows transformed into two dazzling rectangles of white light, flooding the room with their radiance. The explosion of light, followed almost immediately by a roar of thunder, almost threw him off his feet. He fell awkwardly against the mirror behind him.

The thought of what he had just done was terrifying yet exhilarating at the same time. He tried once more, but this time imagined the lightning striking the side of the warehouse in front of him. This time, the force of the blast did send him to the floor, as the whole room shook violently.

Rather than disconcert him, the lightning strike merely spurred him into attempting it once more. Over and over, he summoned lightning out of the dark sky. Some of the bolts struck the ground harmlessly outside. But the more attempts he made, the more accurate he became. Firstly, the two small windows were blown out, showering the floor with glass. Then the wall began to buckle under the bombardment.

Just one more bolt would do it, he kept telling himself. In a mad frenzy of swirling arms, Tom brought down a barrage of lightning, which struck the warehouse in a haphazard way.

Somehow, above the roar of thunder, he heard the roof begin to groan. Looking up, he saw the ceiling rippling and buckling until pieces crumbled away and struck the floor. Just when it looked like the whole thing was about to fall on top of him, he spun round, seized the medallion around his neck and slapped his hand against its reflection in the mirror.

He landed face down on the floor, two pairs of feet in front of him. There was a complete and conspicuous lack of noise all around him, as though someone had just turned off a particularly noisy television.

'Are you okay?' asked Molly, bending down.

Still buzzing from the exhilaration of what he had just been doing, Tom pushed himself up off the floor.

'How did it go?' asked Jake.

Tom was breathing fast, but realised he was smiling. 'That was amazing. It's very hard to control but just ... amazing.'

'That's really lovely, mate,' said Jake. 'But do I need to slap you about the face to shake you out of this?'

Tom blinked. 'What? Yes, probably. Wow, I can see how that could become addictive. I don't know how Tony stays in control.'

Molly frowned disapprovingly at him. 'His mum trained him, don't forget.'

'Yes, of course. Anyway, I think we can go back now. But it might be an idea to use the void to look into the room in case our route is blocked.'

So, Tom removed the backpack from his shoulders, released the Iris into the surface of the mirror, and then they all climbed into the void. Looking through the blurred rectangle back into Tom's world, they could see enough of the room to suggest it was safe to proceed. Since they now had two medallions, Tom insisted on going first just to make sure. Once safely on the other side, he beckoned them through.

Rain was pouring through a large hole in the roof, while a cold wind blew through a great gash in the outside wall. In front of them lay a pile of twisted metal beams and other debris from the roof. Wasting no time, Jake and Tom lifted the mirror onto the two-wheeled sack truck, and then began the awkward task of heaving it over the wreckage before them.

'Can't you make this rain stop?' asked Jake, as they finally pulled the mirror clear of the warehouse.

Lightning flashed overhead, followed by a loud boom of thunder. As the rain poured down on his face, Tom glanced up at the black mass of bubbling cloud. 'I wouldn't know how to. I haven't learnt that bit yet.'

'Well, it might be nice if you did,' said Jake with a grin.

Each boy grabbed one of the handles and began pushing the load forwards, away from the wreckage of the warehouse and into the dark field ahead.

Moving to walk beside Tom, Molly pulled up her hood and asked: 'Where to now?'

'*Lynn Cottage* for now, I guess,' replied Tom. 'We need to keep this away from Miss Doomsday until we figure out what to do next.'

And so off they trudged into the dark, the storm still rumbling overhead.

As the storm closed in around her, Miss Doomsday raced her car along the narrow Cornish lanes, her mind elsewhere. With frequent flashes of lightning illuminating the surrounding countryside and her windscreen wipers straining to maintain a clear view ahead, she drove in a trance, seemingly oblivious to the dangers about her.

She had been betrayed. And now that she had, the slimy Prime Minister was almost certainly going to abandon her and deny all knowledge of their collaboration. It made her furious. The only thing left was to secure the mirror. As long as she controlled that, and provided she could keep the hostages alive, her powers would remain. And with those, she was untouchable. She needed to take the mirror, drive away and spend some time pondering her next moves. And at least with the mirror in her possession, if her stay in this world became untenable, she could always escape through the portal and take her chances in the other world. Everything rested on her maintaining control of the mirror.

Her car screeched to a halt outside the silhouette of the warehouse. The moment she stepped out into the rain, she sensed something was wrong. The security lights should have been on. Instead, the place looked dark and lifeless.

As the rain poured down her face, she looked up at the menacing sky and frowned. With a click of her fingers she made the rain stop instantly; a trick she had read in her books. She moved quickly around to the side of the warehouse and her heart sank. A section of the side wall lay twisted and charred on the ground next to a gaping hole in both the wall and the roof. It looked as though a bomb had gone off inside the warehouse.

She rushed towards the mangled pieces of metal, but already knew what she was going to see. Sure enough, what remained of the room where the mirror had been stored was now empty. She looked around but could see nothing but dark shadows.

Guardians of the Mirror

Looking into the sky once more, she let out a bellowing roar and thrust her hands into the air. A terrible barrage of lightning rained down from the sky, straight onto the roof of the warehouse. Again and again, it was struck, exploding in a giant ball of electricity and fire.

When her rage had been partially sated after several minutes, she stopped the attack. What remained of the warehouse stood battered and buckled in the gloom. A small fire burned in one corner of the building.

She turned around and, in the dim, dancing light from the fire, she saw ruts and footsteps in the muddy ground, heading away from the building. She bent down to take a closer look. Something heavy on wheels had made the ruts, she realised. And they were fresh. What she needed now was a way to track them more easily and to slow them down.

She stood up slowly, racking her brains for the commands she needed. They came to her in no time at all. Raising her hands to the skies, she then began moving them about as though sculpting something invisible in the air.

Chapter Seventeen

The Snow Storm

Progress was slow. The wheels of the sack truck kept getting stuck in the mud and the wind was driving frequent gusts of rain into their faces. As they traipsed along in the dark, Molly had to keep checking on her phone that they were still heading in the right direction.

'Is it me?' asked Jake. 'Or is it getting colder?'

Just as he had spoken the words, Tom felt an icy burst of sleet hit his face. 'I think you're right,' he said.

'The wind's dropping, too,' said Molly.

What had been only moments earlier a swirling, gusting wind dropped to a gentle murmur in a matter of seconds. A chilling silence descended all around them. The air felt suddenly cold, and snowflakes began to flutter down. The three of them stopped for a breather and to look around the dark, shadowy landscape.

'You don't think ...?' began Molly looking worried.

'Yes, I do,' replied Tom grimly.

'But why would she want to make it snow?' continued Molly.

'I don't know.'

'Well, I for one don't mind the snow,' said Jake. 'I haven't seen any since I was a wee kid back in Scotland.'

As the flakes began to increase in both number and size, Tom said: 'Well, you did want a white Christmas, didn't you? Come on. Let's get going again.'

And so off they trudged, Tom and Jake pushing the mirror

along while Molly led the way.

After only a few minutes, it was becoming harder to see where they were going. Giant snowflakes, the size of marshmallows, were pouring out of the sky, obscuring the view. And the dark ground was fast beginning to give way to a blanket of white.

Despite the exertion of pushing their load up and down slopes, Tom was starting to feel cold. The ends of his fingers and his toes were going numb.

'You know what I don't like about the cold?' said Jake. 'When your top lip becomes so numb you can't feel the snot running down it until it runs into your mouth.'

Tom laughed, while Molly said: 'Thank you, Jake, for sharing that lovely image with us.'

'Oh, you're welcome. I've got more if you want to hear them.'

While Tom continued to laugh, he happened to look down at the thin layer of churned up snow beneath him and stopped. He turned around and looked back at the route they had just taken. Even through the heavy snow falling around them, he could see a distinct trail leading off into the distance.

'What is it?' asked Jake.

'I think I now know why Doomsday is making it snow. Look. To slow us down and so she can follow us.'

'Surely the snow will cover our tracks, won't it?' suggested Jake.

'Not quickly enough. Come on, we need to get a move on. How much further, Molly?'

'Less than a mile by the looks of it,' she replied, studying her phone.

On they pressed through the ever-deepening snow, which

had now erased all signs of the grass beneath. Every step they took seemed to plunge down deeper and deeper into the snow. At first, it had come up to their shoelaces, then before long over their ankles, but now it was reaching higher and higher up their shins. Pushing the mirror was becoming more and more difficult, their progress slower and slower.

Finally, they crested a small hill, and began a gradual descent down the other side.

'The cottage is just down there,' said Molly.

It was at that moment that lightning erupted from nowhere, lighting up the whole area, bathing it momentarily in vivid white. The trunk and dozens of tiny branches of the lightning bolt struck the ground to Tom's left, plunging into the snow only a handful of metres from where he was. The shock flung him and Molly to the ice-cold ground, while Jake managed to steady himself against the sack truck and mirror.

Blowing snow from his mouth, Tom rolled over and scrambled awkwardly to his feet, looking back. The snowfall was easing. And there in the distance, perhaps no more than two hundred metres away, was a dark, squat figure, moving towards them, following their tracks. While he watched, the figure began moving its arms about in the air as it trudged through the deep snow.

More lightning arrowed down a short distance in front of him, momentarily obscuring his view of the approaching figure.

'It's her,' he yelled above the thunder. 'You two keep going. I'll try to hold her off.' When Molly looked like she was going to speak, he added quickly: 'Go! Don't worry, I've got these,' he said, holding up his wrists to show the golden wristbands, which were still hanging loosely around his forearms.

Guardians of the Mirror

Without waiting to see whether his two friends would indeed hurry away down the slope, Tom turned back to face whom he knew to be Miss Doomsday. That evil woman stomping towards him, arms waving about, had caused him and his friends so much pain and anguish over the past few months. How many innocent people, including his own father and Tony Singh, had she arrested and thrown in prison? And then there was all that she had done to Molly over the past few days.

Rage was building inside him. He would use that against her, would bring down all manner of vengeance upon her.

Before he had time to react, lightning was exploding all around him. Great shafts of jagged electricity flashed before him, as thick as large tree trunks. A wall of snow erupted close by as the lightning assaulted the ground. Tom found himself blown several metres through the air, before crashing back into the snow, where he lay half buried.

Yet more lightning flashed around him, churning up the snow, showering him with great clumps of the stuff as he tried frantically to scramble to his feet. But moving swiftly in the deep snow was impossible, like trying to run in a dream.

He was a fool. Emotion was not the answer. Anger could never defeat his opponent. Only a clear head could do that. Despite the barrage of lightning and the deafening cacophony of thunder it was producing, he forced himself to concentrate, to relax.

Clawing his hands to the sky, whilst only on his knees, he summoned his own bolt of lightning. It crashed to earth some way short of its mark, but it was enough to throw Miss Doomsday off her stride, momentarily halting her attack on him.

He leapt to his feet, staring for a moment at the deputy head, who was now only about a hundred metres away. Her dark shape was clearly visible through the gently falling snow. She had nearly lost her balance when he had fired back at her, but now her manic hands were preparing to unleash her response.

Tom turned and ran, lifting his feet as high as he could in an effort to move quickly through the deep snow.

She had had more practice than him, had read the books that explained what to do. This was going to be harder than he had expected.

Ahead of him, he could see Molly and Jake struggling with the mirror on the sack truck. But they had at least reached the bottom of the gentle slope. Ahead of them was a short stretch of open ground and then the lake in front of *Lynn Cottage*. Tom had hoped to see lights shining in the house, a sign of potential help for him and his two best friends. But the cottage looked dark and empty.

Sensing that he was about to be attacked again, Tom spun round and without waiting to look for a target, he pulled two lightning bolts out of the sky. They lit up the crest of the hill above him, making the snow all around sparkle like a field of diamonds.

The moment the jagged lines had vanished, he saw the stocky figure of Miss Doomsday emerge at the top of the slope, her knees rising in exaggerated fashion as she moved awkwardly through the snow. She then stopped and seemed to stare down at him, even though it was too dark to see her face clearly.

'You know what I want, Paget.' Her unpleasant voice roared down at him and seemed to echo back off the snow.

Guardians of the Mirror

'Bring it here!'

Tom waved his arms, brought down another streak of lightning, then turned and bounded away once more. Expecting a whole forest of jagged lightning to appear all around him at any moment, he zigzagged down the slope, slipping and sliding through the snow. He lost his footing at the bottom, did a somersault, but managed to spring back onto his feet.

He caught up with Molly and Jake, who by now were making a wide detour around the lake.

'I'm guessing you haven't beaten her yet, then,' said Jake, red-faced and panting.

Breathing heavily himself, Tom replied: 'She's too strong for me. We need to get a move on.' He then leant against the sack truck and helped to heave it forwards.

By now, the wheels were caked in snow, slowing progress to a crawl. Tom spun round to see Miss Doomsday striding down the slope behind them, gaining on them fast.

'Jake,' he said. 'This is too slow. Come on, you and I will carry it. Molly, run ahead and unlock the cottage. There should be a key under the flowerpot by the backdoor.' He knew they would be little safer in the cottage, but for now, it was all he could focus on.

He and Jake lifted the mirror off the sack truck and began carrying it between them. Despite their fatigue, they found they could indeed move much more quickly, marching along with high steps in and out of the snow like a prancing horse.

After several paces, Tom called out to Jake, who was in front, to halt. They dropped their heavy load into the snow where it made a dull thud. Tom turned sharply round, concerned that Miss Doomsday had aimed nothing in their direction for what felt like ages.

An icy gust blew half a dozen large snowflakes into his face. While he was wiping his eyes clean, he heard Jake mutter: 'Oh, no!' When he looked up, he saw the deputy head, still some distance away, but now moving her hands slowly up and down, as though climbing an invisible rope.

Tom sighed. He had seen Harry Singh perform the same ritual only months earlier. He knew what was coming.

The wind was getting up, snowflakes swirling about like swarms of butterflies. And out of the murky grey sky descended a swirling black fang of cloud.

'Quick!' said Tom. 'We've got to move.'

The two boys bent down, picked up the ends of the mirror and began bounding as fast as their cumbersome load would allow. Ahead of them, Molly had reached the cottage and was running around the back. If only they could have gone in a straight line, thought Tom, they would have had a decent chance of reaching the house. But instead, they were having to move in a wide arc around the lake, the cottage tantalisingly close, yet somehow never getting any nearer.

In his haste to move, Tom stumbled, let go of the mirror and collapsed with a crunch into the snow. He rolled over and looked back just in time to see the thin tornado touch the ground. Immediately, it began sucking up the snow and turned into a fast-spinning column of white. Somewhere behind it, hidden from view, the teacher was directing it towards them.

'Jake, leave the mirror,' yelled Tom above the increasing roar of the wind. 'Get back to the cottage.'

'What are you going to do?'

'Try something I saw Tony do once.'

Guardians of the Mirror

As he heard the creak of Jake's retreating footfalls in the snow behind him, Tom rose gingerly to his feet, feeling miserably cold and tired. When this was all finally over, he told himself, he was going to sleep for a week.

The snow tornado was growing, drawing ever closer. Even though every voice in his head was shouting at him to flee, Tom forced himself to stand still, to clear his mind. His breathing was shallow, laboured. He took in a couple of gulps of cold air, then let them out slowly.

The base of the tornado was now as wide as a house, its spiralling, swaying torso reaching high into the sky like an enormous wonky pillar of marble, straining to support the weight of the clouds.

He raised one hand up whilst simultaneously lowering the other one. After one more deep breath, he pictured the whirlwind being squashed, then brought his hands sharply together with a clap in front of his stomach.

A severe, sharp pain shot through his head, like the worst headache he had ever experienced. Before him, the tornado swayed violently, bending over to more than forty-five degrees, then back up again. It seemed to thin, then move left and right in a haphazard manner. Yet, within a matter of seconds it had steadied itself and resumed its inexorable course towards him.

Despite the excruciating pain in his head, Tom tried again to crush the twister with his thoughts, but he could feel some invisible force resisting him, fighting his every move. And what was more, it was winning. Her mind was stronger than his, more focused. He found doubts flooding into his brain, disrupting his concentration.

Looming over him, the whirlwind seemed bigger than

before, now no more than twenty long strides away. It was no use, he had to run, give himself time to think of something else. So he turned and fled, past the mirror half buried in the snow and on towards the cottage, using Molly and Jake's deep footprints to help him speed up.

When he finally reached the cottage, he turned round and rested his back against the front door, gasping for air. Looking out across the lake, he could see that he had at least put some distance between him and the tornado. It seemed that Miss Doomsday had not thought of moving it across the water and was instead directing it around the outside.

He used the time to catch his breath, to refocus. One last attempt, he told himself. He tried to psych himself up, to convince himself he could do this. After controlling his breathing and clearing his mind, he let out a great roar and then brought his hands together sharply once more.

The twister contorted one way then the next, writhing about like a giant fish caught in a net. Then it vanished amid a large noiseless explosion of countless snowflakes, which then fluttered down in silence.

Tom collapsed to the floor, exhausted. His head hurt so much it felt like it would split apart at any moment.

The front door opened. Molly let out a yelp of dismay when she saw him on the ground, before she and Jake hauled him inside the house and closed the door. They carried him through into the lounge and lay him on a sofa.

He was barely conscious, hardly knew what was going on, his face now covered in a cold sweat. But then his eyes shot open and he remembered where he was.

'You need to rest, Tom,' said Molly.

'Where is she?' asked Tom, sitting up, then staggering like a drunk towards the window.

The small, distant silhouette of Miss Doomsday stood on the other side of the lake, apparently studying the cottage.

'Well, at least it'll take her a few minutes to get here now,' said Jake.

'We've got some time to think,' said Molly. 'What are we going to do?'

'I can't stop her,' said Tom, still breathing heavily. 'She's just too strong for me.'

'We should go back and get the mirror,' suggested Jake. 'We've got to stop her getting hold of it again.'

'Or maybe we should just let her take it for now,' said Molly. 'If she has it, she might leave us alone. Then maybe we can get Tony down here.'

While she and Jake continued to discuss their options, Tom stared out across the lake in silence. Miss Doomsday was now moving her arms about once more, waving them at the lake itself. What was she doing? But it was not long before he realised.

'Guys,' he said. 'Look. She's freezing the lake.'

Sure enough, her movements had created a biting wind which was now blowing across the surface of the water, turning it to ice as it went. Sharp creaking noises rose up from the lake as the water froze.

'Why is she doing that?' asked Jake.

When the entire surface of the lake had frozen, Miss Doomsday then stepped onto it and began walking directly towards them. Only moments before, she had been several minutes' walk away from them, but now walking in a straight line, she had halved the time it would take her to reach them.

'I don't think she's interested in the mirror anymore,' said

John D. Fennell

Tom with horror. 'I think she's after us.'

As she strode towards them, occasionally slipping on the ice, but nevertheless getting ever closer, she whirled her arms about and began summoning yet another tornado down from the wintry sky. It touched down at the lake's edge, drawing up vast quantities of snow.

Taking a deep breath, Tom prepared himself to combat her once again.

'You know what?' said Jake. 'It's only a tornado made of snow. What harm can it do? It's not like it's made of fire, is it?'

Just then, the twister began firing icicles towards the house at great speed, launching them like long bullets. Dozens of them flew at the cottage, shattering against the walls and the windows. Instinctively, the three of them dived onto the floor.

A giant icicle, as fat and as long as a large carrot, flew through the window, leaving a hole in the glass with jagged cracks radiating out. It exploded against the wall behind them.

'Okay,' said Jake. 'I take that back.'

More icicles bombarded the window until it exploded in a hail of glass, showering the teenagers below. Crouching down low, they retreated hastily out of the room, while a steady barrage of ice continued to strike the wall.

Once behind the door, Tom steadied himself, poised to leap out and squash the whirlwind before it reached the house. Cautiously, he peered round the door and saw the vast vortex of snow only metres away from the cottage. The wind was howling through a hole where the window had been, pulling objects out of the room, clawing at the curtains. First, a lamp flew out of the window and disappeared into the white tornado. Then a coffee table and a vase.

Tom spread his hands apart, then imagined himself

crushing the whirlwind between them. When he clapped his hands together, there was nothing but sharp pain once more, searing through his head. He dropped to his knees as he fought to control the agony, to battle his mind against that of Miss Doomsday.

Lightning tore down from the sky, exploding onto the house. Even above the noise of the roaring tornado, they could hear tiles being ripped from the roof.

Before Tom had time to react, the twister thumped into the side of the cottage with a deafening bang. The walls and the floor started to shake violently.

'Come on!' yelled Molly, her voice barely audible above the noise. 'We have to get out.'

Jake hauled Tom to his feet and then pulled his exhausted friend towards the back of the house. All around them, pictures were falling off the walls, shelves were collapsing, chunks of plaster were breaking away from the ceiling. An internal wall began to creak, then wide cracks shot along its length.

They darted into the utility room at the back of the house, stumbling over falling furniture and crockery and great lumps of falling ceiling, desperate to reach the back door.

'Head for the tin mine,' cried Tom.

Molly yanked open the door, leapt outside, then turned, beckoning to the other two to hurry up. Just as Tom followed Jake out of the door, the enormous tornado burst through the roof of the cottage, instantly turning the chimney into a swirling spiral of bricks. Sparks flew into the air as the power lines were severed.

The three of them ran for their lives, while the twister tore through the house, cutting it in half. Bricks and tiles and pieces of wood began to fly through the air, thumping down into the thick snow all around them.

Tom glanced back and saw the silhouette of Miss Doomsday standing near the house, directing the twister with her hands as though it were nothing more than a remote-controlled toy.

By now, every step they took disappeared into snow that was so deep it came halfway up their shins, making running almost impossible. In her haste to run away, Molly stumbled and fell forwards. Tom and Jake rushed over to help her up. Then, moments later, Jake lost his footing. At this rate, thought Tom, they were never going to get away.

Razor-sharp icicles began shooting through the air at great speed once more, plunging into the snow around them like flying daggers.

From nowhere, Tom felt the most excruciating pain in the back of his leg. Immediately, he lost all forward momentum and collapsed into the snow, crying out in pain. Jake, then Molly rushed over to him, icicles and roof tiles still raining down all around them.

'He's got an icicle in his leg!' cried Molly as she skidded down onto her knees beside him.

The pain was so much that Tom was screwing his eyes shut, oblivious to everything else but the agony in his leg.

'We've got to move him,' he heard Jake yell. Then there was an even sharper pain, followed by a slight easing. 'I've got it out,' added Jake, before using his bear-like arms to haul Tom out of the snow and onto his feet.

With an arm around both their shoulders and trying to hop along on one leg, Tom was dragged through the snow towards the tin mine. All the while, the giant, white tornado followed their every move, towering over them. But at least for the time being, it had stopped firing missiles at them as it moved away from the cottage.

Still only halfway to the distant tin mine, they all collapsed into the snow with exhaustion. Tom lay on his back, looking back at the twister and the wreckage of *Lynn Cottage* behind it. A thin trail of blood lay on the snow, but at least the cold was now beginning to numb the pain he felt.

As Molly and Jake took in great gasps of cold air beside him, Tom sat up. There was only one thing he could think of doing. He composed himself, emptied his mind of thought, then pictured what he wanted.

Almost immediately, it began to snow heavily again. Thousands and thousands of giant snowflakes fell from the sky, creating a blizzard that blotted out everything around them. But rather than lose focus, Tom concentrated like never before, making wave after wave of heavy snow tumble to the ground. He was not trying to wrestle control of a whirlwind from someone's mind. This was easy by comparison: just make it snow.

Jake dragged him to his feet once more, breaking the spell. 'Come on, mate. Time to move again.'

Molly grabbed his other arm, and on they trudged, scarcely able to see more than a metre in front of them through the falling snow.

Chapter Eighteen

The Final Duel

Through the rapidly thinning fall of snow, the brick engine house and tall chimney of the disused tin mine began to come into view. Behind it, far out to sea where the sky met the water, was a thick band of pale blue where the blanket of angry storm clouds ended abruptly.

Using the compass on her phone, Molly had led them through the blizzard to the old building. Yet it was impossible for her to feel much relief at seeing their destination; Tom had been badly injured, and their stay here was only ever going to be temporary.

By the time she and Jake had dragged Tom through the doorway, there was only a smattering of snowflakes falling. But at least the blizzard had lasted long enough to cover their tracks, and thereby to obscure their progress from Miss Doomsday.

They took Tom through to the small room they had used before with the table and chairs in one corner, and lowered him carefully to the floor, where he sat with his back to the wall, eyes half closed. The small, square window facing the sea and the distant clear sky shone like a light on the wall.

Jake staggered to the table where he found a bottle of water and greedily slaked his thirst. He then collapsed to the floor, his chest heaving up and down. Poor Jake, thought Molly. He had virtually carried Tom all the way from the cottage but had not once complained.

She took the bottle to Tom, who looked weak but was at

least still conscious. He took a swig of water, then looked at her.

'I don't know how to beat her,' he said, his face as pale as the snow. 'We should have—'

'Ssh!' she said softly, placing a hand on his cheek. 'Don't torture yourself. We need to think what we *can* do, not what we should have done.'

He nodded weakly in response.

She smiled and tried to look and sound calm, even though inside, she was terrified. His loss of blood had slowed, but there was no knowing how much he had lost. And somewhere out there, no doubt heading this way, was the vile deputy head.

Still looking utterly exhausted and unable to speak, Jake dragged himself to his feet and went back outside. He returned moments later.

'The tornado has gone,' he said between gasps. 'But I can see her walking this way. She must have guessed we came here. She'll be here in a few minutes.' He looked at them expectantly, pleading with his eyes for either one of them to make a suggestion.

'You two go on,' said Tom. 'Go and get help. I'll try to hold her off here as long as I can.'

Molly clenched her teeth against the cold but also to stop herself from crying. She stood up and went to the window, as much to conceal from Tom the tears she could feel forming. Out to sea everything looked so calm, whilst nearer to them, the shoreline was nothing but grim shades of grey and dirty white. Her eyes followed the crescent shape of the small bay below.

Then she remembered something. Her heart filled with

hope.

Wiping a tear from her cheek, she spun round and dropped to her knees beside Tom. She picked up the small rucksack containing the Iris box and hurriedly put it on her back.

'What are you doing?' asked Tom.

'Give me the bracelets,' she replied.

'No, Molly. That's not the answer.'

She smiled and then began fumbling with one of them until it clicked off his wrist. He was too weak to resist.

'I can't let you do that,' he protested and suddenly gripped her forearm. 'She'll kill you.'

She looked deep into his eyes, kissed him, then said: 'Tom, do you trust me?'

'Well—'

'I'll take that as a yes, shall I?' she grinned, recalling when he had said exactly the same to her not so long ago.

He released his grip, and she hastily undid the other wristband. 'Be careful, Molly,' he said, smiling weakly. 'And don't do anything I wouldn't do.'

'Do you know what you're doing with those things?' asked Jake, as Molly rose to her feet.

She snapped the cuffs around her wrists, then watched as they almost slid off her slender hands.

'Nope,' she replied, with a smirk. 'But if Tom can manage it, how hard can it be?'

She then buried them under the thick sleeves of her coat, hoping that would be enough to keep them in place.

'We can't just leave Tom here,' protested Jake, spreading his arms incredulously.

'Jake,' said Molly, losing patience. 'Do you honestly think I'm going to abandon Tom? He can't walk. So we need to lure

Guardians of the Mirror

Doomsday away from here. Come with me.'

Below a furrowed brow, Jake's eyes flitted from Tom to Molly and back again.

'Go, Jake!' urged Tom with a wan smile. 'She knows what she's doing.'

With Jake following in her wake, Molly rushed into the adjacent small room, where she knew there was another doorway, which led out the side of the building. She burst through the rotting wooden door and out into the cold air once more. Turning to her right, she saw the plump silhouette of Miss Doomsday trudging through the snow towards the tin mine, fewer than two hundred metres away.

Jake stood at her shoulder. 'How do we stop her going in there after Tom?' he mumbled.

'Follow me,' she replied, pulling up her hood. 'Hopefully in this light she won't be able to see who is who.' She then turned and ran away from the building, at right angles to the direction the teacher was heading in. After a dozen or so paces, Molly stopped, turned towards their pursuer and tried to remember everything Tony Singh had told them.

Closing her eyes, she then waved her arms into the air. Even though she had known what to expect, the shock of seeing a vivid bolt of lightning spear down to the ground nearby made her fall backwards onto the snow. Although the dazzling, ragged line of electricity landed some distance from Miss Doomsday, it nevertheless made the teacher flinch and almost lose her balance.

Molly grabbed Jake's arm and urged him to follow her. 'I think we got her attention,' she said, as they bounded through the snow.

'Are you going to tell me what on earth you're up to?'

asked Jake.

Miss Doomsday's response to Molly's wayward attack cracked across the sky and struck a tree only a few metres away, instantly turning it into an explosion of fire. Flames leapt into the dark sky, staining the snow orange and casting long black shadows in every direction.

'There's no time to explain,' cried Molly, as she continued stumbling through the deep snow.

A timely gust of wind blew through the burning tree and sent a pleasant blast of warm air over them. With the fire already beginning to die down behind them, Molly stopped once more and stood facing the teacher. Miss Doomsday's arms were already in the air, preparing her next attack. Knowing that another lightning bolt was imminent, Molly flung her hands upwards, then brought them sharply down. But in her haste to launch her own attack first, Molly directed her own fork of lightning well wide of its mark. It lit up the sky but crashed to earth some distance from Miss Doomsday. Yet the speed of Molly's latest attempt was enough to disrupt the deputy head's composure, as the latter's lightning bolt went soaring over their heads and out of harm's way.

Molly knew she was unlikely to win a shootout with Miss Doomsday, so she wasted no more time, turned to her left and ran towards the sea, imploring Jake to follow her. The snowy ground began to slope down towards the bay in a series of uneven, rocky steps. It was not a man-made path, but rather a natural route that weaved down to the beach between large blocks of snow-covered stone.

Halfway down the path, Molly looked up and saw Jake close behind her, and then the forbidding figure of Miss Doomsday, silhouetted against the snow at the top of the cliff.

Expecting a streak of lightning at any moment, she pressed on until she reached the small beach, stumbling out onto the snow-covered shingle.

'What now?' asked Jake, panting beside her.

'Over there,' she said pointing to her right, where the small bay swept round in a crescent, at the end of which was a small rocky promontory with a number of trees hanging low over the water. 'We're going there, right to the end.'

'But we'll be stranded,' protested Jake, striding after Molly who was already racing along the narrow beach.

'Just please trust me, Jake,' she replied without looking back.

'Why do people always say that when they're about to do something foolish?' said Jake, rushing after her.

Beside them, waves were breaking onto the stony beach, drenching their shoes. But since they had been walking through deep snow for ages their shoes were already soaking wet, so it hardly seemed to matter.

After only a short distance, the beach ended with only rocks sticking out into the water. Molly began climbing across them, moving as fast as she dared over the slippery surfaces.

She was now feeling nervous. She had been telling Jake to just trust her, trying to sound confident. Maybe she had been trying to convince herself as much as Jake, for the truth was, she was terrified her plan would not work. If it failed, she had no plan B.

They were scrambling over wet and in places snow-covered rocks, moving slowly upwards and along, towards the end of the promontory.

A dazzling streak of lightning arced across the sky above them, followed closely by a boom of thunder.

'Come back here!' roared Miss Doomsday's voice across the bay.

Molly ignored her, and kept going, climbing higher up the side of the rocky bay towards the dark trees above. Then she stopped, found somewhere to sit down and removed the backpack.

'Listen to me,' shouted Miss Doomsday, who was now standing on the narrow beach at the bottom of the small cliff down which they had all climbed. 'All I want are the objects — the medallions, your Iris box. Give them to me and I will let you go.'

Jake clambered up and sat down beside Molly on the rocks, looking down into the bay and the menacing figure of the deputy head, who stood glaring up at them in the twilight. Although she now stood facing them no more than a strong stone's throw away, between her and them wave after dark grey wave swept past onto the tight arc of the shoreline a few metres away to their left.

Molly tossed the backpack down onto the rocks directly below the two of them. It came to rest a few metres away, close to the water's edge. If Miss Doomsday wanted it, she would either have to scramble across the rocks as Molly and Jake had done or wade through the dark, icy seawater to reach it.

'What on earth are you doing?' cried Jake, utterly bewildered.

She ignored him. 'They are in that,' she shouted back to Miss Doomsday. 'Come and get them if you dare. I may not be as skilled at this as you are, but you won't be able to climb rocks *and* fight me at the same time. So turn around and just go home. Leave us alone.'

Even in the dim light, Molly could tell Miss Doomsday was

seething. Her dark figure stood motionless for a while, studying them, no doubt plotting what to do next. While nothing but the sound of the surf crashing onto the beach and the rocks filled the air, Molly sat silently willing the teacher to do what she so desperately wanted her to do. Had she goaded her enough? What if the deputy head failed to take the bait? What if she did something unexpected?

Finally, Miss Doomsday began waving her arms about in the air. Immediately, the wind increased, the air became even colder than it had been. The damp on Molly's clothes began to turn to frost. It was so cold it became difficult to breathe. Her fingers, her toes, her whole face went numb.

Then the sea began to freeze. Waves began to slow down, then stopped altogether in mid-motion. Great creaks and cracks rent the air, as though some unseen metal structure were being twisted apart. Soon the whole bay had frozen over, many metres out into the sea. What had once been waves were now undulating ridges of sculpted ice.

Miss Doomsday stepped tentatively onto the ice.

'Oh, now we're in trouble,' muttered Jake. 'I'm not sure you've thought this through, have you?'

'Let's move higher,' said Molly, and began climbing on all fours across the rocks again.

'What about the box?' asked Jake.

'Leave it!' she yelled back.

She chanced a quick glance back and saw Miss Doomsday walking out across the frozen bay, heading in a straight line towards them. She was going to reach the Iris box in no time.

Molly continued clambering up for a few seconds more. Then she turned and looked back down into the bay. The deputy head was now not far from the small backpack, which was still perched on a rock close to the sheet of ice.

Molly cleared her mind. Imagined what she wanted, formed it in her head. When it was ready, she unleashed a single jagged bolt of lightning. Without the requisite practice, her accuracy was poor. But then, she had no need for it to be good.

It hit the ice some metres away from Miss Doomsday, momentarily lighting up her startled and panicked face. The ice cracked. At first, small cracks spread out, followed quickly by much larger ones. The ice sheet around the teacher broke apart into a jigsaw of giant plates of ice.

Miss Doomsday toppled and fell through the ice into the sea water below. For a moment, she disappeared from view, before resurfacing, arms flailing about in a wild panic. 'I can't swim,' she screamed. 'I can't swim.'

'I know,' said Molly, with a grim but satisfied look on her face. She then began scrambling back down the rocks.

'Where are you going now?' asked Jake.

'I won't let her drown,' she said. 'I'm not like her. Besides, she belongs in prison.'

When she reached the edge of the frozen bay, she began crawling on all fours across the ice towards the fountain of splashing water and ice that was Miss Doomsday, as she desperately tried to stay above water. She reached out a hand to grab the teacher's wrist and slowly pulled her out of the water and onto the remaining ice. The moment Miss Doomsday was clear of the water, Molly seized one of her bracelets, snapped it off and stuffed it into one of her own pockets.

Jake arrived and helped drag the deputy head onto the stony beach. There she lay on her back, breathing heavily,

Guardians of the Mirror

staring blankly into space and shaking violently all over. She had lost her glasses and her black hair lay in clumps across her forehead. Her lips were blue.

'She might die of hypothermia,' said Jake in a tone that rather suggested he hoped she would.

'I hope not,' said Molly. 'I want her to stand trial for what she's done.' She then took out her phone. 'Right, let's get an ambulance for Tom. And then we must get rid of this snow.'

'Aw!' said a disappointed Jake. 'Can't we at least keep it till Christmas?'

Izzy and Tony had been stuck for hours in the derelict farmhouse on Bodmin Moor. Every time they were about to move out, another drone or a helicopter would glide into view, scanning the moor for escaped prisoners. But then as dusk approached, it all seemed to go quiet.

Pacing up and down inside the farmhouse in the fading light, Izzy, her mind racing, was trying to fathom out what to do next. She poked her head out of the doorway to look across the barren landscape and to peer at the grey sky.

'What is it?' asked Tony.

She walked back inside, sat back down next to him on the floor and opened her laptop. 'It's eerily quiet out there all of a sudden. Why would they just stop looking for us? I'm going to see if anything has happened.' She brought up the images from a news channel in one corner of her screen, while she searched other sources for clues.

After a few minutes, Tony tapped the small box showing the news. 'Look. What's that about? Enlarge it.'

Izzy immediately filled the screen with the news and turned up the sound. There was an aerial shot of a huge gathering of people in what looked like the centre of London.

'The mass protests have continued all afternoon,' said the newsreader over the images. 'Spontaneous demonstrations against the government have taken place across the country. The biggest of these have been in London, Birmingham, Manchester, Cardiff, Edinburgh and Belfast. In London alone it is estimated that over one million people have taken to the streets.'

The pictures moved from London to another city, where the camera looked down on a sea of people spread along the roads, many of them carrying banners. The camera swept over a large area of the city, yet everywhere it went there were people, thousands upon thousands of people.

'The protesters are continuing to demand the resignation of the Prime Minister and for the reinstatement of free elections. This comes after further footage has emerged showing Prime Minister Sheeran in recent discussions with the disgraced Police Commissioner Livia Doomsday, from the Cornish town of Porthgarrick. In addition, details have been leaked online purporting to show the existence of special prisons dotted around the country, where, it is being claimed, a large number of political prisoners are being kept. Earlier in the day, the Prime Minister vehemently denied the existence of such prisons. However, almost immediately after his statement, the mysterious person or persons behind these recent online posts then released pictures and documents which appear to prove that hundreds if not thousands of people have been held without trial in these prisons.'

A tear ran down Izzy's cheek.

Noticing it, Tony put a hand on hers. 'Hey, what is it?' he asked.

'It's finally happening,' she said, turning to look at him. 'It's actually happening.'

The news bulletin switched suddenly to the newsreader behind her desk. 'We're now going over live to Westminster, where the Independent Party leader, Laurie Adkins, is about to make a statement.'

The picture changed to one of a smartly dressed woman in her thirties, standing in front of a row of microphones.

'Without further ado,' she said solemnly, 'I should like to announce that Prime Minister Sheeran has tendered his resignation.'

Izzy gasped and put a hand over her mouth, scarcely able to believe what she was hearing.

'His majesty the King has asked me,' continued the politician, 'to act as interim leader until elections can be held. It is my firm intention to call a general election at the earliest opportunity.'

The assembled journalists began firing questions at her, until she held up a hand to silence them. 'There are two further brief points I wish to make. Firstly, the matter of these kidnapped schoolchildren in Cornwall. I have asked the local police in Porthgarrick to look into this as a matter of urgency. Secondly, the issue of these alleged prisons will also be investigated immediately.'

Izzy let out an involuntary sob. She felt so overwhelmed, happier, more elated than she had ever felt before. As Tony leant over and put an arm around her shoulders, she looked into his eyes, tears rolling down her cheeks.

'We did it!' she said. 'We actually did it.'

'No,' said Tony with a warm smile. 'You did it, Izzy. You did this.'

Chapter Nineteen

A Happy Christmas

Tom's heart was racing out of control. Despite the cold, he felt clammy and uncomfortable. The anticipation of what was about to happen was killing him.

Standing next to his stepmother and with his baby stepbrother Billy below them in the pushchair, he stood on the windswept pavement outside the tall, imposing gates of the prison. A small crowd of twenty or so people stood alongside them.

It had only been just over a week since Prime Minister Sheeran had resigned, but in that time, true to her word, the acting leader of the country had ordered an immediate review of all prisoners. Since the previous regime had kept meticulous records of all crimes committed, it was decreed that anyone who had been imprisoned for no other reason than they had shown dissent towards the government, was to be released immediately. To Tom's relief this meant that the likes of Harry Singh would remain in prison, whilst his father would soon be free.

Every time the gates swung open, Tom's heart would leap, but then drop again when he saw that the released prisoner was not his dad.

But then at last, he saw the tall, slim figure of his father walking towards them. His stepmother burst into tears and ran towards him. After they had embraced, they walked back towards Tom and Billy.

With tears rolling down his cheeks, Tom stepped forward

and felt his father's powerful, comforting arms wrap around him.

'I guess I've got you to thank for my release,' he said.

'Well, it was mostly Izzy, really,' said Tom. 'But I guess I played a small part.'

'Well, however you did it, I shall be eternally grateful,' said Mr Paget. He then shivered. 'It's Christmas Day tomorrow, isn't it? And it feels cold enough for snow.'

'Oh, don't talk to me about snow,' said Tom with a shudder. 'I've seen enough for one year.'

His father looked at him with a confused expression. 'Okay. Sounds like you've got some tales to tell me over lunch. Come on, let's go home.'

'I'll join you later,' said Tom. 'I need to do something first.'

When Tom and Tony emerged from the concrete bunker, a storm was raging. Frequent flashes of lightning erupted across a black sky, while a blustery wind was driving wave after wave of heavy rain. Every time lightning lit up the barren rolling hills, several writhing tornadoes could be seen swaying across the landscape.

It was hard not to feel a terrible sense of dread at returning to the world of near-perpetual storms, as though the place somehow sucked all hope and joy from the air. But Tom had made a promise to return and he had every intention of fulfilling that promise.

Since Tony was on crutches with a leg in plaster and Tom was limping with one of his legs heavily bandaged, Molly and Izzy had insisted on coming along as well. It was only a few days since both boys had badly injured their legs, so neither of them was able to move freely.

John D. Fennell

'Of course, there's no guarantee this will work,' said Tony, looking up at the menacing, dark sky. 'I can't control normal weather — only the abnormal stuff caused by people travelling through the mirror.'

'I know,' agreed Tom. 'But I'm just really hoping we can do something to help these people.'

'Well, let's give it a go,' said Tony. In an instant, he seemed to put himself in a trance, his eyes unblinking and focused on some distant, unseen point. His breathing looked to have slowed right down until, aside from his open eyes, it appeared as though he were asleep.

Without warning, his arms reached up high above his head, paused for a moment, then began moving rapidly about, left and right, up and down, hands weaving around one another. Sometimes, his hands clapped noisily together, other times they spread wide, then crossed over his chest. And all the while, his face was set like a mask, no emotion, no movement of any kind.

One by one, the tornadoes collapsed, vanishing with a startling abruptness. Streaks of lightning froze halfway down to the ground, then disappeared altogether. And then breaks began to appear in the great mass of cloud. Narrow shafts of sunlight speared down to the ground all over the landscape. Gradually, the sunbeams grew wider and wider, the light stronger and stronger, until they slowly merged together, and large patches of brilliant sunshine burst across the land.

After a few minutes, the hills before them were bathed in a low winter sunlight, with just a few white clouds drifting across a blue sky.

Tom patted Tony on the back. 'You did it.'

Tony blinked and came out of his trance. 'Yes. But I can still feel some force trying to bring the storms back. But if I show the people what to do, they should be able to keep on top of it. And then maybe one day, their climate will return to normal.'

'Right,' said Tom. 'Let's go and find them.'

They began walking towards the ruins of Porthgarrick, a cold but gentle breeze blowing through the sunshine. It felt so alien, and yet so pleasant compared to their previous visit that it seemed like they had arrived in a completely different world.

They had not gone far when a small group of people was seen heading towards them. Even from a distance, the tall, gangly figure of Molly's uncle was unmistakable. As he approached, Tom could see a faint smile on his lips, something he had not seen at all on their previous visit.

'I guess this is your doing,' he said to Tom, looking up at the sky.

'Well, actually you can thank my friend Tony here.'

After they had shaken hands, Tony handed over the Iris box and a sheaf of papers. 'This is yours. Instructions on how to use it are written here.'

The man looked puzzled. 'You'll have to tell me what this is all about.'

'It will allow you to control at least some of the weather.'

Molly's uncle studied the box, then looked up. 'I don't pretend to understand any of this, but we can't thank you enough.'

'There is only one condition,' said Tony. 'This can be a very powerful device. So, all I ask is that you never use it to try to seek revenge against the other world for what they've done to you.'

The man smiled. 'Just as Tom here gave us his word he

would return, I give you my word we will only use it for good.'

'Great!' said Tony. 'Now come on. I'll give you a quick lesson.' With Izzy's help, he hobbled away with Molly's uncle and most of the people who had accompanied their leader.

Only the Molly from that world stayed behind and stood facing Tom and his Molly. 'Thank you for coming back,' she said. 'And I'm sorry again for what I tried to do.'

'No harm done in the end,' said Tom. 'Good luck. And I hope you ... find happiness again.' He hugged her.

When they separated, she wiped a tear away. 'Well, if the climate really can be changed, I'm going to be busy, helping to rebuild this world. Thank you again, Tom.'

It was Christmas Day, and everyone was sitting around a long table enjoying a sizeable Christmas lunch. At the head of the table sat Mr Paget, with his wife on one side of him and Tom on the other, who in turn had Molly next to him. Around the table were also Tony and Izzy, Tony's parents and of course Tom's grandfather Sam.

As Tom looked around the room, whilst holding Molly's hand under the table, he noticed everyone had a smile on their face. Not only was the delicious roast meal and the friendly banter making everyone happy, it was also the sheer relief of being able to relax after the events of recent times.

'When is Jake coming?' asked Molly.

'Should be any minute now,' replied Tom.

In anticipation of his friend's arrival, Tom looked across at the cheval mirror in the corner of the room. In an attempt to soften its rather sinister appearance, someone had draped a long piece of golden tinsel around the frame.

Guardians of the Mirror

In the blink of an eye, Jake appeared in front of the mirror, holding Clare's hand next to him. 'Hello, everyone,' he said. 'Happy Christmas! This is Clare, for those of you who haven't met her. We can't stay for too long in case Clare ... well ... I guess you all know by now what happens.'

'Oh, you should be all right for at least an hour or two,' said Tony.

Jake looked out of the window at the pale blue sky. 'Well, let's hope so.' He and Clare then moved round the table and sat near to Tony and Izzy. 'Hey, are you two an item now?' he added, looking at them suspiciously.

They both grinned back at him. 'Shh!' said Izzy, putting a finger to her lips. 'Don't tell anyone. It's still our little secret.'

'Well, it's about time,' replied Jake. 'We could all see it coming ages ago, couldn't we, Tom?'

'Yeah, absolutely,' said Tom. 'I'm just a bit worried now, in case they ever decide to team up and become master criminals. Then the world really would be doomed.'

After Izzy had thrown a scrunched-up napkin at Tom, and the subsequent laughter had died down, Jake asked: 'Did those poor wee kids get taken back to their world in the end?'

'Yes, of course,' replied Izzy. 'I persuaded the police to hand them over to me and we took them back straightaway.'

'What on earth did you tell the police?' asked Jake.

'Oh, didn't you know, Jake?' said Molly. 'Izzy is now best buddies with the local police chief. They're going to offer her a role in their cybercrime unit.'

'Yes,' added Tom. 'It's what we feared. She's going over to the dark side. She'll be spying on us soon. We're all doomed.'

Izzy picked up her Christmas cracker and threw it accurately at Tom's head. Everyone fell about laughing.

After a few minutes, Mr Paget stood up. 'Forgive me, everyone. I'd just like to say a few words.'

'Oh, no. He's had enough of us already and would rather go back to prison,' someone joked.

Tom's father smiled, then adopted a more serious expression. 'All of you youngsters here have had a pretty traumatic time over the last few months. In fact, most, if not all, the adults in this room as well, come to think of it. So basically, all of us here have had a pretty traumatic time. But ultimately, it's thanks to you guys,' he added, looking pointedly at Tom, Molly, Jake, Izzy and Tony, 'that we're all here today, enjoying this meal together. Without your tenacity, without your love for us and for one another, none of this would have happened. You may not realise yet just what it is that you have achieved. You have succeeded in bringing down an evil and corrupt government. You should all be extremely proud of that. And I for one can never thank you all enough. Thanks, guys,' he said, raising his wine glass.

A chorus of 'Here, here!' filled the room.

As his father sat back down, Tom said: 'Well, I'd just like to propose a toast to Miss Doomsday.'

Amid various startled murmurings, Molly said: 'What? Are you mad?'

'No, seriously,' insisted Tom. 'Without her stupidity in kidnapping those schoolchildren we might not be here now.'

'Well, I for one could never toast that evil witch,' said Molly. 'May she rot in prison.'

'Well, I shall,' said Tom. 'To Miss Doomsday and her stupidity!' he added, raising his glass with fake sincerity.

After the laughter had died down once more and everyone had begun tucking into their turkey and roast potatoes, the

Guardians of the Mirror

conversation turned inevitably to the mirror in the corner of the room. It watched over them silently and continued to draw a constant stream of wary glances, as though no one quite trusted it to just remain there doing nothing.

'What are we going to do with that thing?' asked Jake.

'We have to keep the portal open,' said Tom quickly. 'I'm leading a double life at the moment, so I need it for that.'

'I think we should consider shutting it down for good,' growled Sam.

'Well, at the moment,' said Tony, 'I see no reason to close it. As long as we want to continue seeing our friends Jake and Clare, we're going to need it.'

Tom heartily agreed.

'But it's a very, very dangerous object,' said Izzy. 'How do we make sure it can never be misused again?'

Small conversations broke out around the table, some in favour of Tony, others wavering towards Sam's point of view.

Tom cleared his throat and spoke above the noise. 'We should keep it open.' Everyone stopped to listen. He felt rather uncomfortable with all eyes now scrutinising him but felt compelled to speak his mind. 'I know from personal experience just what it can do, all the bad stuff. But it's also the reason I'm here now. Maybe also the reason the government was toppled in the end. So, I think we should definitely keep it open, as long as we police it carefully.

'For me, they made a mistake two hundred years ago when the Tranter and Trevaskis families went their separate ways. When they formed the Guardians all those years ago to defeat Augustus Doomsday, they should have kept the group going. I can understand they were terrified by what they had seen and wanted to ensure it could never happen again. But surely you don't run away from something like that. You face up to it. Isn't that what all you adults are always telling us?

'So I propose we reform the Guardians. Everyone here, all of us, could become the new Guardians of the Mirror. Tony and his mum can oversee all the teaching. The group would be small enough to keep it secretive, but also big enough that no *one* person could take over and do anything stupid. What does everyone else think?'

There was silence for a moment, and Tom suddenly felt as though he had somehow said something wrong. But then Jake spoke up in agreement, followed by Tony and Molly. Eventually, everyone seemed to agree with the idea. Even Grandpa Sam nodded enigmatically but did not voice any objection.

Tom's father patted him on the arm and smiled warmly at him. 'Well said, son.'

'Well, we know why Tom really wants to keep the thing open,' said Izzy with a mischievous smirk. 'He's got a girlfriend in both worlds now. And he doesn't want to give up either one of them.'

It was Tom's turn to pick up a cracker and throw it at Izzy.

'It's what I've always said about Tom,' said Jake. 'Are you all ready for this one? He always wants ... wait for it ... the best of both worlds.'

Everyone groaned and burst out laughing.

As Tom joined in the laughter, still holding onto Molly's hand, he looked around the room at the smiling faces and could not recall a time when he had ever felt happier.

The End

If you enjoyed this trilogy, why not try my next book?

VESUVIUS

The Roman Time Machine - Book One.

- Winner of the 2021 Incipere Awards for Young Adult fantasy, and second place for children's fiction;
- Red Ribbon winner in the 2021 Wishing Shelf Awards for children's fiction.

'The day after tomorrow, Vesuvius is going to erupt. And when it does, it will completely bury Pompeii ... A lot of people are going to die.'

On Zak's thirteenth birthday, a strange girl called Maia appears in his classroom ... out of thin air. But before he has time to work out where she has come from, the two of them somehow travel back in time and find themselves running for their lives through the streets of ancient Pompeii, chased by sinister hooded figures.

And when they realise they have arrived in the Roman city only days before Vesuvius is due to erupt, their desperation to find a way back home becomes even greater.

But who exactly is Maia? And can Zak really trust her?

John D. Fennell

If you would like more information on any of my books as well as news on new releases, please visit
www.johndfennell.com

I really hope you enjoyed reading this book. If you did, I would be very grateful if you could add a rating and a review on **Amazon** to let others know what you thought.

Many thanks,

John D. Fennell

Printed in Great Britain
by Amazon